RAINBIRDS

RAINBIRDS

Clarissa Goenawan

NATIONAL ARTS COUNCIL
SINGAPORE

Published by
Soho Press, Inc.
853 Broadway
New York, NY 10003

Library of Congress Cataloging-in-Publication Data

Goenawan, Clarissa
Rainbirds / Clarissa Goenawan.

ISBN 978-1-64129-018-0
eISBN 978-1-61695-856-5

1. Brothers and sisters—Fiction. 2. Sisters—Death—Fiction. 3. Murder—Fiction. 4. Japan—Fiction. 5. Psychological fiction. I. Title.
PR9570.S53 G572 2018 823'.92—dc23 2017055165

Interior design by Janine Agro

Printed in the United States of America

10 9 8 7 6 5 4 3 2 1

RAINBIRDS

1

She
Crumbled
and
Turned
to
Ashes

At first, nothing was unusual.

I was on the phone with my sister. She sat at her desk by the window in her rented room in Akakawa. The sun shone through the curtain, casting brown highlights on her long dark hair. She asked me question after question, but I just mumbled one-word answers, impatient for the conversation to be over. But then, before my eyes, she crumbled and turned to ashes.

I WOKE UP IN a black sedan; the dream would have slipped from my mind, had it not been for the white porcelain urn in my lap. Resembling a short cylindrical vase, it was decorated with a painting of a flying cuckoo and chrysanthemums. Inside were the ashes of my sister, Keiko Ishida, who had been only thirty-three when she died.

I loosened my tie and asked Honda, "How much longer?"

He turned the steering wheel. "Almost there."

"Mind putting on some music?"

"Of course not," he answered, flicking a button.

The radio played Billie Holiday's "Summertime."

For a Friday afternoon, the journey was smooth. The sun was high, no traffic jam in sight. Even the music was relaxing, the kind meant to make you drum your fingers to the beat.

My hands tightened involuntarily around the urn, and I stared at it. Honda glanced at me for a second before turning his eyes back to the road.

"Keiko used to love jazz," he said.

I nodded, unable to speak. The small stack of cassettes that made up her collection—what would happen to them now?

"The funny thing was, she couldn't name a single jazz musician," he continued.

I cleared my throat. "You don't need to be knowledgeable to appreciate jazz."

"Well said, Ishida."

Actually, it was my sister who had first spoken those words to me.

Even now, I could picture her sitting at her desk, her hand twisting the phone cord. A self-satisfied smile on her face as she murmured, "You don't need to be knowledgeable to appreciate jazz."

Strange that this image was etched in my mind, though I'd never seen her rented room—I had no idea what it looked like.

"We're here," Honda said as the car pulled up to the entrance of the Katsuragi Hotel.

"Thank you for your help arranging the memorial service," I said.

"Don't mention it. Keiko's done a lot for me in the past."

I nodded and got out, still clutching the urn. I was already heading through the entrance when I heard him call after me.

"Ishida."

I turned. Honda had already wound down the passenger window.

"What are you going to do with . . . ?" He scratched the back of his neck, looking at the urn.

"I haven't decided yet."

"If you want the ashes scattered at sea, we can ask the crematorium staff. They'll handle it for a small fee."

"That won't do," I said. "My sister was afraid of water. She couldn't swim."

HONDA AND MY SISTER had taught at the same cram school. It was he who had arranged my accommodations.

"It's sparsely furnished, but cheap and livable," he had said, a completely accurate description. A queen-sized bed, a small television, a wardrobe, and a dressing table with matching chair—that was all. The furniture was dated but functional. Relatively clean, the room had an en-suite bathroom and a slightly musty odor.

I placed the urn on the dressing table and looked at my watch. It was two-thirty, so I had an hour to make my way to the police station. I took off my suit and left it hanging over the back of the chair. I needed to shower, to wash away the smell of the funeral incense.

Sliding the bathroom door, I glanced at the dressing table. The urn stood there silently.

I ARRIVED AT THE police station to find a lone young officer manning the counter. I was the only visitor. When I gave the man my name, he stood to open the office door.

"Follow me," he said, and I did, surprised he would leave the counter unattended.

The officer led me down a cramped corridor and gestured for me to enter a room on the right. I knocked on the door twice, took a deep breath, and turned the knob.

"Excuse me," I said.

A middle-aged man sat behind a desk piled high with folders. His hair was thinning, and he wore a faded black suit over a crumpled white shirt. For a police officer, the man dressed sloppily.

The room we were in was windowless and smaller than I'd expected. Perhaps it was designed to make visitors feel claustrophobic. The desk ran from wall to wall, dividing the office in two. I wondered how the officer managed to get to his chair each morning. Did he climb over the desk, or crawl underneath it?

He looked at me. "Mr. Ren Ishida?"

"Yes."

"Please, have a seat." He motioned to the two empty chairs in front of the desk. "I'm sorry for what happened to Miss Keiko Ishida. This must be a difficult time for you and your family." He shifted the folders over to one side and handed me his business card. "I'm in charge of Miss Ishida's case. You can call me Oda."

I nodded and read the card: HIDETOSHI ODA, SENIOR DETECTIVE.

"Mr. Ishida, I need you to tell me as much information as you can." He took out a tape recorder. "May we proceed?"

"Yes."

The detective pressed the record button, looked at his watch, and began a well-rehearsed script. He gave the time, date, and location of the interview before introducing himself and me. I confirmed my identity, and he started with the official interview.

"Tell me about your sister," he said. "Were you two close?"

"I suppose so. She called at least once a week," I answered.

"When was the last time you spoke to her?"

"Last Monday."

He turned his table calendar to face me. "That would have been the sixth of June?"

"Yes."

"June 6, 1994," he muttered into the tape recorder. "And what did you talk about?"

I stared at the blank wall behind him. "Nothing much, just the usual stuff."

"Can you be more specific?"

I took a moment to recall our last conversation. What had we talked about? Yes, of course. We'd talked about my date.

"Did you go out with Nae this weekend?" my sister asked.

"Uh-huh," I answered. "The obligatory Saturday night date."

"Where did you go?"

"An Italian restaurant."

"The fine dining kind?"

"I guess it counts as one."

"Really?" she exclaimed. "I wasn't aware you had such refined taste."

"It was Nae's idea, not mine. She learned about it from a fashion magazine."

"Was it good?"

I snickered. "Far from it."

"What happened?"

Where should I start? "Service was slow, the pasta was bland, and it was expensive. I should have known what to expect when taking restaurant recommendations from a fashion magazine."

She laughed. "Are you sure your expectations weren't too high?"

"Trust me," I said, "it was bad."

"And where did you go after that?"

I paused. "Nowhere."

"What?" She raised her voice. "That was all?"

"Yes." I echoed, "That was all."

"Are you for real?"

"Is it me, or do you sound disappointed?"

"I *am* disappointed," she said. "You're so boring for someone so young."

"Don't talk like you're an old woman. We're only nine years apart. Anyway, what were you expecting?"

"People your age would usually go for a romantic walk after dinner. Or are you withholding the best part from me?"

"Sorry to disappoint you again, but she went straight home."

I wasn't lying, but that was only part of the story. Nae and I had had an argument during dinner. To be fair, I was already in a bad mood. The restaurant's lackluster food and poor service made it worse. So when Nae kept pressing me with questions about my future plans—*our* future plans, according to her—I became agitated.

"You're so desperate to get married," I said. "Are you afraid you're going to be the only one left on the shelf?"

I realized I'd gone too far when she stood and grabbed her bag. She hadn't even touched her main course.

"Don't expect me to talk to you again until you've apologized," she said before storming out.

I sighed. Nae was stubborn. She would carry out her threat, but that was fine. I needed a break. Lately, all of our conversations were about marriage, even though I'd told her I wasn't ready. A little distance could be a good thing.

I left the restaurant soon after she did. On my way to the train station, I saw a bar across the street. I went in and ordered a beer. A woman took the empty seat next to me. We started talking, and I ended up having more drinks than I intended to. She was attractive enough, though I believe the alcohol and dim lighting played a part. One thing led to another, and I found myself in the bed of her upscale studio apartment.

After we were done, she drifted off to sleep while I showered.

The last train had gone, so I stayed for the night. She was still sound asleep when I woke up around four in the morning. Not wanting to get any more involved with her, I left quietly.

Of course, I didn't share any of this with my sister. She would've asked about the woman, and I hardly remembered her face, let alone her name. We had talked for hours, but the memories had evaporated. The only thing I remembered was that she had a tiny mole at the nape of her neck.

"Ren, why so quiet?" my sister asked.

"I'm tired," I lied.

She continued as if she hadn't heard me. "But you like Italian food, don't you? I remember you used to polish off the spaghetti Bolognese I would make."

"I only like it if it's done well."

"I know a good Italian place. It's not fancy like the one you went to—just a small, homey eatery run by an elderly couple. I'll take you there when you come to Akakawa. It's outside of town, but worth the trip."

I smiled, sensing her excitement. "All right," I said, and that was the last time we spoke.

"IS SOMETHING ON YOUR mind?" the detective asked.

I doubted my personal life had any bearing on my sister's death. "We talked about my studies. Nothing important."

"Did she mention anything that was troubling her? Work or relationship issues?"

I shook my head. "Not that I remember."

"Do you know why she came to Akakawa? It's more provincial than Tokyo, and she lived here all by herself."

I hesitated before answering. "My parents don't get along with each other. My sister couldn't take it."

He checked his file. "She left Tokyo right after graduation, when she was twenty-two. Is that correct?"

"Yes."

"So she had been living here for eleven years." He looked at me. "Why were you the only family member who attended her memorial service?"

I couldn't bring myself to answer. He gazed directly at me, waiting for my reply, but I kept my mouth shut. I didn't want to divulge too much about our family problems, which should be kept private and were irrelevant to my sister's death. The detective sighed and scribbled something on his pad. The paper was full of notes in his illegible handwriting.

"Your sister, was she in a romantic relationship?"

"No."

I was sure my sister hadn't been in a relationship recently. Not because there was anything wrong with her—she had a sweet disposition, quite a slim frame, and the air of someone with a good upbringing. In short, Keiko Ishida was the type of woman the average salaryman wanted as his wife. During her high school and university years in Tokyo, a few decent guys had asked her out, but she turned them all down politely.

"There's no point if I'm not in love with him," she told me.

"Don't be a hopeless romantic," I said. "You'll never be married at this rate."

She laughed it off, but though she would never admit it, she knew there was a seed of truth in what I'd said.

"Are you sure?" the detective asked, interrupting my thoughts.

He took some photographs from his drawer and spread them across the table. One of them was of a beige handbag, which I recognized as my sister's. The handbag was soaking wet and covered in blood. The fabric was torn, and there were deep scratches all over it. Looking at it, I should have felt sad, but I didn't. I was numb.

I examined the rest of the photographs. Nothing unusual. Her wallet, a red scarf, keys with a dangling rabbit trinket, some medicine, a planner, and pens.

"Take a look at this." The detective pointed at the medicine. On closer inspection, it was a pack of birth control pills.

"And this." He singled out the photograph of the scarf. "What does it resemble to you?"

"A scarf," I answered, without giving the matter much thought.

"Forensics found one of her eyelashes on it. We also found deep marks on her wrists, as if they had been tied with a rope."

I felt a lump in my throat. "So she was blindfolded and tied up when she was killed?"

"Our investigation suggests that it happened well before the murder. From her injuries, it appears she tried to block her attacker with her handbag." He pursed his lips in thought for a moment. "I'm sorry to be insensitive, but it's my job to look at this from every angle."

I went silent, awaiting his next question.

"Is it possible that Miss Ishida was involved with some organization? Or a group engaging in . . . a certain sexual inclination?" He shifted his eyes awkwardly. "I only mean, she was attractive and, as you've mentioned, had no romantic ties."

The idea was so absurd, I withheld a laugh. "I knew her well enough. She didn't sleep around."

He sighed, but didn't press the subject any further. "She never mentioned anyone she liked?"

I struggled to recall anything of the sort from our years of weekly phone conversations.

"Maybe an ex-boyfriend?" he continued.

"There was a man," I said. "Around four years ago. I'm not sure if he was her boyfriend, but she told me she was spending a lot of time with someone."

The detective leaned forward and reached for his pen. "Tell me his name."

"She didn't say, but it was the only time she ever mentioned seeing a man. A few months later, they had a disagreement."

"What kind of disagreement?"

"I have no idea."

He tossed his pen back on the table. "What else do you know about this person?"

"He drives," I said. "They went on a few trips out of town together."

The detective scratched his chin. "Do you know where they went?"

"She never told me."

"Anything else?"

I shifted uncomfortably in my seat. I knew so little about my sister's friends, or the men she dated. She had never confided in me, but I'd never asked enough questions. Had I always been so uncaring?

"I'm sorry," I said. "I wish I could be of more help."

He turned off the tape recorder. "To be honest, it's the same with everyone I've spoken to. Her supervisor, her colleagues, her landlord. No one knows anything about her personal life. She must have been very private."

No, that wasn't it. My sister cared too much about the people around her; she was always the one asking after others, never putting herself at the center of the conversation.

Or maybe he was right. Maybe she *had* been a private person, and it was I who'd had it wrong the whole time. I mean, I didn't even understand why she'd been carrying birth control pills and a blindfold around in her handbag.

"We'll do our best," the detective said. "Call me if you think of anything that might help our investigation. Anything at all, just call me. Got it?"

I gave a vague nod. If this was their method of investigation, they would never solve the case.

"Do you have any questions for us?" he asked.

I had so many, I didn't know where to start. I still couldn't believe she was gone.

Three days earlier, I had received the call from the police. The next thing I knew, I was standing in front of her coffin. The undertaker had done a good job. She looked like she was sleeping.

"I would like to know what happened," I told the detective.

He tilted his head forward. "Meaning the details surrounding her death?"

"Yes."

"It's more or less what was in the papers," he said. "Miss Ishida was walking alone at night when she was assaulted with a sharp object. We found a bloodied knife at the crime scene, and her injuries are consistent with stab wounds. The DNA from the knife also matched hers."

Could it be? I cleared my throat. "May I see the knife?"

"It's a common kitchen knife."

He took out another photograph from his drawer. The knife, as he had said, was ordinary. Not the one I had in mind.

"Did you find any fingerprints?"

"Only your sister's."

"Is it possible that the knife was hers? Perhaps she was carrying it for self-defense, and the attacker snatched it."

He pursed his lips. "We can't discount the possibility, but Akakawa is a safe town. We have some petty crimes, but nothing that would warrant a young lady carrying around a knife for self-defense."

I kept quiet. If the town were so safe, then my sister would still be alive.

"Nothing was missing from her bag," the detective said. "Her wallet and jewelry were untouched. It didn't look like a case of robbery gone wrong. The attack was vicious."

I remembered a sentence from one of the newspaper articles I'd read: *Aside from her face, the victim was covered with severe stab wounds.* But I hadn't seen any of her injuries. As I stood next to the coffin, where she lay pale and composed, I wanted to shake her and shout, "Wake up, will you? What are you doing here?"

Keiko Ishida had always been so thoughtful and well liked. I didn't think anyone could hate her enough to kill her in such a gruesome way. Or was I wrong about her? If I had made an effort to understand my sister, could I have changed her fate?

It was too late for these questions to matter. Keiko Ishida had fallen into an irreversible sleep. Even a tsunami couldn't wake her from her eternal dream.

2

How
to
Make
Curry
Rice

I woke up at half past eight. Disheveled and still in the same suit I'd worn to the police station, I took a few seconds to remember I wasn't in Tokyo. Then the hunger hit. I would have preferred to sleep in and skip breakfast, but my body wouldn't compromise.

Although the guests could help themselves to tea, coffee, and orange juice in the lobby, the Katsuragi Hotel didn't serve breakfast. I'd seen only one other guest, a balding middle-aged man. Judging from his formal suit and beaten-up leather briefcase, he was probably on a business trip.

According to Honda, the hotel only used the first and second floors. The remaining three floors were empty.

"Don't worry, it's not haunted or anything," he had said. "There would just be no point to the additional upkeep. Akakawa isn't a tourist spot or business hub. No hot springs, beautiful parks, or green mountains. To be honest, I'm surprised a small operation like the Katsuragi Hotel has managed to last."

I guessed it had to do with their low overhead. I'd only seen two staff members during my stay. One was a svelte middle-aged lady who worked the reception desk. She wore a different kimono every day. The patterns were always simple, which made her look elegant and refined. The other employee was the cleaner. Her trolley of detergents and toilet paper rolls was her constant companion, following her like the faithful dog Hachiko.

My stomach growled again. Left without a choice, I begrudgingly got up, put on a fresh set of clothes, and headed out.

ALTHOUGH IT WAS MORNING rush hour, not many cars were on the road. Most of the commuters rode bicycles. No wonder the air felt cleaner than in Tokyo.

I walked to the convenience store at the end of the block. A bell pinged as I opened the glass door. The shop was small, with items cramped against each other on the shelves. I grabbed a tuna sandwich from the refrigerated section and went to the cashier, picking up the morning newspaper, and, on a whim, a *Guide to Akakawa* booklet.

A group of high school students entered as I left the store. One of them knocked into me, then apologized with a flustered face as the rest of her friends giggled. These schoolgirls brought back memories of my sister when she was their age. In those days, she and I always had convenience store food. Our parents were hardly at home; they refused to deal with each other or their failing marriage.

"If they hate each other so much, they shouldn't have gotten married in the first place," I told my sister as I helped her sort the laundry.

"They used to get along better," she said.

That must have been a long, long time ago, because I couldn't recall it at all. "Then how did things turn out this way?"

My sister took a deep breath. "The first quarrel was because of the hair. After Mother had you, her hair started to fall out. One morning, Father casually mentioned that the loose hair was clogging the bathroom drain. Mother snapped and screamed at him. They shouted at each other, and Father walked off."

"I don't remember any of that."

She loaded the light-colored laundry into the washing machine. "You wouldn't. You were still a baby. You cried because of the yelling, but Mother wouldn't pick you up, and I was too scared to approach her."

"Did Mother become bald?"

She laughed and pressed the start button. "It wasn't that bad."

"What happened next?"

"I thought everything would be fine when Father returned home the next morning, but I was wrong," she said. "His company was going through a difficult period, and it looked like he was going to lose his job. Things went downhill after that first argument. He would get angry at the tiniest things, like when the meat was slightly overcooked, or he found the smallest crease in his shirt."

"So Father is to blame?"

"Not really, Mother played a part too. She was too emotional," my sister said. "But I admit, I might be a little biased. I'm closer to Father. He's always been nicer to me than Mother. Sometimes I feel like Mother picked on me unfairly. Am I being oversensitive?"

"Maybe." I looked down. "So I'm the cause of their problems."

She tilted her head. "What makes you say that?"

"You said their first argument was after she had given birth to me."

"Don't be silly, Ren. It's not your fault." She patted my head.

"Don't you *ever* think about it that way. You just happened to be born during a difficult time."

"But Father has a good job now, so why are they still quarrelling?"

"Maybe they've become used to arguing. Both of them are so stubborn. If only they would learn to make peace with each other. Sometimes it's all right to agree to disagree."

"You should tell them."

"Yes, I should."

To be honest, even when I was only eight, I knew my sister would never dare to confront our parents. We kept our thoughts to ourselves. We hoped these problems would disappear on their own if we ignored them long enough, but that wasn't the case.

Things got worse. Both of them avoided home. Father often returned past midnight, staggering in reeking of alcohol and sweat. Mother spent her time playing mahjong or singing karaoke at her friends' places. On the rare occasions when both of them were home, they shouted at each other and threw things.

When that happened, I slipped into my sister's room and we played board games. We pretended not to hear the loud noises. She remained silent, as did I.

MOTHER EVENTUALLY STOPPED COOKING, and we ended up eating takeaway food from the convenience store. She would leave money next to the TV console, and my sister was in charge of buying the meal. It couldn't have been easy for her either, but one day I decided I'd had enough.

"I'm not eating," I told her when she placed the two lunch boxes on the table.

"Not hungry?" she asked.

"Not for this. Seriously, who eats takeaway food every day?"

She forced a smile. "But today is the special eel set. Or if you want, you can have my chicken set instead."

"I don't want either of them."

Her smile disappeared. "Ren, don't be—"

"I said I'm not eating!" I shouted.

"Fine, suit yourself." She opened my lunch box and snapped her wooden chopsticks apart. "Are you sure?"

I kept quiet and clenched my fists. She wouldn't be able to talk me out of this. My sister took a bite of the eel before putting down her chopsticks. Her expression hardened. I flinched, thinking she was going to yell at me.

"You know what, I think you're right. I'm sick of this too." She smiled. "Let's get ingredients. I'll cook something."

I thought I'd heard her incorrectly. "What did you say?"

"I said I'll cook something," she repeated. "Put on your shoes. We're going to the supermarket."

It was already dark when we left the house. When we reached the neighborhood market, a few of the shelves were almost empty, but it didn't dampen our mood. That night was the most exciting trip to a supermarket I've ever experienced. I remember grinning as we walked through the vegetable section.

"What do you want for dinner?" my sister asked.

"Curry rice," I answered. It was one of my favorite dishes.

"All right. I'll cook the most delicious curry rice you've ever tasted in your life."

Then it occurred to me that I'd never seen her cook. "Do you know how to make it?"

"Of course," she said without hesitation, filling the basket with various ingredients.

The problems started when she tried to cook the rice. The first batch was still uncooked, the second one watery. I watched her struggle with the rice cooker for over an hour. It was so late I was no longer hungry.

"Do you know how to use the rice cooker?" I asked.

"Give me some time. The setting is different from the one I use in home economics," she said. "I wonder where the instruction manual is."

My sister checked the cabinets one by one but couldn't find it. Looking at her, I felt bad for shouting earlier. I wanted to apologize, but she spoke first.

"I'm sorry, Ren. You must be starving."

I lowered my head. Her words made me feel worse. I didn't want to cry, but I couldn't control it. I wiped my tears away, but they kept on coming.

"Don't cry," she said, "I will cook you something."

Her voice was shaky. When I looked up, I realized her eyes were red and swollen.

"Stupid, you're crying too," I said.

She wiped her tears. "Shut up."

A pain rose in my chest. I had never seen my sister cry before. She was always mature and composed. Averting my eyes, I went to the bathroom and washed my face.

When I returned, the rice was cooked, warm and fluffy. My sister was smiling and humming. I breathed a sigh of relief. She heated some oil in the pot to sauté the onions. Her movements were slow and clumsy. She wasn't good at it, yet she kept telling me everything was under control in a cheerful voice. I sat on my chair and watched her back. She looked smaller than usual. By the time she finished cooking, it was already ten.

She placed the curry on the table. "Give it a try. Tell me what you think."

I examined her masterpiece. It looked like mushy potato and

carrot soup with floating meat chunks. She took a plate and scooped the rice onto it, then poured the curry on top. The food was still steaming, but I dug in my spoon and ate.

"How is it?" she asked, eyes gleaming.

I gave a thumbs-up. "Delicious."

"Really?"

I nodded. Her satisfied smile was all I cared about. "How about you? Why aren't you eating?"

"Later," she said. "I want to watch you eat first. You look so happy."

"It's good, so of course I'm happy." I took another big scoop. "Can you cook again next time?"

"No problem. Starting now, I'll cook every single day. What else do you want to eat?"

"I'll eat anything you cook if it's as good as this."

She blushed. I don't remember how the food tasted, but I know it felt good.

My sister went out and bought a few cookbooks the next day. As time went by, she got better and better. Her dishes were simple, but they never failed to give me a warm feeling. I owed it to her for making the house feel like home.

For her twentieth birthday, I bought her a kitchen knife. A chef's knife with a wooden handle and white bolster, the most expensive gift I've ever bought anyone. She used it every day and took it with her the day she left Tokyo.

WHEN THE DETECTIVE MENTIONED the knife, I thought about the one I had given my sister. It was probably still in her rented room. A few months ago she told me she had moved out of her previous apartment. She hadn't given me her new address, but her workplace would have it. I should give them a call anyway, to see if there were any personal belongings to collect.

My watch showed nine-fifteen. Cram school wouldn't be open so early.

I returned to the hotel and got myself a cup of coffee in the lobby. Settling into one of the chairs, I glanced at the cleaning lady. She ignored me when I took out the packed sandwich. Peeling the plastic seal off, I sank my teeth into the soft bread. The celery was cold and crunchy, the tuna filling oozing out the sides. Tasty. My coffee was still steaming by the time I'd guzzled the last crumbs, so I picked up a newspaper and skimmed the headlines.

Two masked men on a motorbike had stolen a purse, but the owner reported that the only thing inside was a bible. An article on road safety, and another one about the opening of a shopping mall. Nothing memorable. As the detective had said, Akakawa was a safe town. I couldn't find anything about the murder. People moved on so quickly.

I put the newspaper back into its plastic bag and took out the guidebook. The first page had a pop-up city map full of colorful icons. I found a useful list of bus routes. Next were a few pages about the town's highlights: temples, historical buildings, public parks, and shopping districts. The town had a total area of 252,136 square kilometers and was located on high ground. No wonder I felt chilly.

I had always wondered why my sister had chosen Akakawa, of all places. She had never been here before. I'd wanted to ask her, but it was never a good time somehow.

Flipping the pages, I saw a lot of education-related advertisements. A hostel for students, a few cram schools, a private music teacher, and two specialized English courses. She had probably seen the job opportunities and decided to try teaching.

I reached for my coffee again, but it was already cold. I threw it away and returned to my room to rest.

WHEN I CAME DOWN to the lobby at one o'clock, no one else was there. A desktop pay phone was perched at the edge of the counter. I inserted a coin into the slot and dialed my sister's workplace. My palms began to sweat. Since my sister's death, I'd avoided making phone calls; they reminded me of her, and I almost expected to hear her voice. Luckily, I didn't have to wait long. A woman with a cheery voice answered after the first ring.

"Thank you for calling Yotsuba," she said. "This is Abe speaking. How may I help you?"

"I'm Ren Ishida," I said, "Keiko Ishida's younger brother."

A brief silence followed before she said, "I'm so sorry about what happened to Miss Ishida. Is there anything I can do for you?"

"May I come over to pick up her personal belongings? And do you happen to have her home address on file? I understand she had recently moved."

"Please give me a moment."

She must have covered the receiver with her hand, because I could hear muffled voices in the background. She was talking to another woman.

"Mr. Ishida?"

"Yes."

"You can come tomorrow any time after one. We close at nine."

"Thank you."

I put down the phone and saw the kimono lady behind the counter. Had she heard me talking on the phone? The murder case would have been all over the local news last week.

The woman bowed to me. "Good afternoon."

If she had heard my conversation, she was very professional about it. I couldn't detect the tiniest shift in her serious expression, which matched the somber tone of her kimono. I relaxed, comforted by her apparent lack of interest.

"Erm."

I made the noise out loud without realizing, and now she was looking at me.

"I was wondering if you were familiar with the recent murder case. The victim was someone I knew," I said.

"So you're here for the funeral."

I nodded.

"Please, wait a minute." She disappeared into her back office and returned with a newspaper from a few days prior. "Here, you can keep it."

"Thank you." I took the newspaper. The murder article splashed across the whole front page. I put it under my arm while trying to maintain my composure. "My apologies, you are . . . ?"

The kimono lady smiled. "I'm Natsumi Katsuragi. Let me know if there's anything else you need."

I thanked her again and headed out for lunch at the nearby café. On my way back, I dropped by the convenience store and stocked up on instant noodles.

Thunder rolled across the ashen gray sky as I left the store. I hurried back and reached the hotel just before it began pouring. The tension and miserable weather had exhausted me. I returned to my room for a nap. Six hours later, hunger woke me again. Filling one of the ramen cups with hot water from the bathroom, I waited for the noodles to soften.

The rain was still heavy when I dragged the curtains open. If it carried on like this, I would never get anything done. Tomorrow, I decided, regardless of the weather, I'd head out to the place where my sister had died. I never gave a thought to what might be waiting.

3

The Man She Loved Had the Smell of Cigarette Smoke

Gray clouds loomed in the sky, blocking the rising sun. The dark asphalt road glistened in the aftermath of yesterday's downpour. I opened the guidebook and studied the map of Akakawa before slipping it inside my parka.

A well-dressed lady in front of me teetered in her high heels. The pavement was narrow so I had to match her pace. I looked around at the row of still-closed shops. Nothing seemed familiar. Then again, I'd only visited the town once for a few hours, and that was seven years ago.

On a windy day in April, my sister had picked me up at the train station. We went for a short walk before settling at a nearby café. I'd told my mother I was going to a friend's house to study, so I could only stay for a few hours.

While we waited for our order to come, my sister asked about my studies. Mostly, I gave one-word answers. School was nothing more than a routine.

Then she asked, "So, do you have a girlfriend yet?"

"I do," I answered. Just like most seventeen-year-olds.

She looked surprised. "Why didn't you tell me?"

"I'm telling you now, aren't I?"

I didn't bother mentioning that I'd already dated several girls, even before she'd left Tokyo. I wasn't trying to hide it. She had never asked, and I didn't see the need to bring it up.

"What does she look like?" my sister asked.

I shrugged. "She's okay."

"Promise me you'll introduce her to me soon."

"All right."

I never fulfilled this promise. In the end, I broke up with that girl before my sister had the chance to meet her, and it was the same with all the other girls until Nae.

Nae was different. I told my sister about her before she asked. I had wanted them to meet. But now, my sister was gone, and I was in a bad situation with Nae. I hadn't spoken to her since the Italian restaurant incident. My sister's death had made our argument seem distant, unimportant. I didn't feel like talking to Nae, or anyone. I wanted to be left alone, all by myself, in this unfamiliar town.

I WENT TO A flower shop—just a short walk from the Katsuragi Hotel—and asked the florist for lavender, my sister's favorite flower.

"I'm sorry, but we don't have that," she said. "May I know the occasion? Or perhaps who the flowers are for?"

I hesitated before answering. "They're for a woman."

Her face brightened. "A special lady? Let me see." She picked up a bunch of tiny white flowers. "How about baby's breath? They symbolize everlasting love."

I smiled. "Okay, I'll get those."

The florist arranged them into a bouquet and tied that with a satin ribbon.

Walking out of the shop, I felt a nip in the air. I could hear thunder in the distance. How could I forget it was already June? The six-week rainy season had started. I thrust my hands into my pockets and quickened my pace.

I walked for another fifteen minutes before reaching a wide, gradually declining slope. On one side of it was a deep valley, and on the other lush greenery. Perhaps it was because I was early, but not a single vehicle passed by. From where I stood, it looked as if the path went on forever, but having seen the map, I knew the road would bend left toward the end and merge with the highway.

The police had put up a sign calling for witnesses in the exact spot where my sister had died. Realistically, what were the odds? If anyone had seen the murder, they would have gone to the police long ago, unless they didn't want to get involved. If that were the case, they would never come forward, no matter what the sign said.

Life was such a mystery to me. Who would have guessed that my sister, of all people, would have gone so early, and so tragically? Though I hadn't seen her in seven years, she was still the person closest to me. No one could ever take her place. My life would never be the same again.

I crouched and placed the bouquet on the ground. A white trail of smoke rose up from behind the sign. What was that? I leaned forward to take a closer look. On the damp soil lay a Seven Stars cigarette.

MY SISTER USED TO love a man who smoked Seven Stars, though I wouldn't have known he was a smoker if it hadn't been for her.

Mr. Tsuda was my homeroom teacher in the third grade. He was the youngest teacher in school, and one of the few who used tricks to make the lessons fun. It was no surprise he was popular.

My sister first met him when she went to my school to collect my report card.

"Ren, you did a great job," she said on the way home. She always said that, regardless of the marks I got.

"Thanks for coming," I said.

"Don't mention it." She ruffled my hair. "It's what all big sisters do."

I brushed her off. "Stop that." I knew she was lying. I hated my parents for making her do their duty, but I didn't want to trouble my sister, so I said nothing.

"Your teacher seems understanding," she said. "He didn't ask any unnecessary questions when he saw me."

"Yeah, he's not bad."

"Mr. Tsuda looks too young to be a teacher. Do you know how old he is?"

"He's thirty-three."

"You know, he's exactly my type. Tall, nice, with a friendly smile."

I stopped walking. "Don't tell me you like him."

"Come on, you said he's not bad."

"He's too old."

She shrugged. "Age is just a number."

"And he's getting married soon."

"Is that so?" She sighed, though she didn't look too disappointed. "Too bad, but I guess it would be surprising for someone like him not to have a girlfriend."

"It's not like he would like you. To him, you're just a kid."

She nudged me. "Don't be rude."

I glared at her, but I didn't give much thought to the conversation afterward.

When a classmate told me he had seen my sister with Mr. Tsuda,

I dismissed him. "You must have mistaken someone else for her," I said. Soon, several of my schoolmates told me they had seen them together. But still, I thought there was no way she would ever go out with him. By then, Mr. Tsuda was married. My sister wasn't the type to play around. It had to be a misunderstanding.

ONE DAY, I SAW Mr. Tsuda and my sister together in a café in Koenji. They were laughing and smiling, not realizing I stood right across the street.

I didn't know my sister drank coffee. And Mr. Tsuda looked different. Instead of his usual formal clothes, he was in a T-shirt and jeans. But most disturbing of all was the look on my sister's face. I'd never seen her so happy. She was different from her usual self, and I didn't like it.

Years later, I recognized this as the look of someone in love. But at the time, I didn't know any better. Standing wide-eyed in the middle of the street, I felt like an invisible hand was stirring and knotting my gut. I couldn't confront them. My feet were heavy. I went back home as if I'd never seen them, but the memory constantly returned.

Whenever I saw Mr. Tsuda at school, the scene would replay itself in my mind and the awful feeling would return. I tried not to think about it, but it was no use. I figured I might as well bring it up.

"Do you still like Mr. Tsuda?" I asked my sister.

We were having beef spaghetti for lunch, just the two of us. It seemed like the right time. Funny how I still remember what we ate that day after all these years.

Her expression didn't change. "Why do you ask?"

"You told me he was your type."

"He *is* my type. Don't you think we would make a good couple?"

I was quiet, but she continued to look at me, awaiting a response. She was challenging me.

"He's old." I twisted the spaghetti around my fork. "It'd look like you were dating your father."

"Don't be silly. For that to happen, he'd have to have become a father at sixteen."

"You just admitted he's almost twice your age."

"It's not such a great difference when you're older," she insisted. "Like a fifty-three-year-old woman and a sixty-nine-year-old man."

I couldn't believe she'd said that. "But you're seventeen, and he's thirty-three. It's disgusting."

She stared at me.

"And he's married," I added.

My sister stood abruptly and left. I shrugged and continued eating. In my mind, I'd stopped her from sinking deeper into a problematic relationship. Some things are not meant to be.

The next day, she acted as if we never had the conversation. She said nothing, and I said nothing. Neither of us brought it up again. Everything was good, or so I thought, until a few weeks later when she cooked an extra portion during lunch.

"I can't join you for dinner tonight," she said. "I've made curry rice. Can you heat it up yourself?"

I nodded. "I'll manage."

It was unusual for her not to have dinner with me, but it didn't occur to me to ask where she was planning to go. I should have guessed something was amiss.

Around six o'clock, I reheated the food my sister had cooked. My plate looked small on the table, and the curry rice didn't taste as good as usual. I scraped half of it into the garbage bin before starting my homework. Spreading my books over the whole table,

I tried to fill up the empty spaces. I studied until I could no longer stay awake. She still wasn't home when I went to bed.

A NOISE WOKE ME up in the middle of the night.

I got up and traced it to the kitchen. The lights were off and the curtains were shut, but my eyes slowly adjusted to the darkness. My sister was sitting on the floor. I ran to her.

"What's wrong?" I asked.

"Nothing's wrong," she whispered. "I'm fine, Ren. Go back to sleep."

Even in the dark, I could see glistening streaks on her face. "Why are you crying?"

"I'm not." She wiped her face with her wrists. "I'm not crying."

"What happened?"

"Nothing."

I clenched my fists. "It's him, isn't it?"

She didn't answer, but continued crying. I returned to my room and got dressed. I was on my way out when my sister grabbed my arm.

"Where are you going?" she asked.

"I'm going to find Mr. Tsuda," I said. "I'll make him apologize."

She looked down. "Ren, he's done nothing wrong. It was my idea, and I have no regrets. No one needs to apologize, so please don't make things more complicated than they are."

I tried to pull my hand away, but she held on tightly. I wondered where that strength came from. She wasn't much bigger than me.

We stood near the door. Neither of us said a word. The cicadas were loud in the warm summer night.

"Let go of my hand, will you?" I eventually said. "I won't go anywhere."

My sister released her grip and we returned to the kitchen. She sat at the table and buried her face in her arms. She didn't make any sound, but her shoulders were shaking.

What was I supposed to do? Should I have wrapped my arms around her shoulders? That would have been awkward, so in the end, I did nothing.

That night, she cried herself out without a sound. I'd never seen anyone cry like that before, not even in a television drama. It must have been a few years' worth of tears.

When the sun shone through the gaps of the thick brocade curtain, she wiped her face and asked me, "What time is it?"

I glanced at the clock behind her. "A quarter past five." Parroting her usual question, I asked her, "Tell me, did you learn anything?"

She mustered a smile. "I learned that he smokes Seven Stars."

"You're weird," I said, "or stupid, or maybe both. You're weird and stupid."

My sister burst into laughter. Her expression told me she was sad and happy at the same time.

She got up and stretched. "Can I make you some breakfast?"

"Yes, please," I said, feeling glad the night was over. "And it'd better be good. Thanks to you, I didn't get enough sleep."

My sister laughed and cooked omurice. She drew a smiley face with the ketchup, and that image helped me graduate from elementary school without punching my math teacher.

I KNEW MR. TSUDA didn't have anything to do with her any more. I doubted he knew she had left Tokyo, let alone that she was dead. He might not even remember her. Yet the Seven Stars cigarette brought a strange comfort.

The cigarette was halfway burnt. Whoever left it had been there not long ago. I looked around but saw no one.

Across the valley stood rows of modern two-story houses. All bland and compact, with hipped roofs and stone garden walls, they gave only a passing nod to traditional Japanese architecture.

I imagined a family of four living inside one of those houses. Father, mother, and two children. The father was a surgeon, and the mother was a housewife who loved baking cookies. The older daughter played the piano, the younger son loved Verdy Kawasaki. How did it feel to be a part of a picture-perfect family? If we had been born into such a family, would my sister still be around?

Drops of water pattered onto my skin. Ominous black clouds covered the sky and the rumbles of thunder signaled an approaching downpour.

I flicked up the hood of my parka and ran down the slope to a gazebo overlooking the valley. I wasn't the only one seeking shelter. A girl in a white pullover and black leggings was already there. Her long, wavy hair fluttered in the strengthening wind. I smiled at her, but she turned away. Sitting on the bench, I wiped droplets of water off my hands. The rain was getting heavier. It didn't look like it was going to stop anytime soon.

The girl took a box of Seven Stars from her pocket. My heart skipped a beat. Could she be the one whose cigarette I had seen earlier? She put one to her lips and lit it with a gold Zippo lighter. Narrowing her eyes, she took a deep puff. The smell of tobacco mingled with the scent of rain. She blew the smoke straight into the wall of rain a few inches from her face, twisting the cigarette between her long, slim fingers. She was a real beauty. Mid-twenties? Early twenties? No, even younger, too young to be smoking.

She looked at me and I averted my eyes. My palms had begun to sweat, so I wiped them inside my pockets.

"Want one?" she asked.

I shook my head. "I don't smoke." I'd tried it a few times in high school, but it reminded me of Mr. Tsuda, so I could never bring myself to enjoy it.

The girl continued to smoke facing the rain. Maybe it was the atmosphere, but she seemed shrouded in an air of elegance. I couldn't take my eyes off her.

When the cigarette was almost finished, she dropped it on the floor and used her Converse sneaker to crush it. Then she lit another. She did it over and over. A chain smoker. I counted eight cigarettes in total. She walked away when the rain was about to stop. Left alone, I lingered for a while before returning to the hotel.

Somehow, I was unable to shake her presence from my mind. If I didn't know better, I would've mistaken it for love at first sight. But no, it wasn't that simple.

4

How
I
Ended
Up
at
Yotsuba

My sister had worked in a four-story building of an educational complex. It would be hard to miss the place. A huge sign in front bore the name YOTSUBA, and testimonials from successful students were displayed prominently behind the glass panels.

A group of girls in sailor uniforms entered the school. I took a deep breath and followed them. When the automatic glass door opened, a gust of cold air blew into my face. I detected the scent of jasmine.

The reception area was filled with a couple of plastic chairs and a two-seater sofa. A plump older lady sat behind the counter.

"Miss Abe?" I asked.

She stood and looked at me through her glasses. "Are you Mr. Ishida?"

"Yes." I mustered a smile.

She stepped forward past the counter. "I'll take you to the office."

We climbed all the way up the staircase, jostling against the students. They were laughing and teasing each other, alive and carefree. I found it strange I'd once been like them.

The fourth floor was an open office area. Low dividers separated rows of desks piled with books and papers. My sister's workspace was located near the window. Compared to the others, her desk was neat and tidy, but it looked impersonal. Not a single photograph or plush toy. No one would be able to guess she used to occupy the place. Anyone could have sat there.

"Take your time," Abe said. "If you want anything to drink, feel free to help yourself from the faculty lounge. The principal is still in a meeting. As soon as he's done, he'll get Miss Ishida's file for you."

"Thank you," I said.

She bowed and took her leave.

Sitting at my sister's desk, I flipped through her documents. Teaching handbooks, student worksheets, and notebooks. Which ones were hers, and which belonged to her workplace? I had no idea what to take and what to leave.

I stood to stretch, only to realize people were staring at me. One of them was a petite woman sitting nearby. When our eyes met, she quickly shifted her gaze down to her keyboard. They all kept their heads low, and it suddenly felt like I was the one watching them. Taking a deep breath, I returned to my seat. I could still feel their sidelong glances.

Whenever people look at me, I become uneasy. I'd never realized it until my sister pointed it out. Almost fourteen years ago, she had taken me to Ueno Zoo on my tenth birthday, just the two of us. We watched a sea lion bask in the sun atop a stone platform.

"Do you think the animals hate us?" my sister asked.

I shrugged. "Why would they?"

"Look at this sea lion. He lives in a confined space, all eyes on him. Wouldn't it be uncomfortable to have so many people staring at you every day?"

She turned to me and I looked away.

"Especially for you, Ren," my sister said. "Whenever people look at you, you get nervous and avert your eyes."

"I'm not nervous. I just don't like being stared at," I said. "And these animals have a good life, sleeping and eating the whole day. No homework or exams to worry about. They shouldn't complain."

She put her arm around my shoulders. "You've got a point."

Another sea lion leapt up onto the platform from the water and looked over at the visitors before diving in again.

"Maybe to them, a zoo is a place where animals see human exhibits," she continued. Even then, my sister had her own way of thinking.

I WENT OVER TO the petite woman.

"Excuse me," I said, startling her. "I'm sorry to disturb you, but can you tell me where the faculty lounge is?"

"Umm, go straight then turn left." She pointed toward a doorway flanked by two battered file cabinets.

As I walked, I felt the eyes of my sister's former coworkers following me. Most only snuck a quick peek, but a few openly stared. I wiped my sweaty palms on my trousers.

The faculty lounge itself was pretty basic: a small table, a sink, a water dispenser, and a mini fridge, but no chair to sit on. A box of Sencha sachets and a jar filled with packets of instant coffee sat on the table.

"Need help?"

I turned around and saw a woman holding a Hard Rock Café mug. She wore a white blouse paired with a beige pencil skirt, and her hair was tied in a high ponytail.

"Is there a cup I can use?" I asked.

"Of course." She bent down and opened the cabinet under the counter, revealing a dozen ceramic cups. "If I were you, I would rinse it first. You never know who used it last, or whether they cleaned it properly."

I took one cup and ran it under the tap. I couldn't find a towel to dry it, so I gave it a couple of shakes over the sink.

The woman rinsed her mug next to me. "You must be Keiko's younger brother."

Unsure of what to say, I simply nodded and reached for the instant coffee.

"I'm sorry to hear about what happened. She was such a sweet person," she said. "Are you a teacher, too?"

"I'm still in school." I filled the cup with hot water from the dispenser. "I'm finishing my graduate studies."

"Must be busy. How long are you planning to stay?"

"Maybe a couple of weeks. I've submitted my thesis, so I can afford to take a break." She had smooth skin and a radiant complexion; I guessed she was in her thirties. "Are you a teacher here?"

She sighed. "Yes, but only as of very recently."

I hadn't expected her to be new, since she'd referred to my sister by her first name. Only lovers and close friends did that.

"What are you studying?" she asked.

"British and American Literature," I answered. The same as my sister.

Her eyes widened. "Are you studying at Keio, too?"

"Yes. Are you an alumna?"

"No, it's not that." She flashed me a wide smile. "Say, would you consider working here?"

This caught me by surprise.

"Don't give me that stunned look," she teased. "Keiko was one of our few permanent teachers. She was in charge of most English classes. We've tried to divide her work among ourselves, but each of us already has plenty of things to handle. It would be great if you could join us on a temporary basis as a teacher. We should be able to find a permanent replacement by the winter break."

"Umm . . ."

She tilted her head. "You don't like the idea?"

"It's a bit sudden, isn't it?"

"I know, but we're having a tough time." She didn't bother hiding her feelings. "It's not a bad deal. The pay is decent, I can assure you. Keiko was a senior staff member, so she had Sundays off. If the job is unsuitable, you can just quit. But I'm sure you'll do well. Younger teachers are always popular amongst the students."

I was at a loss for words. "It sounds like a great plan, but the school's owner might not want to hire me."

"Don't worry, the owner's getting desperate," she said, laughing.

She made it sound like an offer with no downsides. I had to admit, it sounded better than spending my days eating and lying around like a sea lion.

I creased my brow. "So you'll introduce me to the owner and . . ."

"Head over to the principal's office after you finish your coffee. It's right around the corner, behind the tall partition. I'll go talk to him now." She took her mug and walked off. Before she left, she turned and said, "I'm the owner, by the way."

Oh, nice.

I took a sip of the coffee. It tasted horrible.

To call the principal's room an office was an overstatement. In truth, it was a small section of the fourth floor, walled by moveable panels.

The principal was a middle-aged man with white hair—more likely from genetics than a stressful lifestyle—but what caught my eye was the potted plant on top of his desk. I'd never seen anything like it, with its bright, peculiar multicolored leaves.

"You must be Ren Ishida." He gestured to me to take a seat. "I've heard from Hiroko that you're finishing up your graduate studies at Keio."

"Yes."

"Excellent. Keio is a top university. You can't go wrong with Ryutaro Hashimoto's alma mater. Personally, I think he's going to be the next prime minister." The principal opened his desk drawer and rummaged through it. "Can you start a week from tomorrow?"

That was *very* soon. I didn't even have a permanent place to stay yet. "Would it be possible to start on Wednesday instead?"

"Wednesday it is." He singled out two identical copies of a booklet and opened one. Pressing the spine, he placed it on the desk and drew a tiny X. "Please sign here."

He wanted me to sign the contract without reading it? Against my better judgment, I did as instructed. The principal took the copy I had signed and handed me the other.

"I almost forgot." He removed a folder from the same drawer. "Here is Keiko's file."

"Thank you."

He gave me a firm handshake. "Welcome to Yotsuba. We'll see you next week. Please arrive before two-thirty."

And that was it. I had my first white-collar job. In the end, I didn't take home a single item from my sister's desk.

HONDA CALLED ME THAT evening.

"I hear you'll be working with us," he said, sounding upbeat.

I laughed. "A surprising turn of events, don't you think? It'll just be for a few months."

"Give it a try. You might end up liking the job."

"Maybe," I said. "Is the owner really that lady, Hiroko?"

"In a way, yes. Why do you ask?"

"She looks young."

"The school is a family business founded by her grandfather," he said. "Her father used to run the business. Recently, he was unwell, so Hiroko took over. But don't worry—despite her age, she's capable of doing the job."

So it was a position she'd inherited, not one she'd chosen. "I'm not worried. Just curious."

"So she was the one who recruited you? Well, she's been telling us we need to hire more young, handsome men to motivate the female students. Most of the male teachers are way past their prime."

I replied with a dry laugh.

"Hey Ishida, are you free this coming Sunday? It's my day off. Let's go for lunch to celebrate your new job."

I sighed. "Sunday isn't good. I have an appointment in the morning with my sister's landlord, so I can collect her belongings. I'm not sure what time I'll be done."

"I can drive you. It's easier to move things with a car."

Honda had been extremely helpful, but I didn't want to trouble him further. "It's all right, I can take a taxi."

"Don't waste your money. I've got nothing planned, anyway. Or how about this, you can treat me to lunch afterward."

It didn't sound as if he would take no for an answer. "If it's not too much trouble."

"No problem at all," he said. "Where's the place?"

I took out the paper in my wallet with my sister's address scribbled on it in my hastiest handwriting. "It's in Segayaki."

"Segayaki?" He sounded surprised. "That's quite an upscale district. I wouldn't have guessed Keiko lived there. Her landlord must be wealthy."

"Someone named Kosugi Katou," I murmured, staring at the piece of paper.

"Kosugi Katou?" Honda said, his voice slightly raised. "You must be kidding."

"Do you know him?"

"Of course I do. Everyone in Akakawa knows him."

"Is he a celebrity?"

He laughed. "I guess you could say that."

5

The Politician and His Wife

Kosugi Katou was, indeed, a kind of celebrity.

"He's a politician. Everyone here knows who he is. He comes from a family of high-ranking officials and established politicians," Honda said. "Have you heard of Ryu Katou, the Diet member? That's his uncle."

The name sounded familiar, but I wasn't into politics.

"Look at this house. It's huge."

I nodded and pressed the doorbell. We stood in front of a white, Western-style terrace house located in a pleasant neighborhood, peaceful and quiet.

The door opened and a middle-aged man greeted us. He wore a crumpled formal dark suit, oddly paired with beige house slippers. I caught a glimpse of thick white socks around his ankles.

Kosugi Katou looked unhappy that we had turned up at his house. But after a while, I realized it was just the deep wrinkles around his forehead, causing him to look perpetually grumpy. We introduced ourselves. He nodded once before beckoning us in. A man of few words apparently. We took our shoes off and followed him.

The living room was spacious. All the furniture was Western-style and painted or upholstered in white. The giant windows were adorned with thin lace curtains. They waved around as the wind blew, reminding me of goldfish tails.

Walking through a passageway, we passed a reading room and a home office. Rows of oil paintings hung on the wall. All were pictures of rural landscapes, and judging from the similar style, they were done by the same person.

"Did you paint these yourself, Mr. Katou?" Honda asked.

"No, my wife did," he answered, the first time he'd spoken.

His tone was exactly the same as the one he'd used on the phone, flat and serious. He came across as cold to me. I heard somewhere that politicians are the loneliest people on the planet. There must be some truth to it.

The room my sister had occupied was spacious for one person. A bed with a matching nightstand stood in the middle of the room, both adorned with stencils of English roses. There was also a white wooden wardrobe near the door and a desk over by the window, exactly as I had always pictured. My chest felt heavy.

"I'll be in the reading room," Mr. Katou said before leaving us alone.

We stood there awkwardly and looked at each other.

"So, what's the plan?" Honda asked.

"I'll sort through her belongings," I said. "Most of them will probably go to charity."

"Are you sure your folks at home won't want her stuff?"

I thought about my parents. "No, I don't think so." They would want nothing to do with her, or her memories.

I started with the wardrobe. It had a main compartment, a shelf on top, and a drawer below. Formal dresses filled the compartment. My sister had hung them by color. Black to gray to white, followed by brown and beige, and finally, the more brightly colored ones. A systematic, yet appealing arrangement. Beneath that, blouses, T-shirts, and pajamas were folded neatly and divided into four stacks. Most of her clothes looked completely unfamiliar, which reminded me how little we had seen each other after she'd moved to Akakawa.

I noticed that my sister hadn't owned any pants or shorts. I tried to recall whether I'd ever seen her wear any. No, I never had, except for her school sports uniform.

On the shelf, she kept towels, bedsheets, and handbags. She had stuffed all her bags with tissue paper for them to retain their shapes. I knew my sister had always been organized, but was surprised by this level of meticulousness.

I opened the drawer below and found underwear, stockings, and scarves. They were also ordered by color. Remembering what the detective had said, I shuddered at the thought that the scarves might have been used as blindfolds. Would it be better if I'd never known that?

As I was about to close the drawer, I caught a glimpse of something shiny amidst the rolled stockings. I took it out for a closer look. A half-empty bottle of Estée Lauder perfume. I opened the cap and sniffed it. It had a cool, musky scent, a classic American elegance. The fragrance reminded me of the crispness of clean sheets on a breezy early summer day.

After the wardrobe, I moved to the bedside table. The top drawer had a divider. The left side was filled with batteries and cables, while the right side contained several neat piles of jazz cassettes. I opened the door to the shelf below and found a stereo. I pictured my sister lying on her bed, listening to jazz with her eyes closed. I took a deep breath to quell my emotions.

The surface of the desk was empty, except for a study lamp

and a red phone. The phone was smooth and shiny, reflecting the sunlight. The side facing the window had faded, and the cord was slightly tangled. It was hard for me to look at. Just last week, my sister had used that phone to call me, and now she was gone.

"Are you okay?" Honda asked.

"Yes," I answered.

Pulling out the drawer on the left underneath, I found a couple of books and folders. I took them out and put them on the desk. They were all work-related.

"Do you think I need to return any of these?" I asked Honda.

He peered over my shoulder. "I doubt it. Everyone has a copy of their own. The school will give you a new set when you start working."

Still, I inspected them one by one. As I was flipping through one of the books, a piece of paper fell out. Something told me it might be important. Without looking at it, I slipped it into my pocket. I glanced at Honda, who was facing the other way and hadn't seen what I'd done.

I circled the room to make sure I hadn't missed anything. There was a rubbish bin under the desk and a laundry basket near the wardrobe; both were empty. That should be it.

"I'm done," I said.

"That was fast," Honda said. "What are you planning to keep?"

"Probably the stereo and jazz cassettes. I need some cardboard boxes to pack everything else."

"We have some of those at the office, but that means we can't finish up today. Why don't you talk to Mr. Katou to see if he minds?"

We left my sister's bedroom and went to the reading room. The gentle tinkle of wind chimes echoed through the house whenever the wind blew. I wouldn't have heard the sound if the place hadn't been so incredibly still.

"What's on your mind, Ishida?" Honda asked.

"It's so quiet here," I answered.

"I think it's because he doesn't have a television."

Now that Honda mentioned it, I hadn't seen one. But everyone had a television in this day and age. I figured it must be hidden inside one of the rooms.

But later on, I learned there really was no television. Mr. Katou had made the house his sanctuary, where he could be free from the pressures of the outside world. He'd gotten rid of anything that might upset him; he didn't want to be disrupted at home by news about his political rivals or recent changes in the cabinet. Indeed, politicians are the loneliest people on the planet.

The reading room was impressive for a private collection. Floor-to-ceiling bookshelves covered the walls. In the middle of the large room, four leather couches encircled a coffee table with a jeweled keepsake box on top.

Mr. Katou was on the couch reading a book. Seeing us, he put it down and invited us to sit. "Have you settled everything you needed to?"

"My apologies, but we came unprepared," I said. "Would you be willing to give us a few days? We'll return with cardboard boxes to pack the items."

"There's no rush, since the room isn't occupied."

"Is there any rent I need to settle?" I didn't have much money on me, but I figured I should ask.

"Don't worry, there was no rent in the first place."

"Excuse me?"

He was silent for a while. "I had an agreement with Miss Ishida."

I wondered what this implied, but he had stopped speaking, and I could tell he had no desire to talk about it. The atmosphere became tense. I turned to Honda, who was already looking at me. The three of us remained silent for some time.

"Is your wife at home?" Honda eventually asked.

The creases on Mr. Katou's forehead deepened. "Yes, she's here."

"We should greet her then."

"There's no need. She prefers to be alone."

"I see." Honda's voiced trailed off.

I took the time to look around at the bookshelves. The collection consisted of mostly English hardcovers, a set of English encyclopedia, and a few English-Japanese dictionaries. He must have an interest in the English language.

"You said you were Miss Ishida's colleague," Mr. Katou said to Honda. "By any chance, do you also teach English?"

"We were colleagues, but I teach math," Honda said.

"Do you like English literature?" I asked. "There are a lot of English books here."

Mr. Katou shook his head. "Those are my wife's."

"You should introduce Ishida to her," Honda said. "This young man here is studying British and American Literature at Keio."

"Is that true?"

I gave a slight nod. "Yes, but I'm graduating soon."

Mr. Katou kept his eyes on me. He looked as if he wanted to say something, but his lips remained shut. He made me uncomfortable. I excused myself to the restroom, just to get away.

Walking through the corridor, I looked at the oil paintings. They didn't seem like Japanese landscapes. Despite the fine technique, they were lifeless. They gave the impression of being copied from a calendar.

I stopped in front of the kitchen and peered through the glass door. No one was inside. On a whim, I pushed the door and entered.

The kitchen looked like it had been lifted straight from an interior design magazine. It was spotless, with not a single dirty dish or a drop of spilled food. I ran my fingers along the bottom of the shiny cabinets. I was about to open one when I heard the sounds of footsteps approaching. Turning around, I saw Mr. Katou. Was he angry that I'd wandered in here without permission? I couldn't tell; his expression remained unchanged.

"Your kitchen is so beautiful and clean," I said.

He nodded. "It's hardly used."

"Your wife doesn't cook?"

"Not now. She used to." He rubbed his nose. "Honda tells me you're going to be working at Yotsuba?"

"Yes, that's the plan for now."

"Where are you staying?"

"The Katsuragi Hotel."

He raised his eyebrows and nodded slowly, but I had the feeling he wasn't listening.

"Say, do you like this house?" he asked.

"Yes." I supposed if the owner of the house asked you the question, the answer should be yes no matter what, though I did like the place. "It's bright and airy."

"My wife used to work in a hospital. She insisted a house must have plenty of sunshine and air circulation." He paused before asking again, "Do you really like it here?"

"Yes, yes," I said, unsure why he kept pursuing the subject.

"I have a proposal," he said. "If you want, you can use any of our spare rooms in exchange for a favor."

I paused, waiting for him to explain.

"My wife has a condition that prevents her from leaving her bedroom. A cleaner comes twice a week to do the housework, but I still need to sort out her meals. It would be great if you could help her with lunch so I don't need to take time off from work on weekdays."

I was surprised by this revelation. Was this the arrangement he'd had with my sister? It made sense since she loved cooking, but it wouldn't do for me.

"Mr. Katou, I'm afraid I'm a terrible cook," I said.

"I'm not asking you to cook for her. You're welcome to use the kitchen if you want to, but otherwise, buying the lunch is fine."

I didn't know what to say. The idea was both logical and bizarre. Why would anyone invite a stranger he had just met to stay in his house?

"You might be thinking, if it's only lunch, why wouldn't I ask my secretary to do it? The truth is, there's something else. I need someone to read to her."

My brow furrowed, matching his. "Read to her?"

"My wife is fond of English books. She would be very happy to have someone read a few pages to her every day."

"Your wife, may I ask . . . ?" My voice trailed off.

"She's unwell, but her illness isn't contagious or life-threatening."

"I see." I nodded slowly, struggling to find an appropriate response. "Mr. Katou, your offer is generous, but you see, right now . . ."

"I don't expect you to decide right away." He cut me off. "But I would appreciate if you could give your answer soon."

We agreed to meet again the following Sunday. He gestured to me to follow him out, seeming to forget my original excuse of going to the restroom.

Before I left, Mr. Katou shook my hand and said, "I hope you'll consider my proposal seriously."

I could sense Honda looking at us.

Once we were both sitting in the car, he asked, "What proposal is he talking about?"

"Free lodging at his house," I answered.

Honda looked at me skeptically. "There's no such thing as free lodging."

"Well, not exactly free. He wants me to buy lunch for his wife, since she's sick and unable to go out on her own. Do you know her?"

"Not on a personal basis, but I've seen her a couple of times. She was always smiling. It's a small town, after all. Everyone knows everyone." He changed gears. I do remember hearing his wife suffers from depression. They had a young daughter, but she passed away a few years ago."

"I see."

"Ishida, you should take the offer. It does sound too good to be true, but someone like Mr. Katou wouldn't do anything dodgy that could ruin his reputation. News travels fast here."

"I'll think about it." Honda could be a little patronizing at times, perhaps because he was older than me.

"What are your reservations?"

"It's the house." I rested my left hand on the window. "I don't mind quiet, but something feels strange."

"The place is too neat and orderly, that's what makes it odd."

"What did you think of my sister's room?"

"It suits the kind of person she was."

I didn't disagree; Keiko had always been organized and focused. But her room was so cold and distant. People usually personalize their space with their favorite books, photographs, mementos. You can learn a lot about a person by looking at their bedrooms. They have the signature of their occupiers.

In contrast, my sister's room lacked color. Apart from those jazz cassettes and a bottle of perfume, there was no mark of individuality. The room, just like her office desk, was faceless, as if she had wanted to erase herself.

I thought about the job at Yotsuba and Mr. Katou's offer. If I traced the paths my sister had taken in life, maybe I would finally understand the things she had never said.

6

The
Missing
Knife
and the
Traffic
Light

In the privacy of my hotel room, I retrieved the paper I'd taken from my sister's bedroom. The page was crumpled, as if it had been read over and over again. I recognized the handwriting as hers.

She wrote:

Love comes when you least expect it. That's why people call it falling in love. You cannot learn to fall, nor do you ever plan to. You just happen to fall.

It captures you like a pitcher plant, in a split second. There's no room to think, let alone react. When you realize what has happened, you know there's no way to escape. You've already fallen too deep.

I stared at the paper. Had she come to Akakawa to chase after someone, or to escape them? But the fact that she'd left home after graduating shouldn't have come as a surprise. I'd always known it was coming.

ON HER NINETEENTH BIRTHDAY, my sister had bought nineteen birds from the pet shop. I recalled it well because I'd gone with her after we'd had dinner.

I couldn't remember what the birds were called, but they had black feathers. The pet shop owner put them in three birdcages. My sister carried two, and I carried the third. I had no idea what she was thinking. The birds weren't very attractive and made annoying noises.

After we left the shop, I couldn't contain my curiosity any longer and asked, "Why did you buy these?"

A faint smile played across her lips. "It's my birthday and I feel like buying birds."

"What do you need them for? They're so noisy. Mother will be angry, and I don't want to get involved."

Her smile vanished. "I'm not planning to bring them home."

"Are we going to eat them?"

"Don't be silly."

I followed her to a canal in the neighborhood. There were grassy fields on both sides of the water, where I often went to play soccer with my friends. In the afternoon, the place was full of joggers and children, but it was evening now, and the area was nearly empty.

We put down the birdcages and my sister opened them. We waited for the birds to fly away, but they didn't. They stayed put inside the open cages.

"Strange," my sister said, half-whispering. "Why don't they leave?"

She whistled to coax the birds out, but they didn't budge. She clapped her hands loudly. Still, nothing happened. Frustrated, my sister lifted one of the cages and shook it. One of the birds flew away. The rest followed. She watched them soar into the sky with a satisfied smile.

An old man who was walking his golden retriever came over and told her, "Young lady, you shouldn't release those birds. You're not doing them a favor. They don't know how to find food and shelter. They will die soon." After saying that, he walked off with his dog.

My sister looked upset.

"It might not be a bad thing." I tried to cheer her up. "Even if they die soon, they'll have lived a happier life than if they'd been caged for their entire lives. Plus, that old man is probably wrong. Birds adapt too, don't they?"

She didn't reply. We returned home in silence.

I often felt that incident was the catalyst.

Three years from that day, my sister packed her belongings and bought a one-way ticket to a place neither of us had ever been. Perhaps she wanted to free herself. And like those birds, she ended up dying too soon.

The day my sister left Tokyo, I returned from school to find the house in chaos. Loose papers, cutlery, broken plates and glasses scattered all over the floor. One of the table lamps was missing its shade. In the middle of the living room, my mother was sweeping the floor.

"What happened?" I asked. "What's with the mess?"

She ignored me and continued to clean.

I stood still near the door. I didn't dare to move. Tiny fragments of broken glass were everywhere. "Where's my sister?"

"What are you talking about, Ren?" She turned to me. "You're my only child."

Her answer sent shivers down my spine. I dashed to my sister's bedroom on the second floor. I opened the door, but she wasn't there. Some of her belongings lay on the bed and floor. The wardrobe door was open and half her clothes were gone. Reality came crashing in. My sister had left.

My knees felt weak. I sat on the floor of her room for hours, dumbfounded. I only came out when my mother called me for dinner. Surprisingly, she had cooked. She didn't say anything about Keiko, and I didn't ask either. I kept my head low the entire time I ate the miso ramen. I couldn't taste anything.

Eventually, my mother spoke. "Why are you still in your school uniform? It's already seven. Go and shower, I can smell your sweat."

LYING IN BED IN my hotel room, I went through the list of people I needed to contact.

Who would I need to inform? My parents, of course, though I doubted they cared. After my sister had left, it became an unspoken rule not to talk about her. I shouldn't need to report to Keio, since I'd completed all my assignments for the semester and was simply awaiting my diploma. What about Nae? I had to make up with her eventually, but I didn't think now was the right time. I decided for now that my parents would be all.

Initially I wanted to call them, but it was easier to write a letter. I went downstairs for an envelope and a few sheets of paper from the reception counter. The blank white pages were intimidating, but once I'd penned the first couple lines, the rest flowed easily.

To Father and Mother,
I trust both of you are well.

The wake, funeral, and cremation are complete. There are still some minor arrangements to be made, so I'm going to stay on for another six months. Don't worry about me. I have found a temporary job and lodging.

Please take care of your health. I'll let you know my new address soon.

After finishing the letter, I read it one more time. Why had I written six months? I could leave Yotsuba sooner without penalty. But this seemed like long enough to tie up my sister's loose ends, and I had enough savings to sustain myself if teaching didn't work out.

I signed the letter and put it inside the envelope. After dropping that off at the convenience store mailbox, I returned to the hotel lobby and used the pay phone to call Mr. Katou. I told him I'd decided to accept his proposal. I knew I wouldn't be able to find a better deal. Even if things didn't go well, I figured I could move out anytime. Nothing to lose.

"I'm glad you've decided to take the offer," Mr. Katou said in his usual monotone voice. "When are you planning to move in?"

As soon as possible, so I could stop spending money on the hotel room. "When would be a good time?"

"How about today?"

I had no complaint.

"The thing is, the only available guest room right now is the one Miss Ishida stayed in," he said. "If you're uncomfortable with that, I can arrange for another room in a couple of days."

"Don't trouble yourself, that room is fine," I said.

The arrangement was perfect for my objective of digging into my sister's life in Akakawa. I checked out of the Katsuragi Hotel and moved to Segayaki that afternoon. Before I left, I gave the kimono lady some cakes from a nearby patisserie. Her pink kimono matched the sakura illustration on the cake box, and she looked pleasantly surprised.

MY SISTER'S ROOM WAS exactly as I remembered, spacious with plenty of sunshine coming in through the window.

"Please make yourself comfortable," Mr. Katou said. "I need to go to a meeting now. Feel free to use the kitchen, and help your-self to food and drink in the fridge. I'll introduce you to my wife tomorrow morning."

"Thank you." I bowed to him.

He left the room and I set down my belongings. Since I hadn't planned to stay in Akakawa for more than a couple of weeks, I hadn't packed much. I had only a suitcase and Boston bag with me. I unzipped the bag and took out the porcelain urn. Opening the wardrobe, I rearranged my sister's clothes, clearing a shelf.

"Welcome back to your room," I whispered, placing the urn there.

I closed the wardrobe and climbed onto the bed. Arms behind my head, I lay staring up at the white room. An opaque white lampshade encircled the ceiling light. The afternoon sun cast faint shadows, gradually getting longer and darker. I took a deep breath, catching a waft of sweet fragrance. Was it from the flowers in the garden, brought in by the afternoon breeze? Or had it lingered from her presence in the room? The scent vaguely resembled that of the Estée Lauder perfume I'd found in her drawer. I didn't recall her using any fragrances back in Tokyo. But people changed.

I shut my eyes, and before I knew it, I was in a dream.

I STOOD BY THE side of a busy road, waiting to cross. I expected the little green man on the traffic light to appear, but the light remained red, and the stream of passing cars never ceased. Was the light faulty? Should I walk to the next one? Perhaps it wasn't too far ahead.

As I contemplated this, I noticed a little girl across the road. She was about four or five years old and stood around three feet tall. She wore a kindergarten uniform—a white shirt and dark-blue pinafore—and had her hair tied into pigtails. Without hesitation, she walked toward me.

The light was still red, and cars were speeding past. One of them would hit her. I wanted to shout at her to stop, but I was paralyzed. The girl walked calmly. Her small steps were constant, like the ticking of a metronome. Despite her lack of caution, she reached my side of the street unharmed. She stopped a few steps away from me, and we looked into each other's eyes.

I tried to ask, "Who are you?" But once I opened my mouth, my voice evaporated. From the way she looked at me, I knew my thought had reached her. She said nothing, though the corners of her mouth curled up a little.

WHEN I OPENED MY eyes, the shadows had taken over the entire room. It felt as if I'd only closed my eyes for a couple of minutes, but several hours must have passed.

I usually forgot my dreams as soon as I woke up. But I couldn't erase the image of the girl's pigtails, bobbing up and down as she walked through the traffic. I'd never seen her before, though she was strangely familiar.

Hungry yet again, I got up and went to the kitchen. In the fridge, I found a box of chocolate milk. I searched for a mug and poured the milk into it, finishing the cold drink in a few big gulps. I washed the mug and placed it on the drying rack. It was the only item there, which reminded me of the knife I'd given my sister for her birthday. I knew she'd brought it with her to Akakawa, so it should've been here somewhere.

I checked the three drawers attached to the cooking station. The top was filled with silver cutlery, the second with kitchen utensils. The lowest one had chopping boards and a classic five-piece stainless steel knife set housed in a wooden block. But the knife I was looking for wasn't there.

Opening the rest of the cabinets, I discovered more cooking equipment, from frying pans to bamboo steamers. All of it looked new. But I still couldn't find my sister's knife.

I gave up and returned to my room. I wondered where the knife could possibly be. I knew she had treasured it. She wouldn't have given it away.

The streetlight crept through the curtain, dimly illuminating the red phone on the desk. As I stared at it, I missed my sister. Her voice, her laughter, her phone calls. Why had I only realized how much she meant to me after she was gone?

I picked up the receiver and pressed it to my ear. The plastic felt cold. I could hear a *tuut*, *tuut*, *tuut* before it went *piiiiiiiiiip*, and I put it back down. Who was I kidding? I would never hear her voice again. She was dead. Her life had been abruptly cut short, and she was in a place I couldn't reach.

Ren Ishida, what do you want to do?

7

The
Woman
Who
Stopped
Speaking

Mr. Katou introduced me to his wife the next morning. They had separate bedrooms. Hers was the farthest from the entrance, and it was even bigger than mine. Through her window, I could see a Western-style garden, where purple irises and white roses bloomed.

Mrs. Katou sat on her bed, supported by a pillow. She wore a long-sleeved beige cardigan on top of a white blouse. I'd imagined her as thin, with sunken eyes. But apart from her blank expression and pale skin, she looked relatively healthy.

"This is my wife," Mr. Katou said, before turning to her. "This is Ren Ishida. He's going to help us starting today."

"Nice to meet you." I bowed to her.

I waited for her to respond, but she remained silent. She wasn't paying attention to us. To be more precise, it was as if she didn't notice we were there, right in front of her.

We stood still, watching her quietly. She shifted a little from time to time. One moment, she would gaze out the window. The next moment, she would turn to the wall in front of her.

"I'll have a word with Ishida about the arrangement," Mr. Katou said before walking out.

I bowed one more time to Mrs. Katou before leaving the room.

"My wife isn't deaf, blind, or mute, if that's what you had in mind," Mr. Katou said. "She has a psychological issue that has made her choose to stop speaking."

"Psychological issue?"

"Yes. I would appreciate if we could leave it at that."

He rummaged in his pocket and took out a bunch of keys. "These are duplicates because the police kept the originals, but they should work fine."

I took the keys and put them in my pocket.

"Let me give you a rundown on what you need to do," he continued. "You can purchase a packaged lunch each day from the nearby convenience store. If you follow the main road east, you'll see it on your right side. Miss Ishida used to buy the food before she went to work."

That was unusual. "My sister didn't cook?"

"Not to my knowledge. It's too much trouble to cook just for two people."

I knew that wasn't the case for her, but I didn't correct him.

"Before I forget, you don't need to bring the food into my wife's room. Just knock twice and leave it in front of her door. Money for the food is inside the keepsake box in the reading room."

I nodded. "Should I keep the receipts?"

"There's no need. I don't have time to go through them."

"All right."

"As for the reading, choose whichever time is most convenient for you. Pick any book from the reading room. I would say, perhaps read a few pages every day. She may not be responsive, but I know she'll love having someone read to her." He nodded a couple times, satisfied with his explanation. "I think that's it for now."

He then excused himself and went to his office. I returned to my room, feeling the weight of the keys inside my pocket. What an odd arrangement I had followed my sister into, but perhaps it would somehow lead me to her.

AT NOON, I BOUGHT two deep-fried chicken rice sets from the convenience store. I left Mrs. Katou's packed lunch in front of her bedroom door, then went to the kitchen to eat alone.

Putting the plastic bag on the table, I took a can of lemonade from the fridge. The cold drink refreshed me after walking in the sun. I took out my lunch box and lifted the lid, which was wet with water droplets.

After my sister had moved out, I'd gone back to eating takeout every day. Like most teenagers, I often had fast food. By that time, I didn't hate it as much. I had to eat out anyway, since most of the time I was out with one of my girlfriends.

Nae was my ninth girlfriend, if I didn't count the girls I'd randomly hooked up with. A few of them, including Nae, could cook well. Once, I'd even dated the daughter of a chain hotel chef. Her dream was to study at Le Cordon Bleu, and she trained hard. She whipped up all kinds of fancy meals for me, but somehow, I still preferred my sister's dishes.

"Your cooking is the best," I'd once told my sister as she was making miso soup.

She laughed. "That can't be true."

"But it is."

"Is that so?" She dropped a handful of chopped tofu into the soup. "Maybe I should open a restaurant."

"Don't," I quickly said. "Cooking is subjective. Other people might not have the same weird taste as me." But really, I wanted her to cook only for me. I was that selfish.

My sister turned to me. "I'm not sure whether you're complimenting or insulting me."

"Consider it a compliment, then."

She laughed again and stirred the soup.

I enjoyed watching her cook. Those moments were special. No matter how bad my day was, I felt at ease whenever we were together in the kitchen. Perhaps I thrived on the comfortable routine of it.

Sometimes, my sister would steal a glance back at me. Realizing I was looking at her, she would say, "I know you're hungry, but stop staring. I'm almost done," and we would burst into laughter.

Keiko Ishida—she always misunderstood me.

AFTER I'D FINISHED EATING, I went to the reading room to choose a book.

The Katous' selection was huge. From Shakespeare to Virginia Woolf, Ernest Hemingway to George Orwell to F. Scott Fitzgerald. Rather than giving the impression of a well-read person, Mrs. Katou came across as a classics collector.

Singling out Salman Rushdie's *Midnight's Children*—one of those books I'd always wanted to read but never gotten the chance to—I walked to Mrs. Katou's room. The packaged lunch in front of the door was gone.

I knocked on the door twice and waited. After a few seconds passed, I entered.

"Excuse me," I said.

Mrs. Katou was sitting on her bed, in the same position I'd seen her in earlier, her empty lunch box on the nightstand. Her eyes were fixed on the wall.

I sat on the wooden chair next to her bed, waving the book awkwardly. "I'm going to read this today."

Again, no response.

Looking at her made me uncomfortable, so I quickly flipped open the book and began to read. My voice came out trembling, and my palms were sweaty. I glanced over at her a couple of times, but she still appeared in a daze.

After the third paragraph, I couldn't continue. I left the book on the nightstand, picked up the empty lunch box, and excused myself. I felt uneasy. Had it been a mistake to move here? Even then, I could tell the house was full of dark secrets.

8

The
Girl
with
the
Beautiful
Fingers

The cram school was just a single bus ride from Segayaki. Even if I counted walking time, it took less than half an hour to get there. As I entered Yotsuba, I caught a waft of lavender. So jasmine on my first visit, and this time was lavender. I wondered what would come next. Cherry blossom, perhaps?

"Good morning, Mr. Ishida," Abe said brightly from behind the reception counter. "The principal is waiting in his office."

I climbed the staircase to the fourth floor and walked past the cubicles. Some of the staff members were already in. A few of them nodded, and I nodded back. Were they aware I was going to be working here? Walking into the principal's office, I saw him sitting opposite a slender woman with shoulder-length hair.

"Ishida," he said, "please come in."

He and the woman both stood. She had no makeup on, a rarity these days.

"This is Maeda. She'll be guiding you as you transition into the new job."

I bowed to her. "Nice to meet you."

She did the same and led me out of the office. "I'll get you the schedule and teaching materials."

Despite her high heels, Maeda moved swiftly. Going straight to the file cabinets near the faculty lounge, she took out a stack of files and passed them to me.

"Your working hours are Monday to Saturday from two-thirty to nine-thirty. You'll be teaching three classes a day, an hour and a half each. There's also a break for you to have dinner."

We went to my desk—my sister's few possessions still there— and I put my things down. Maeda signaled me to sit and pulled out another chair for herself.

"You're lucky to be taking over a senior teacher's slot," she said. "New hires don't usually get such a neat timetable and end up having to work both days of the weekend."

I could tell she was making an effort not to mention my sister's name.

"Don't worry, just follow the syllabus. It's pretty straightforward," she continued. After that, she explained how to use the teaching materials.

"Will I be teaching today?" I asked.

She smirked. "No, not so fast. Today, I'll be the one teaching, so you can observe. But from tomorrow, you'll be on your own, so pay close attention."

I nodded. "Of course."

"Great. Now then . . ." Maeda took a quick look at the large circular clock in the middle of the office wall. A quarter past three. "Follow me."

She fished some files from the stack before walking off. I put my bag down and followed her. I wanted to help her carry everything, but she walked so fast, I barely managed to keep up.

As we walked down the staircase, streams of students rushed

in the opposite direction, making it difficult for us to get through. Several of them glanced at me as they passed. I told myself it was nothing to be anxious about. A new face always attracts curiosity.

THE FIRST OF MY classrooms was on the second floor. Shortly after we reached it, the bell rang and the session began.

I stood in front of the blackboard next to Maeda. The class had around twenty students; several wore the same uniforms. Some were busy with their books, while the rest chatted with each other.

"Good afternoon," Maeda said. "This is Mr. Ishida. He will be joining us to teach English."

The room went quiet, their expressions all going solemn once they heard my name. I should have expected this. After all, my sister had been their teacher.

"I'm Ren Ishida." I weakly attempted to hide my nervousness. "I hope we'll get along well."

A few of them whispered to each other.

Maeda slammed her hand on the desk. "Quiet!"

The class was once again silent.

"I'm taking attendance now."

She called off the names one by one. Three were missing. Five minutes into the lesson, they appeared together, huffing and puffing. They apologized and quickly settled into the remaining empty chairs.

To be honest, I hadn't expected these teenagers to be so obedient. They listened to Maeda's explanations and took notes. None of them talked out of turn again. When it came to the question-and-answer segment, most participated. And it was back to silence during the written exercises.

The second bell rang and everyone packed their belongings. On the way out, they turned in their answer sheets.

After they had all left, Maeda asked me, "How was it? Not so bad, right?"

"They're so well-behaved and hard-working," I said.

"That's to be expected. Yotsuba has a high acceptance rate into prestigious universities, so we can afford to be selective and charge a premium. In fact, we're the most expensive cram school in town. I might be overgeneralizing, but our students are serious. They're here because they want to get into good places."

"So all of them are seniors?"

"Not all, but most. They're either second- or third-years. We don't take freshmen."

Our conversation was interrupted by the next group. This class was bigger than the first, proved to be just as quiet and studious. Such a contrast to how I'd been six years ago at my neighborhood high school in Tokyo. My classmates, especially the boys, were boisterous at times. I wasn't used to seeing teenagers behave so well.

More students poured in, and then, I saw her.

She came with a group of girls, all wearing the same navy uniform. She looked slightly different. Her hair was shorter and tied in a high ponytail. With this hairstyle, she looked much younger. I couldn't believe it, but I knew I wasn't mistaken. She was the girl who had been smoking under the gazebo. Based on what Maeda had said, she was about seventeen or eighteen.

The girl sat in the back row. I took a deep breath and tried to gauge her reaction. Our eyes met, but she made no acknowledgment that she recognized me. I then pretended to be unaware of her presence, but she must have realized I'd seen her. I was shocked to find her in my class. Was it fate?

When Maeda introduced me to the class, the girl stared at me intently, but only for a moment. After the lesson was over, she left the classroom with the rest of her friends. It wasn't the best time, but I hurried after her.

"Excuse me." I tapped her on the shoulder. "It was you, wasn't it?"

She turned and settled her gaze on me. Up this close, I was sure I had the right person.

"Last week," I said, "at the gazebo."

She shook her head. "You must have the wrong person. I've never seen you before."

"But—"

"I need to go to my next class." She cut me off. "Will you excuse me, Mr. Ishida?"

She walked away, leaving me speechless. It might have been my imagination, but she'd sounded unfriendly, especially when she'd said my name.

"Is everything all right, Ishida?" Maeda asked me, the lesson folders in her arms.

"Yes." I went to Maeda and helped her. "Are we returning to the office?"

"You were talking to Nakajima just now. Do you know her?"

"I mistook her for someone else."

"I'm sorry; I was worried you were trying to make a pass at her. I know you're still young, but we aren't supposed to have any romantic ties with the students or other staff." She shifted her eyes uncomfortably. "Also, about that girl . . ."

"Yes?"

"I've heard she dates older men for money."

Nakajima certainly was pretty, but she hadn't come off as materialistic. If anything, she was dressed plainly, especially compared to other girls her age in Tokyo.

"That's probably just a rumor."

Maeda lowered her voice. "Actually, I saw it myself. She was leaving a high-end jewelry store with a well-dressed man, old enough to be her father."

"Maybe it was her father."

"They didn't look alike."

Our conversation made me uncomfortable, and luckily, Maeda seemed to notice. We returned to the fourth floor without another word. I sat at my desk and stretched my neck.

"For you, Ishida." Honda put a canned iced coffee in front of me. "How's your first day?"

I mustered a smile. "I've managed to survive so far."

"Good. I know you can do it," he said. "Do you want to grab dinner together?"

I looked around for Maeda; to my relief, she had gone elsewhere. I didn't dislike her, but she wasn't someone I wanted to spend my break time with. "Why not," I told Honda. "What's good around here?"

We went out for a quick bite at a nearby ramen stall before returning to Yotsuba for the day's final session. The students looked exhausted. A few of them had trouble paying attention, and so did I. Throughout the lesson, I couldn't focus on Maeda's teaching. All I could think about was the girl who had held the Seven Stars cigarettes with her beautiful fingers.

9

The
Lingering
Smell
of Rain
and
Carbon

After my first day of work, I arrived back at the Katou household around eleven at night. I dropped my bag on the floor and sat down to take off my socks. My eyes were immediately drawn to the red phone on top of the desk.

Get a grip, Ren Ishida. The phone can't connect you to a dead person.

"Shut up," I hissed. "I know that already."

Reaching for the cord, I unplugged it from the wall. She would never call me again, so I didn't want to hear the phone ring. I closed my eyes. What was I doing here, all by myself in this town?

REN . . .

It was my sister's voice—warm and clear, the way I remembered it. I opened my eyes and found myself standing alone in the middle of a vast white space.

"Is it you?" I shouted, but there was no answer.

Above me, gigantic bubbles were suspended in the air. What were those? I jumped and managed to reach one. When the tip of my index finger touched the surface, I felt a chill. The bubble burst like summer fireworks, splitting into millions of tiny balls that dropped to the ground.

I rubbed the thin film on my finger with my thumb. It was water.

Slowly, it dawned on me that I was inside a dream. But something about it wasn't right. I had to get out. If I couldn't escape, I would be stuck there forever.

No matter where I walked, the sea of whiteness and water bubbles was uninterrupted. Was I closer to the way out now? Or farther from it?

"Ren," someone called.

I turned around and saw the little girl with pigtails staring at me. She wore the same dark-blue pinafore from my previous dream, when she'd walked through traffic.

"Who are you?" I asked. "What do you want?"

She was quiet for a moment, then shook her head and pointed up. A school of giant goldfish swam through the air. Hundreds, maybe thousands. Each of them the size of a soccer ball. Their vibrant scales painted the sky a golden orange.

The flying goldfish danced above us, sweeping their translucent glittering tails while avoiding the balls of water. I was dazzled. They looked so elegant.

Suddenly, the goldfish charged at the bubbles, bursting them. Cold water splashed everywhere, and a bright light flashed from the distance. I shielded my eyes with my hands. Squinting, I remembered the little girl and looked for her, but she'd run off. I should have chased after her, but my feet felt heavy.

Before I woke up, I heard my sister's voice.

Ren, you shouldn't be here.

I'D FALLEN ASLEEP WITH my head on the desk and the window open. It was pouring outside, and water sprayed into the room. I could hear thunder amidst the sound of rain.

Getting up, I closed the window. Half of the desk, including the phone, was already wet. I took a face towel and wiped off the rainwater. Good thing I hadn't taken out the day's work papers from my bag.

My watch showed two in the morning. I knew I should shower, but I was too tired. Tossing myself on the bed without changing my clothes, I pulled up the blanket, but it was too thin to warm me. I got up and threw on a jacket before climbing back in. I fell sleep again, and this time, I didn't dream.

When I awoke, the sun was already high. Tiny droplets made their way down the glass panel to the wooden frame before disappearing. I opened the window, taking a deep breath.

Once, when Nae was staying over at my place, I asked her if rain had a smell. She gave me a puzzled look while brushing her hair. Her long, black hair fell down to her elbows; she always pulled it up when she slept with me. Her ponytail would end up messy, but I didn't care. I liked her messy look.

"I don't think rain itself has a smell," Nae said, "but there's this unmistakable fragrance that lingers after the rain. A fresh, earthy scent. Do you know what I mean?"

I nodded. "I think so."

"Maybe it's the smell of wet soil. Whatever it is, I like it."

Me too, I love the distinctive after-rain smell. Thinking about rain always reminds me of Nae.

I sent another letter to my parents on my way to Yotsuba, giving them Mr. Katou's address. But I hadn't contacted Nae. I didn't know how to talk to her. It was the first time we'd had such a prolonged argument.

On the bright side, I enjoyed the feeling of being single. No one to call, no one to plan dates for, no special occasions to remember. It suited my personality. I never had liked commitment—perhaps I shouldn't have had a girlfriend in the first place.

OVER THE NEXT FEW days, I developed a new routine to match my teaching schedule.

I would wake up around eight and go for a one-hour jog on a path leading to the slope where my sister had died. It was as if I hoped to trick myself into thinking I was visiting her every morning. I really should have tried to see her more often when she was alive.

On my way home, I would stop by the convenience store and buy two lunch boxes, leaving one in front of Mrs. Katou's room. I would eat my lunch alone in the kitchen. After my meal, I'd stop by Mrs. Katou's room and read a few more pages of *Midnight's Children* to her before heading to work.

The schedule didn't change much on my days off. Instead of going to work, I took the bus into town. Most of the time, I wandered aimlessly around the shopping mall or sat down for a cup of coffee. Every day was predictable.

Contrary to my expectations, after two weeks I grew to enjoy the time I spent with Mrs. Katou. I could choose books I'd always wanted to read, but never found the time to. I could also reread books I loved. If I wanted to, I could repeat the same line over and over. No matter what, she would listen to me without a single word of objection. I felt like I had a captive listener. And if I got tired, I could stop at any time.

The house itself was always quiet. While sitting on the chair next to Mrs. Katou's bed, I could pick up the tiniest noise in the air, like the sound of the breeze caressing the wooden window and the tinkling wind chime, or the rhythm of Mrs. Katou's breath colliding against mine. If I stayed still long enough, the air came alive and sealed us in an invisible film.

Whenever I felt stifled, I walked to the window and traced the shadow of the pine tree in the garden. Birds were always flying by.

I didn't know what breed, but they had dark-bluish feathers. So dark they were almost black. Were they the same kind of birds that my sister had bought on her birthday? I couldn't tell. I couldn't remember them well, apart from the fact that they were black. Or had they been dark blue?

I seemed to forget the things I wanted to remember, and remember things I wanted to forget. Like my sister's death. I wished everything that had brought me here had been a dream.

I'd expected a prominent politician like Mr. Katou to receive plenty of guests, but that wasn't the case. The only visitor I'd seen so far was the white-haired housekeeper who came every Monday and Thursday. Each time, it took me a while to notice her presence, the way she blended into the house. She was quiet and discreet—or rather, I'd never heard her speak—and somehow entered the premises without anyone noticing. The only thing that gave her presence away was the whirring of her vacuum cleaner.

Whenever I saw her, I bowed to her, but she ignored me. Was she upset that I noticed her? What a bizarre thought. No one would think that way. But when she was around, I made it a point not to read aloud. I would slip into my room and wait there until it was time to leave for work.

"Have you tried talking to her?" Honda asked me after I'd told him about the housekeeper.

I shrugged. "It doesn't seem like she wants to talk."

"You could test it out, start a conversation."

"Maybe," I said, knowing I never would.

The last class had ended. Honda and I were at my desk, having cup noodles for supper. It had been drizzling all day. Cold weather makes people hungry, so stocking up on instant noodles in the office during the rainy season had been a wise choice.

"What about that Mr. Katou?" Honda asked.

"I rarely see him," I said. "He leaves the house before I wake up, and by the time I return from work, he's already in his room."

"Does he spend time with his wife?"

"Not when I'm around."

"He's a workaholic, then?"

"Probably."

"Or maybe he prefers to be alone."

"Could be."

Though I had once seen him in his wife's bedroom.

It was a Sunday, and I was about to do my daily reading. The door was open, and I stayed outside when I realized Mr. Katou was inside. He sat on the wooden chair next to his wife's bed, the one I usually used, and both of them looked out the window in silence. I left to give them some privacy.

Though they were quiet, I sensed a strong connection between them. It was as if they had their own special way to communicate. A secret language. Strange, yet beautiful.

I drank the soup and threw the Styrofoam bowl into the bin. Peering out of the window, I saw that the rain had stopped. Seven Stars—or Rio Nakajima, as I'd learned—walked out of the building. The students around her were laughing and smiling, but she looked detached from the rest.

At that moment, I realized what drew me to her. It was those beautiful fingers. The way she had moved them gracefully while smoking her cigarettes that rainy day still captivated me.

"Are you done, Ishida?" Honda asked. "I'm going near Segayaki. I can give you a lift."

"Don't worry, I can take the bus. It's not that far."

"Since it's not that far, let me drive you back."

I grabbed my bag and followed him to the basement parking

lot. His car always smelled faintly of citrus, but I couldn't see an air freshener anywhere. He probably spritzed the interior every morning.

Honda released the handbrake and the vehicle slowly rolled forward. Feeling a chill, I rubbed my nose and sneezed.

"Are you sick?" Honda asked.

"No, I'm fine," I answered. "Must be the weather."

"When you live alone, you need to be careful with your health."

I mumbled in agreement.

"Am I being too preachy?"

I wasn't thinking properly when I said, "You remind me of my sister sometimes."

As soon as the words were out, I regretted them. The atmosphere became awkward, but thankfully, Honda pretended not to notice.

I looked at the streetlights and squinted. The red traffic light in the distance turned to green. At night, the road felt wider, probably because fewer cars were around.

Recalling the dream I'd had, I asked Honda, "Is there a public aquarium around here?"

"Not in Akakawa, unfortunately. The nearest one is in Tokyo," he said. "Why? Feeling nostalgic?"

"I had a dream about goldfish."

"Goldfish?" He laughed. "What made you dream of goldfish? And if you're only looking for goldfish, you can go to the pet shop."

"That's true."

"When was the last time you saw one?"

I thought about it, but couldn't recall.

When my sister was still in Tokyo, we used to go to the summer festivals together. She loved the goldfish-scooping game stall, even though she wasn't good at it. She always moved the paper net too quickly and ended up breaking it. After two or three failed attempts, she usually asked me to do it instead.

I never failed to catch at least two fish. With a proud smile, my sister would walk away with the goldfish in a plastic bag half-filled with water. But after the festival, she always made a detour to the canal to release them. I told her it was a waste, but she wouldn't listen. Keiko Ishida didn't let anyone else make decisions for her.

"Do you like fish, Ishida?" Honda asked.

"I don't particularly like them, but I don't hate them either," I said. "Fish are just fish."

"What about goldfish?"

"They're pretty. I think it's their colors."

"It's hard not to like goldfish, isn't it? Like with dolphins. Everyone loves dolphins."

The car pulled over in front of Katou's house. I thanked Honda for the ride and got out.

"See you tomorrow," he said.

I watched the black sedan get smaller and smaller before disappearing in the distance. The carbon smell from the exhaust still lingered when I opened the gate. The cold and quiet night provided a false sense of tranquility.

1 0

The
Bubblegum
World and the
Woman with a Mole
on the Back of
Her Neck

The next morning, I went for my usual jog.

I now knew the location of all the electricity poles. I could pinpoint the corners where the stray cats hid. One of the spots was where a brick wall had crumbled, wild grass sprouting from it.

On my way back to the Katou house, I stopped at the convenience store. Wiping the sweat off my forehead, I pushed the glass door open and went to the lunch box section. I checked the day's selection: chicken cutlet, deep-fried octopus ball, salted salmon, and mini hamburgers. Which should I go for?

The bell pinged, and I saw a familiar face. It was Seven Stars, still in her school uniform. To be here at this time of day, she had to be skipping class. I was about to approach her when a young man I'd seen before entered the store.

He went to the magazine rack, but his eyes were locked on her. Though he wasn't in uniform, I recognized him as the officer who had been manning the police counter on my visit. Could he be on a mission to catch students who were ditching school?

Standing in front of the candy shelf, Seven Stars slid her fingers over the packages as if she were looking for something. Then, with a sudden flick of her index finger, she knocked a bubble gum tin into her schoolbag. I gasped. She'd done it in a second, with delicate precision. From the way she'd carried it out and her unchanging expression, I knew this wasn't her first time shoplifting.

Seven Stars was about to walk out when the officer put down the magazine he was holding. No longer thinking straight, I ran over and grabbed her arm. She looked at me in surprise.

"What are you doing?" she hissed, after the initial shock wore off.

"I saw what you just did," I whispered. "Return the bubble gum now."

She averted her eyes, staring off into the distance. "I have no idea what you're talking about."

"You do know what I'm talking about, and so does the plain-clothes police officer over there."

I glanced at the young officer, and Seven Stars went pale.

"It's all right, you're still inside the store," I continued. "Don't panic; just put it back onto the shelf."

"I can't." She looked down. "I need it."

"Then pay for it."

She shook her head. "That would defeat the purpose."

I sighed in frustration. "What do you want to do? Spend the night in the police station?"

No answer. She kept her head low. It was apparent that she was prepared for the consequences. I wondered if she was being rebellious to get someone's attention. But surely, that wasn't worth risking a criminal record.

The officer approached us. "Is there a problem?"

"Everything is fine," I said, forcing my hand into Seven Stars' bag.

I took the bubble gum to the cashier to pay for it. Seven Stars remained standing next to the officer. Her eyes followed my every movement. I didn't know what she was thinking, but I had to save her. I returned to her and put the bubble gum in her hand.

She shoved it back at me. "No one asked you to buy it."

I couldn't tell what she wanted. "Fair enough," I said, putting the gum inside my pocket.

Seven Stars gave me a defiant look before walking off. Once she had left, the officer caught up with me at the corner of the block.

"You're Keiko Ishida's brother, aren't you? I don't know what you're trying to do, but you're not helping that girl. I've been watching her, and I saw what she did. She won't learn unless we catch her red-handed."

"I understand, but please overlook it this time," I said. "I'll talk to her and make sure she won't do it again. She's still young. Her future prospects will be hurt if she has a criminal record."

His forehead creased. "May I know what your relationship is to her?"

"She's my student." I bowed to him. "Let me apologize on her behalf. Please, give her another chance."

"Mr. Ishida, don't apologize to me. I'm sorry, but I can't let her off. I have to take down her particulars in case she reoffends. I hope you don't think badly of me. I'm only doing my duty."

The officer left and chased after Seven Stars. I watched them from a distance as they talked. She took something from her schoolbag, probably her student ID. The officer copied the information from it into his notebook. Once he was gone, I went to her.

"Are you all right?" I asked.

She remained silent and crossed her arms.

I had to find a way to get her to talk. "Why do you like bubble gum so much?"

"What's wrong with bubble gum?"

"Nothing. Bubble gum is fine, but I prefer chocolate," I said.

"My favorite is Ritter Sport milk chocolate with cornflakes. You've probably never seen it. They don't seem to sell it around here."

She looked into my eyes. "I appreciate your help, but you have no right to be patronizing."

"Fine, I'll leave you alone," I said, raising my hands. "But don't push your luck. They're not going to let you off next time."

Seven Stars was quiet, but she looked at me hesitantly, like she wanted to ask a question.

"Is there something you want to tell me?" I asked.

She pressed her lips together. "You have the same surname as our previous English teacher."

"Of course I do." I forced a smile. "She was my sister."

Her expression changed a little. I waited for the usual words of condolence, but they never came. Instead, she turned around and walked away. I returned to the convenience store to get a newspaper and two lunch boxes.

BECAUSE OF THE CONFUSION from that morning's incident, I left the Katous' house earlier than usual. I had some time to kill, so I went to a café. A mere five-minute walk from Yotsuba, the place served strong coffee. I ordered a cup and sipped it slowly.

"Ren?" a soft voice called.

I looked up and saw a woman standing in front of me. Wearing a peach blouse and white skirt, she looked like a typical office lady in her mid-twenties.

"I knew it was you." Her smile widened. "Are you alone? May I join you?"

"Of course," I said, trying furiously to recall who she was.

She wore natural-looking makeup, the right amount to give her a pleasing glow. Her long hair was secured with a black clip above her right ear. Could she be someone from work? But no one there addressed me as Ren.

The woman pulled over a chair. "Are you surprised to see me here?"

"Kind of," I said. "Can I get you a drink?"

She smiled and got up. "Don't trouble yourself. Let me order something, then we'll talk."

As she walked to the counter, I weighed the various possibilities. Was she a former classmate? Perhaps a distant relative? No, I was certain I didn't know this woman. But she might be important, someone I ought to remember.

She returned to my table with an iced coffee. I still couldn't figure out who she was.

"I'm here for our company retreat," she said, playing with her straw. Her nails were painted beige, and none were chipped. "It's a three-day, two-night trip. We're leaving tomorrow."

I decided to play along. "What have you done so far?"

"The usual—shopping, monuments, temples, more shopping. To be honest, I don't know why we chose Akakawa instead of someplace like Nara or Kyoto. I do think small towns have their charm, but they don't necessarily appeal to everyone."

I nodded.

"This place certainly doesn't appeal to me. I was hoping for a hot spring, like the previous years." She stirred her drink with the straw and took a sip. "What about you, Ren? What are you doing here?"

"I'm working. I teach English at a cram school nearby."

"That's good," she said. "I mean, back when we last spoke, you were having a hard time figuring out what to do after graduation."

"Right. That was . . ."

She counted on her fingers. "Three, four weeks ago?"

I felt like I'd been walking in a fog so thick I couldn't tell the color of my shoes. And then a gust of wind blew, clearing it away when I realized who she was.

Starting from the mole behind her neck, the memory of the night I'd spent in her apartment came flooding back. I could even recall the fragrance she wore. A refreshing blend of tangerine and cherry blossom—she had the scent of spring on her warm skin. I remembered her curved back, illuminated by the moonlight, her loud, sensual moans, and her perfectly painted fingernails, digging into the pillow. Flustered, I took a sip of my coffee.

"Do you think I was too forward?" she asked. "Usually it's the man who approaches the woman, but I walked up to you that night and talked to you first."

I shook my head. "It doesn't matter."

"Really?"

"Really."

She stirred her drink again. "This might sound odd, but I had a dream about you last week. I swear, I wasn't obsessing or anything. Somehow, you just slipped into my sleep."

I wasn't sure how to react to this, so I shrugged and said, "Sometimes it happens."

"When I woke up, I wanted to see you. I had this strong urge to pick the phone up and call, but it would be weird for me to be the one asking you out. What do you think? Be honest."

"Like I said, it doesn't matter. This is the nineties—it's completely normal for the woman to make the first move."

"Do you prefer women who take the initiative?"

That depended completely on the situation, but I didn't want to go into detail.

"Anyway, that's beside the point," she said. "Even if I'd decided to call you, I couldn't. You didn't give me your number."

I forced a smile. "Is that so? It must have slipped my mind. I was quite drunk that night."

"You looked perfectly fine."

"I hardly ever look drunk, no matter how much I've had. To be fair, you didn't give me your number, either."

"I did. I wrote it on a piece of paper and slipped it into your pocket." She covered her mouth. "Don't tell me you didn't realize. Who did your laundry?"

"I did it myself, but I never check the pockets before tossing my clothes into the washing machine."

"That's too bad," she said. "Still, it was cruel of you to leave without a word. If you had waited until I'd woken up, I would have made you breakfast."

"I had an early appointment, and you were sleeping so well. It would have been a crime to wake you up."

"A crime? What a charming way to put it."

We both laughed. She knew my excuse was lame, but appreciated the attempt enough to go along with it.

"Do you regret it?" she whispered. "Is that why you left so quietly?"

"You're mistaken," I responded quickly, not wanting to hurt her feelings. "It's not like that. You looked peaceful, so I didn't want to wake you up. That's all."

Leaning closer, she stared at me for a moment, as if searching for something in my face. I cleared my throat and stared into the distance. I didn't want to meet her gaze.

She let out a heavy sigh. "I don't know why, but I feel like I can trust you. You seem sincere. I guess it doesn't hurt that you're pretty good-looking."

I mustered a smile. We were just humoring each other at this point. What else could you expect from someone you'd had a one-night stand with? Were we supposed to become friends? Continue to have sexual encounters?

She leaned in toward me. "My hotel is down the block. Do you want to come over?"

I couldn't answer. I'd seen it coming, but I hadn't expected to be asked so quickly, or so straightforwardly.

"Let me guess," she said, sensing my hesitation. "You're married."

"No, but I'm in a relationship."

"That's fine. I have a boyfriend, too, even though he's overseas most of the time."

This wasn't surprising; I hadn't gotten the sense that she was looking for a relationship.

"That puts us in the same position, doesn't it?" She took a notebook from her purse, tore a page out, and scribbled on it. Shoving it into my hand, she said, "Let's be clear about it this time. Here's my number. Don't lose it."

I nodded. "I won't."

"I was joking about the hotel. I'm sharing my room with a colleague, but you can stay over at my apartment anytime you want. My boyfriend comes only once or twice a year, usually for less than a week. Most of the time, I'm on my own."

I wanted to ask whether this open arrangement with her boyfriend was mutual, but stopped myself.

"When you're in Tokyo, give me a call. We can keep each other company," she continued.

"And you can make me breakfast."

"Right. I make an excellent omurice."

My heart skipped a beat. One of my sister's specialties. I cleared my throat. "Sounds like a good plan."

She gave me a coy smile. "The sex or the breakfast?"

"Both."

"It's a deal, then." She stood and bent over to pick up her bag. Her white lacy bra peeked out from the gaping neckline of her blouse. "I would love to talk to you for longer, but I have to go now. I'll wait for your call."

After she left, I realized I hadn't given her my number. I folded the paper she'd given me in half and slipped it into my pocket.

11

You're Going to Be Fine

I had another dream about Pigtails.

I stood in the middle of the street I didn't recognize, a fine mist coating my skin. The place appeared deserted, with not a single soul in sight. There were puddles everywhere. It must have rained recently.

Slow, gentle waves formed on the surface of the water. The ripples intersected with each other. It was starting to rain again; I had to find shelter.

A screeching noise came from above, shattering the silence. I saw a flock of black birds high above me, but they weren't moving. They were suspended, frozen in the air. Time had stopped for them. I wondered if they would ever fly again, or would they remain there forever?

The gray clouds in the distance moved closer. The sky was getting darker, but the birds were still as stone.

"Ren, is that you?"

I looked around, recognizing the soft voice. No one was nearby, but I knew it belonged to the woman with the mole behind her neck. She spoke as if she was whispering a secret song.

"Hey, are you alone? Mind if I join you?"

Her voice came from behind me. I turned and saw Pigtails. As I was about to say something, she brought her index finger to her lips.

Not now, Ren, not now. It's not the right time yet.

THE POUNDING OF THE rain against the window woke me up. I wanted to go back to sleep, but it was too noisy. Eyes wide open, I recalled a paragraph from the article in the newspaper the kimono lady had given me.

> *The estimated time of the attack was around 11:30 P.M., just before the rainstorm. Due to heavy downpour and poor visibility, no one noticed the victim. The postmortem established her time of death at approximately 1:00 A.M., the cause being a massive hemorrhage. A jogger found the victim's body at 5:40 A.M. and alerted the police.*

An hour and half had passed between the time of the attack and the time my sister succumbed to her injuries. How had it felt for her, lying on the street in the rain in the middle of the night, sinking slowly into death? She had bled out as the water washed her wounds clean. And she had always been so afraid of drowning.

Getting up, I glanced at the clock. A quarter past eleven. I should have enough time.

I changed into a sweater and jeans and left the house. The bus service had already stopped, and hardly any cars were on the road. I picked up my pace and ran along the main road in the pouring rain, passing deserted alleys and empty fields. In no time, I was completely drenched. The rubber soles of my sneakers had worn off. I tripped and fell twice, but got up and continued to run until

I reached the declining slope. The police had removed the yellow sign, but I still remembered the exact spot. It was etched in my mind, never to be forgotten, no matter how hard I tried.

I lay down on the ground, panting. The rain hit my face, but I stayed still and closed my eyes. All I could hear was the sound of rain.

My sister should have been able to guess nobody would come in this kind of weather. She would have known she was about to die. What was on her mind in those final minutes? Had she thought about Mr. Tsuda, or the guy she had gone out with in Akakawa? Had she thought about me?

Since the day my sister had left Tokyo, I'd hoped for her return, but I'd never told her that. Had I been too proud, or too indifferent? If I'd asked her to come back, would she still be alive?

I clenched my fists. No use in asking myself that now—no answer would bring her back. The day my sister died, a part of me died, too.

The rain got heavier, and I stayed there, losing track of time. I waited until it stopped before opening my eyes. I turned over to face the road. The puddles shone, reflecting the streetlights. So this was what she saw before she died. I got up and walked back with an unbearable heaviness.

It was still dark when I reached the house. I took off my wet clothes and grabbed a towel from the bathroom, wiping up the water that had dripped all over the floor before taking a long shower. By the time I was back in bed, it was already four in the morning. I was tired, but I stayed awake until the sun rose. I needed its warmth. With the bright rays shining on me, I finally fell asleep.

I AWOKE AROUND NINE with a terrible headache.

My body was burning, but I forced myself to get up. I dragged myself to the convenience store to buy lunch. I also grabbed some medicine, a thermometer, and a pack of face masks. Using the pay phone near the shop, I called the school to let them know I couldn't turn up for work that day.

"What happened, Mr. Ishida?" Abe asked.

"I got caught in the rain last night," I answered. "It's just a common cold. I've bought medicine already. I should be returning to work tomorrow."

"All right. If the medicine doesn't help, please go and see the doctor."

I thanked her and hung up. Wearing one of the masks, I returned to the Katous' house. After putting down my stuff in the kitchen, I took my temperature: 102.5 degrees. No wonder I felt terrible. I had no appetite. I ate only half of my deep fried breaded pork cutlet, throwing away the rest. After popping a pill with some water, I returned to my room.

I was usually lucky with illness; I didn't fall sick easily. As far as I could remember, it had happened only once before. I was down with a high fever the entire first week after my sister left Tokyo.

At the time, I'd been angry. I felt betrayed and abandoned. I hadn't expected her to disappear without a word, so I walked out in the heavy rain to get sick. It was so childish. I went to play soccer at the field near my school, alone in the storm. It was a challenging feat, running on the sloshy, slippery grass. The ball's movement became unpredictable, and it often skidded farther down the field than I intended.

The next day, I had a high fever and terrible headache, as expected, but my sister didn't return. Mother bought porridge and medicine, but she had to leave at the usual time.

"I'm sorry, but I promised my friends I would come over." She wrote down a phone number on the calendar. "If your fever gets worse and you need me to take you to the hospital, just call Mrs. Koyama and ask for me."

I nodded, knowing I wouldn't call. She was going for mahjong, and they needed four players. They couldn't continue with one player missing, just like my sister and me. We needed each other; or had it just been me?

I remember lying on my bed with that horrible cold, feeling alone. When I think about it now, it's so embarrassing. But so many years later, I ended up in the exact same situation. This time, too, I felt she had abandoned me. And this time, too, she wouldn't return.

Keiko Ishida, why did you always leave without a word?

I closed my eyes and drifted to sleep.

I STOOD IN FRONT of a white, Western-style mansion when the bell rang and the door opened. Hundreds of men in dark suits stormed out of the building, each carrying a black briefcase. The sudden rush caught me by surprise. I tried to avoid the onslaught, but was pushed farther and farther from the building.

Amidst the crowd, I saw a familiar face. A bald man with his beaten-up leather briefcase, he'd been the only other guest at the Katsuragi Hotel.

"Excuse me," I shouted, but he couldn't hear me, and kept walking.

I followed, but the sheer number of people around us made it hard to cut through to him. Giving up and going with the flow of the crowd, I felt a gentle tug on my sleeve. Pigtails stood next to me, her hand grasping tight onto my right cuff.

"It's you again," I said.

She nodded before letting go of my shirt.

"Wait." I tried to stop her. "I need to talk to you."

But the little girl had already walked away.

More people shoved against me. I felt like a salmon, caught in an upstream migration. I had no choice but to move with the crowd. Tripping on someone's shoes, I lost my balance and fell to my knees. I thought I would be trampled, but the crowd around me simply vanished.

Picking myself up, I saw a white coffin, circled by rows of mourners. Honda, the principal, Abe, Hiroko, and other teachers from Yotsuba. Everyone was dressed in black. Not far from me, the kimono lady sat beside the hotel cleaning lady, whose trolley was nowhere to be seen.

The bald man came and sat next to the kimono lady. Opening his suitcase, he took out a white handkerchief. "I'm sorry for arriving late," he said to me, wiping sweat from his face. "I was caught in a traffic jam."

I nodded at him.

The funeral ceremony began. A Buddhist monk in a black robe bowed to the coffin before lighting the incense. With gentle movements, he waved the burning stick through the air, disseminating a sweet and musky fragrance.

The monk read the sutra and invited me to pay my respects. I stood and bowed. Taking the granular incense from the bowl, I held it in front of my forehead and dropped it into a burner. After that, I took a step back and bowed one more time. Pigtails came up and reached for my hand. She pulled me toward the coffin, but I stood still. She turned to me and stared, as if saying, *You've got to see it.*

I obliged, despite knowing my sister would be inside the coffin. Leaning closer, I saw a sleeping face surrounded by flowers. I held my breath and froze.

It wasn't my sister's face. It was my own.

I WOKE UP DRENCHED in sweat. My T-shirt was wet, and it clung to my skin. I took it off and went to the bathroom, splashing cold water on my face.

I looked up, and the man in the mirror stretched his hand out to me. Our fingers met on the shiny hard surface. In my own voice, I heard my sister say, "It's okay, Ren. You're going to be fine."

Closing my eyes, I was my thirteen-year-old self again, crouched in the living room in my pajamas and holding the phone tightly.

"I heard you were sick," my sister said. "Are you all right? Have you gone to the doctor?"

I sulked. "Why don't you come here and see for yourself? I'm telling you, I'm going to die."

"Stop that. It's bad luck to talk about death," she said. "Actually, I want to see you too, but I can't yet. I need to find a job and save up first."

"All the more reason for you to come back."

She forced herself to laugh. An awkward silence ensued.

"Your new place, is it really better?" I asked.

"I don't know," she said, a slight hesitation in her voice. "Only time will tell."

"You shouldn't have left. We were doing all right here."

"Don't worry, Ren. I'm fine, and I know you're going to be fine too. You have to trust me."

I couldn't believe she was saying this. "You would have been better off staying here."

"You really think so?"

I didn't answer.

"Hey, Ren," she said softly, "I'm going to call every week, I promise. So you won't be lonely."

"Who says I'm lonely?" And I didn't believe she would call every week, but she kept her promise until the day she died.

Keiko Ishida, you were such a liar. You would have been better off staying in Tokyo. And you told me we were going to be fine.

I dried my face and wiped my body with the wet towel, then put on a fresh T-shirt. I knew I should go back to sleep, but I was afraid of slipping into another nightmare.

Sitting at the desk, I took out one of my sister's notebooks and opened it to a blank page. I drew horizontal lines, stretching all the way from the left to the right of the paper, over and over until there was no more space. I tore it out and did the same thing on the next page. My sister was the one who had taught me to do that.

That day, I'd had a minor squabble in school. I couldn't recall what it was about any more. But my teacher had called my sister, and she went to my room to talk to me.

"Whenever you're feeling sad and frustrated, don't keep it inside," she said. "You need to write it out."

"But I'm not good with words," I said.

"Then draw it."

I looked at her in disbelief. "You know I can't draw, either."

"Just draw a line. A straight line. You can manage that, can't you?"

"How's that supposed to make me happy?"

"I didn't say it would make you happy. But you'll definitely feel better after letting off steam, and you're not harming anyone in the process. It's a form of self-expression."

My sister gave me a blank piece of paper and a pen. Halfheartedly, I drew some lines.

"Honestly? I don't feel any better," I protested.

My sister didn't seem to hear me. Looking out the window, she said, "Remember this, Ren. Sadness alone can't harm anyone. It's what you do when you're sad that can hurt you and those around you."

Even now, her words lingered in my mind.

1 2

What
She
Couldn't
Say

"Abe told me you were sick," Honda said. "Didn't I tell you to take care of your health?"

I laughed. "Stop nagging, I'm all right now."

Neither of us felt like going out, so we'd settled on instant noodles for dinner again. I dispensed hot water into the cups and waited for the three minutes to pass.

Recalling my dream, I asked Honda, "Have you ever dreamt of the same person more than once?"

"Yes, one of the teachers in my primary school. She was so fierce, she gave me nightmares."

"That's not what I mean." I searched for a better way to phrase it. "Not someone you know, but a total stranger."

He thought about it for a while. "I'm afraid not. Though I did once dream of a memorable stranger."

"Tell me about it."

"Well, I dreamt that I'd met a girl in a park. We got along fine, and I knew somehow that I was inside a dream. But hey, I liked this girl and thought maybe I could find her in real life. So I asked for her name and promised to look for her after I woke up."

Intriguing. "Did you manage to find her?"

"That's the thing." He sighed. "I couldn't remember her name. I know it starts with an M, but that's about it."

"Maria, Mariko, Mai, Maki, Manna, Mina, Mika, Michi—"

"It's no use, Ishida." He gave a dry laugh. "I won't remember."

"But you have a girlfriend now?"

He shook his head. "I'm not seeing anyone. I've only had one girlfriend before, and her name doesn't start with an M."

"Really? Only one?" That seemed impossible for someone his age.

"I do have some close female friends, but I've never see them as potential girlfriends. Only this one woman. I met her a few years back and was convinced that she was the one. But things didn't work out."

He seemed solemn about this, so I didn't probe further.

"What about you?" Honda asked. "Did you meet your perfect girl from your dream?"

"I'm not that lucky; the stranger in my dreams is a five-year-old girl with pigtails."

"How odd. Perhaps she's someone you've seen before, but don't remember?" Honda checked the instant noodles. "Let's eat now before they turn soggy."

"Uh-huh."

Slurping the noodles, I came up with a few possibilities.

In my bereavement, I could simply have invented Pigtails. But Honda had a point, and the more I thought about it, the more unlikely it seemed. Why would a total figment of my imagination consistently be invading my dreams?

Another possibility was that the girl was my sister, whom I hadn't known at that age. Pigtails had appeared after my sister died. If she knew who her murderer was, and had the power to do so, she could reveal who was responsible in this way. Yet, for some reason, I was certain Pigtails wasn't my sister. Both of them had similar bright, intelligent eyes. But unlike my sister, Pigtails didn't smile much.

One more possibility entered my mind. What if Pigtails had something to do with the Katous and their deceased child? The dreams had started after I moved into the politician's house. I had no idea how their child had died. What if she had a message to pass along? Then again, why through me? Why not go to her parents instead? The more I sought an answer, the more questions I found.

"Do you believe in reincarnation?" Honda asked.

"Not really," I answered. "Do you?"

"I'm not into any particular religion, but I do believe in reincarnation. It's a convincing explanation of how things turn out. For instance, why someone has good luck. Maybe he was charitable in a past life."

"In that case, you probably dumped a lot of girls in your past life."

He laughed. "Maybe. But it's comforting to be able to think that, maybe in my next life, I could be with that girl."

"The one from your dream, or your ex-girlfriend?"

"My ex," he said. "This way, it would be sort of a happy ending."

I nodded in agreement.

If reincarnation existed, what kind of life would my sister have next? She had been caring and gentle. Maybe she would be given something better. Born to doting parents. Knowing her penchant for jazz, she would go for piano classes. She had always wanted to learn to play. Then, she could moonlight at a hotel jazz lounge, where she would meet the kind manager with a gentle smile. They would date for a couple of years, get married, have three kids. She would live a long, fulfilling life and pass away from old age, surrounded by her loving family.

A happy ending did sound comforting.

I HAD SEEN THE book in the reading room a number of times, but never picked it up. I thought it might seem too childish. But that day, I decided to read from Hans Christian Andersen's fairy tale collection. I needed something with a happy ending.

"I hope you don't mind a children's story," I told Mrs. Katou.

As always, she was silent.

The gentle wind rippled her thin blouse. The tips of her fingers peeked out from the long sleeves. I sat next to her and opened to the index page. After some deliberation, I chose "The Little Mermaid."

A young mermaid gave up her life in the sea to gain the love of a human prince. But when I reached the last few paragraphs, I remembered that Andersen's version concluded with the little mermaid dissolving into foam.

I closed the book. Not a happy ending after all.

Another gust of wind blew. It was getting chilly, so I closed the window. Hearing Mrs. Katou cough, I picked up the glass of water that had been left on the bedside table and placed it in her limp hands. As she sipped it, her sleeves dropped to her elbow, revealing the blue veins under her pale skin and the scars on her left wrist. Some looked like old wounds, faint and fading, but others were fresh.

I felt a lump in my throat. How had I failed to notice it for so long? She always wore long sleeves, regardless of the weather.

Fifteen years ago, one of my sister's classmates had committed suicide. She'd downed a bottle of sleeping pills and slashed her wrists with a kitchen knife while soaking in the tub. When her family found her, she was already dead, and the bathwater was a deep red. The case was reported in the national newspapers. My sister had said the school was in a frenzy.

I knew the girl. She was a friend of my sister's who had come to our house twice. My sister told me she was good in school and at sports. Everything was going well for her, except that her boyfriend had just left her for another girl.

"It must have hurt a lot," my sister said to me.

"I guess so. You need to cut deep to die from massive loss of blood, and it's a slow death. It takes a lot of courage to commit suicide that way." If it were me, I would have preferred to jump off a building. Not that I ever planned to do that.

"I wasn't talking about that. I meant the pain she must have felt inside." My sister cracked her knuckles. "The trouble with emotional pain is, you can't see the wound. But it's still there. It's real."

Her serious tone made me uneasy. "Hey, you sound depressed."

She ignored me and continued talking. "She probably wanted to express her pain. It was her attempt to communicate her feelings. She needed help, but nobody noticed until it was too late."

"It sounds like you need help, too."

"Shut up." She nudged my shoulder.

To my relief, my sister returned to her usual self. Back then, I didn't fully grasp the meaning of what she'd said or how she could understand that girl so well.

I took the glass from Mrs. Katou's hands and put it on the table. Leaving her alone, I returned to my room. I sat on the bed and tried to get over my discomfort, but couldn't.

Even at work, I kept thinking about Mrs. Katou's bony left wrist. Her skin was so thin, almost translucent. And those scars . . . What was she thinking? Whatever had caused them—was that also why she refused to speak?

Knowing Mr. Katou's background and profession, it was likely that he was hiding his wife's condition from the public for the sake of keeping up appearances. Perhaps that was why his wife was cloistered at home instead of receiving medical help. It pained me to think about it. Was she less important than his career? I hoped someone would see her pain, before it bubbled over.

THE BELL RANG, AND I stood up. The first session had ended.

"That's all for today," I said before reciting the usual wrap-up lines. "Please leave your answer sheets here, and make sure nothing is left behind. I'll see you next class, and don't forget to study hard."

Conditioned to this routine by now, the students packed their belongings, grabbed their bags, and walked to the front to pile their papers on the desk. A few nodded at me as they left the classroom. Soon, only one was left. Seven Stars came to me and laid her answer sheet squarely on top of the pile.

"My father would like to invite you to our house this weekend," she said carelessly.

"Your father?" I asked, taken aback by the offer. "But why?"

She shrugged. "How should I know?"

I looked at her, and she narrowed her eyes at me defiantly. She had laid out a challenge.

"I'm free Sunday morning," I said. "What's your address?"

She gasped, probably not expecting me to accept so easily. But in a split second, she regained her usual cold demeanor. "You know where it is," she said. "You pass our house every morning on your jog."

I forced a laugh. "So you've seen me. Still, I cover quite a long route, so you need to be more specific."

"It's one of the two-story houses across the valley. Ours is number twenty-three."

1 3

The
Days
of
Bubbles

That Sunday, I made an effort to dress smartly: beige sweater over white shirt, khaki trousers, and brown leather loafers. I'd informed Mr. Katou that I had an early appointment and couldn't buy lunch for his wife. He said nothing, only nodding once.

I left the house and walked along my usual jogging route. When approaching the valley, instead of going down the declining road, I turned into the residential area. All the houses in the complex looked identical. White walls, tall windows, a garage, and perfectly tended gardens. Without the numbered gold placards, it would be difficult to tell them apart.

I found house number twenty-three, pressed the bell, and waited. The door swung open and a bespectacled man appeared. He looked to be in his mid-fifties. He should have been the father, but his soft features and remarkably wide-set eyes bore no resemblance to Seven Stars.

We looked at each other. Neither of us spoke. For a moment, I thought I saw his eyes widen as he stared straight at me. I kept my eyes on him, unable to move.

"You must be Mr. Ishida," he finally said, breaking into a gentle smile. "I'm Nakajima, Rio's father. Thank you for coming."

I lowered my head. It must have been my imagination. "Pleased to meet you."

"Come in and make yourself comfortable."

I took my loafers off and entered. The place wasn't large, but it was cozy. Not much furniture either, yet the arrangement was aesthetically pleasing. A tall wooden shelf separated the living room from the entryway, stairwell, and door to the kitchen.

"Take a seat, Mr. Ishida."

I did as he asked, looking around for Seven Stars. There was no sign of her. I assumed a comfortable sitting position and waited for Mr. Nakajima to speak.

He shook his head and sighed. "I heard about what happened at the convenience store. One of the police officers is a friend of mine, and he saw Rio's name in the daily list of write-ups. I didn't believe it at first. How could my daughter steal? She's only seventeen, and I give her enough pocket money. But when I asked my daughter, she didn't deny it."

So this was what the invitation was about.

"They let her go with just a verbal warning, since they couldn't catch her red-handed. Thankfully, a family acquaintance is quite a high-ranking officer here, and he managed to convince his colleague not to file Rio's particulars. Regardless"—he bowed to me—"thank you for helping my daughter. I'm in your debt."

"Don't mention it." I felt awkward. "It seemed like the right thing to do as her teacher."

"This is my failure as a parent. She's my only child, and I've spoiled her too much. From now on, I'll be more strict."

I kept my opinion to myself. Knowing how strong-willed that girl could be, she wouldn't behave just because of a stern warning from her parents.

"Have you had breakfast, Mr. Ishida?" Mr. Nakajima asked.

"I'm going to grab a sandwich later," I answered.

"Why don't you let me fix you some sandwiches instead?"

I hesitated. "Please, don't trouble yourself."

"It's no trouble at all. I need to make breakfast for Rio and myself anyway," he said. "Do you prefer chicken or tuna?"

He looked determined, so I relented. "I'm fine with either."

"I'll do a mixture, then. And to drink? Coffee? Tea?"

"Coffee, please, no sugar."

"Got it."

He went to the kitchen, leaving me alone. Without anything to do, I glanced around aimlessly. Photographs lined one of the walls; I counted twenty-five in total. Printed in eight by ten and framed in black wood, most were photographs of women. A few were of food, fashion accessories, and electronic gadgets. I guessed Mr. Nakajima was a photographer, but he didn't strike me as the artistic type.

I heard clanking noises, followed by the sound of a coffee grinder. Mr. Nakajima returned with a tray of sandwiches and two cups of coffee.

"Long black," he said, placing a cup in front of me.

I thanked him and took a sip. The flavor was rich. It felt good to have a cup of freshly brewed coffee after weeks of drinking the instant kind. He took the first sandwich, and I followed suit. He had cut them into uniform bite-sized pieces and secured them with toothpicks.

"Are you a photographer?" I asked.

He smiled. "What makes you think so? Is it those prints?"

"Uh-huh."

"You're mistaken, Mr. Ishida. Those are photographs of my wife."

I wanted to ask which one, since they showed different women, but I didn't want to be rude, so I kept quiet.

"She's in all of these photographs, somehow or another," he explained. "My wife is a hand model."

"A hand model?" I'd never heard of that, but an image flashed into my mind of Seven Stars, holding a cigarette with her beautiful fingers, looking vacantly at the rain.

"Yes, sort of like a body double, but only for hands."

He gave me a quick tour of the highlights of her career. She had graced the cover of this fashion magazine and that, her hands passed off as those of famous supermodels and actresses. I'd heard of a few, but most I didn't recognize. I'd never been into celebrity culture.

"Your wife has an interesting job," I told him after he'd finished talking. "How did she get into the profession? Was she already a model?"

"No, she was an ordinary housewife. An agent spotted her in the supermarket and convinced her to give it a try," Mr. Nakajima said. "At first, she just did it for fun. It was a nice outlet, an activity of her own. Then she got a job in a national hand soap campaign, and her popularity shot up. Are you familiar with the Matsuyama Corporation?"

"The milk soap?"

"Yes, that's the one. She became sought after and earned more than me. I used to work as a salesman, but was ill suited for the job. When her income doubled mine, she came up with the idea for us to switch roles. She enjoys her assignments and can't afford to damage her hands doing housework, and I'm more than happy to do domestic chores."

"Sounds like an excellent arrangement."

"Indeed. I'm more of a homebody, and the better cook," he said. "Most people find this setup unusual, but I've learned not to care about what they think. You can't please everyone."

"What's important is that both of you are happy."

He replied with a thoughtful nod.

I took another sip of the coffee. "Is your daughter at home?"

"She's in her room," he said. "I asked her not to come out at first because I wanted to talk to you privately."

"Is there anything else I can do?"

He cleared his throat. "Actually, I'm wondering if my daughter is doing okay."

"Yes, her marks are above average. She should get into a good university."

"I'm not worried about her academic results." He shifted his eyes. "I'm more concerned with how well she gets along with her peers. She never talks about school, and I never see any of her friends. A girl her age should be socializing a lot, shouldn't she? Having sleepovers and things like that."

I wasn't sure how to respond, so I stared at my coffee.

"I might be overthinking it," he said.

I needed to change the topic. "Does your daughter look like your wife?"

Mr. Nakajima smiled, back to his comfortable self. "You must be asking because Rio and I don't look alike."

Well, I couldn't deny that.

"My wife has the good looks. My daughter did take after her," he said. "A few modeling agencies have scouted Rio, but she's not interested. It's such a pity. She has the potential."

"Do you want her to follow in your wife's footsteps?"

"It might help her to open up," he said. "She's a good kid, but she lives in her own world. She doesn't let anyone get too close. I worry about what will happen to her in the future."

"Maybe she prefers to keep to herself."

"Yes, perhaps . . ." he muttered. "Actually, Rio did try modeling once. My friend, a jewelry designer, asked her to model for their shop catalogue. To be honest, I was surprised she agreed. Too bad the photographs aren't ready yet, or I'd love to show them to you."

I recalled what Maeda had told me—that she'd seen Seven Stars leaving a jewelry store with an older man. So that one incident had sparked the rumor about Seven Stars and older men, probably compounded by the fact that she habitually skipped class.

"Can I get you more coffee, Mr. Ishida?"

"Thank you, but I'm good."

"Then I'll clear the table and ask Rio to greet you."

Mr. Nakajima stood and went off with the tray, disappearing behind the wooden shelf. I heard him call his daughter. Seven Stars appeared in a loose knit top and shorts. Her hair was pulled up into a high bun.

"You're here," she said, peering behind the shelf to check if her father was nearby. "Come with me."

I reluctantly stood up and followed her. The dining area was behind the partition. Through the glass door that separated it from the kitchen, I could see Mr. Nakajima washing the dishes.

"Stop spacing out," Seven Stars whispered.

She led me up the stairs, opened a door, and pulled me into her bedroom. It was unexpectedly girly, with walls painted pastel pink. There was a twin bed full of stuffed animals, a desk piled with books and anime figurines, and a white wardrobe with a full-length mirror next to it. She had decorated the furniture with glittery stickers.

"How long are you planning to stand there?" Seven Stars asked, sitting on the bed.

"You shouldn't bring men into your room." I stayed there but kept the door open. "It will give people the wrong idea."

She gave a chuckle. "Don't worry, old men don't count."

"Age is just a number," I said. "Where's your mother?"

"She won't be back any time soon. She ran away from home a few weeks ago. Abandoned my father and me."

I was impressed by her ability to deliver such a crude joke with a straight face. Pulling out the swivel chair, I sat in front of the desk, the only available seat in the room.

Her desk was next to the window. It was open, but a faint tobacco smell lingered. I could imagine her standing by the window, languidly lifting a cigarette to her lips, the white smoke dancing around her before vanishing with the wind.

Resting my elbow on the desk, I looked outside. I had a clear view of the road. The window faced the site where my sister was murdered. I thought about the night I lay down on the side of the road in the pouring rain. She could have seen me, but I doubted it. It had been late, and the weather awful.

"Want to see something interesting?" Seven Stars asked.

She pulled out a drawer under her bed. I walked over to get a better look. Inside were hundreds of bubble gum packets of various brands, all still sealed.

"You're crazy," I said. "Did you steal all of these?"

She nodded, her expression unchanged.

I couldn't tell what was on her mind. Was she proud of her conquests?

"Look carefully, Mr. Ishida. A few of them aren't available in Japan." She fished out one of the packets. It had a circular yellow dispenser with a face printed on it. "I got this in Copenhagen."

"You must really love bubble gum," I said. "Or you've got a screw loose in your head."

"Or both," she said.

"Or both," I repeated. "This amount is insane. Can you even finish them before they expire?"

"I've never opened any of them. I imagine some have already

expired." She used her right hand to sweep the packets around. "I started building this collection when I was twelve, so that makes it six years' worth of effort."

"Why did you do this? Do you like collecting gum?"

"Not particularly. I just have the urge to take things that don't belong to me."

"Kleptomania?"

"Maybe," she said nonchalantly. "Or curiosity. I don't know."

That would be an unhealthy level of curiosity. "Why bubble gum?"

"Why not? It's everywhere and it's small, one of the easiest things to steal." She took a packet and twisted it around her fingers. "The first time I stole was from a convenience store near my school."

"With serial crime, the first offense is usually done on impulse."

"True," she said. "Where'd you learn that?"

"From a TV drama."

"Uh-huh." Seven Stars looked into my eyes. "Well, the first time I did it, it felt great, so I ended up doing it again. The second time too, it felt good. Not quite as much as the first, but still a nice feeling. One thing led to another, and it became a habit. Now I'm a serial bubble gum thief."

"You're twisted."

"What about you, Mr. Ishida? Have you ever had the urge to steal?"

"No."

"You've never stolen anything in your life? Not even once?" She dropped the bubble gum back into the cabinet. "Don't bluff. There must be at least one occasion. Like, maybe you stole someone's girlfriend. Or you took another teacher's pen. That counts too, you know."

I took a moment to think about it. I had many failings, but stealing was against my principles. Then I remembered that I had stolen before, unintentionally. "Fine. I did take something once."

She smiled. "Now you're talking. What did you steal?"

"A car."

Her eyes lit up. "Are you kidding me? A real one?"

I wasn't joking, though I wished I was. "Yes, a real car. A Toyota Celica. Yellow coupe."

"That's flashy. I assume you didn't end up in jail?"

"My friend and I took it for a joyride. We returned it to where it had been parked. The owner never realized it was gone."

Her excitement wore off. "That's borrowing, not stealing."

"It's still stealing," I insisted. "When you borrow something, you get the owner's consent first. My friend and I took it without permission."

"The owner didn't lose anything. The car was returned, wasn't it?"

"That doesn't make it less of a crime. Whether the car stayed missing or not isn't the issue here."

"All right, all right," she said. "Let's count it as stealing. How long ago was it?"

"I was seventeen."

"I can't believe you were a better thief than me when you were my age. For real, stealing a car. I guess I'm learning from the best."

I ignored her sarcastic remarks.

"So you like sports cars, Mr. Ishida?"

"Most people do, don't they?" I said.

She shrugged. "I don't. They make me sick. All cars, not just sports cars."

"You get motion sickness? So you can't ride in cars?"

"I can if I really want to, but I try to avoid it. No point in torturing myself," she said. "Why don't you tell me the full story of The Great Toyota Celica Heist?"

I shook my head. "It's not something I'm proud of."

"Then why did you do it?" she asked.

"It was my friend's idea, to celebrate my birthday."

14

A
Flashy
Yellow
Toyota
Celica

The friend I'd mentioned, strictly speaking, wasn't really a friend.

One summer in high school, I worked as a pizza deliveryman. I met her when I was delivering an order to an apartment in Den-en-chōfu. I was standing in the lobby next to her while waiting for the elevator.

The girl looked younger than me. She sported a short bob, which made her stand out. Most girls at my school kept their hair long. I thought she looked stylish in that haircut, though way too skinny to be called athletic. Her thin T-shirt was stained with sweat, revealing the outline of her bra. She wiped the sweat from her forehead and turned to me. I didn't want her to think I was staring at her chest, so I quickly looked at something else. It happened to be the outdoor parking lot.

It was a weekday afternoon, so many of the spots were empty. But since the apartment was located in a pricy complex, a few nice vehicles were still parked there.

"Do you like that Honda coupe?" she asked.

There was only one sports car in the lot, but it wasn't a Honda. "The yellow one?" I asked.

"Yes. That's the one you're looking at, isn't it?"

"It's a Toyota Celica."

"I see," she mumbled. "You certainly know a lot about cars."

This was because my classmate Jin had spent an entire year obsessed with cars. He'd brought dozens of automotive magazines to school, and I'd inadvertently picked up the knowledge.

"Do you think the elevator's broken?" The girl pressed the button repeatedly. "We've been waiting for so long."

I didn't answer. I wasn't in the mood to talk. It was supposed to be a special day. And here I was, sweating under my scratchy pizza uniform next to an impatient girl.

When the elevator doors eventually opened, two workers came out with a black upright piano. That must have been what held it up. A tanned boy followed them out. He was a deliveryman at the same pizza joint as I was. He went out as the girl and I entered.

"Ishida?" He looked at me in surprise. "I thought you were taking today off."

"Change of plans," I said. "I took the morning shift."

"Anyway, happy birthday. Enjoy your date later."

I forced a smile and pressed number nine. Turning to the girl, I asked, "Which floor?"

"Same as you," she said.

The number on the panel gradually increased. It stopped at nine and the doors opened.

I held the button. "After you."

"Let me guess," she said. "You got dumped by your girlfriend, so you went to work instead."

I was shocked by her bluntness, but couldn't refute what she'd said.

"Poor thing," she said, though her straight face didn't match her words. "How about this—I'm bored and I've got nothing planned today. When your shift is over, why don't we spend some time together? I promise it will be fun."

I hadn't expected her to ask me out, but I wasn't complaining. She was quite good-looking. Prettier by far than most of the girls at my school, including my very recent ex-girlfriend. Her advance seemed too good to be true, in fact, but I didn't care. Even if it was crazy to go out with a girl I barely knew, it beat being home alone on my birthday.

"Once I deliver this, I'm done for the day," I said.

"Excellent." She gave me a satisfied smile. "In the meantime, let me go grab something. I'll see you here in five minutes."

She turned right and I went left. I delivered the pizza to a young man who complained that I'd taken too long to arrive. I apologized and had no choice but to listen to his rant. He went on and on, making a fuss that his pizza was cold. It wasn't even true. The pizza had still been hot when I'd arrived, but he had wasted so much time scolding me, it had gotten cold. Eventually, he slammed the door in my face. One of the many occupational hazards of a pizza deliveryman.

Returning to the elevator, I expected the girl to be there, but she wasn't. I waited another ten minutes. Had she gotten tired of waiting and left? I was about to give up when she finally appeared.

"Sorry to keep you waiting," she said, pressing the down button.

"What took you so long?" I asked.

The elevator doors opened and we went in.

"Stop complaining." She pressed the button for the lobby. "You should be thankful—I'm giving you a birthday present."

Really? "You don't need to."

"Don't be ridiculous. You can't reject a gift. It's impolite."

The door opened and we stepped out.

She took a car key with a Toyota logo from the pocket of her shorts and dangled it in front of me. "You like it, don't you?"

I was at a loss for words. This had to be a joke.

The girl walked straight up to the parked yellow coupe before opening one of its doors. "What do you think?"

My mind was blank.

"Get in, pizza boy."

I walked over to the passenger side while she took the driver's seat. The car was lower than I'd imagined. It didn't have much legroom, but the fittings were luxurious. I ran my fingers over the soft leather seat.

"Your dad's car?" I asked.

"No, it belongs to Gouda," she answered.

Who was that? "And he let you borrow his car?"

"I didn't ask."

"What?"

"Stop shouting," she shushed me. "It makes my ears hurt. And don't worry. This Gouda, he's just a spoiled, rich brat. He's always drunk and never locks the door. Anyone can just walk in and take his car keys. It's a miracle no one besides me has ransacked his apartment yet. He's such an easy target."

Aren't you a spoiled, rich brat yourself, I wanted to say, but of course I didn't.

The girl turned on the engine and the car made a loud roar.

"What are you doing?" I raised my voice. "You're not planning to drive this, are you?"

She arched an eyebrow. "Cars are meant to be driven. Don't tell me you just want to sit around and enjoy the air conditioner."

"I can't believe this. How old are you?"

"I'm fifteen this year."

"You don't have a driver's license."

She rolled her eyes. "Of course not. Fifteen's too young to qualify for a driver's license."

She released the hand brake. It was too late to be asking, but . . .

"Do you know how to drive?" I asked.

"Of course," she answered. "I practice almost every day."

She switched to first gear and pulled out of the parking space. Her handling was rough. The car jerked a little and I cursed.

"Shut up, pizza boy," she hissed. "I've been driving for two years, so sit still and relax."

"And where exactly have you been driving?"

I regretted asking as soon as I heard her answer.

"Just down the road." She stepped on the accelerator. "At the arcade."

I THOUGHT I WAS going to die on my seventeenth birthday, but I didn't.

"My boyfriend let me drive his car a couple of times," the girl said.

That wasn't so bad. At least she'd had some experience. "Then why are you here with me? Let me guess, he just dumped you."

I was teasing her, but she was silent, so it must have been true. I felt bad for saying it now, but couldn't take it back. It would be more awkward for me to apologize.

We stopped at McDonald's to order food to go and drove toward Yokohama. She pulled over at a quiet beach before we reached the city. The two of us got out. She took off her shoes and ran barefoot toward the sea. I sat on the warm sand, enjoying the breeze and watching her kick the waves.

When she got tired, she walked back and joined me. We ate our double cheeseburgers, staring at the ocean. The sunset painted the beach in warm golden hues.

"Do you think Gouda's reported us to the police?" I asked, crumpling the wrapper.

She shook her head. "He won't be awake until noon tomorrow."

Other than that, we were quiet. I guessed we both needed company, but neither of us wanted to talk. We just wanted to be with someone so we wouldn't be alone.

After it got dark, we drove back to Tokyo.

Looking at her profile as she drove, I felt a peculiar connection to this girl. She wasn't wearing any particular expression, but she looked lonely. Perhaps it was a reflection of my own state.

When the car stopped at a traffic junction, I reached for her hand that rested on the gear switch. She didn't react. When the light turned green, I moved my hand away. She shifted gears and the car moved off.

We reached the apartment complex around nine. Half the parking lot was full now, but the original spot was still unoccupied. After she returned the yellow coupe, we went to the back of the building where I'd locked my bicycle.

"Thank you for today," I said, undoing the chain.

"Don't mention it," she said. "Did you have fun?"

"I did." It was special. Not that I ever planned to pull any stunts like that again. "I won't ever forget it."

She smiled. "That's great."

I pushed my bicycle through the gate and she walked behind. Once outside, I got onto my bicycle and looked at her. She waved goodbye.

"I know the order is mixed up, but we haven't introduced ourselves." I extended my hand. "I'm Ren Ishida."

She folded her arms and averted her eyes. Feeling embarrassed, I withdrew my hand.

"You're a good guy, Ren," she said. "If we meet again, I'll let you know my name."

"So I just have to turn up here tomorrow."

"It's not that easy. I don't live here."

"Where do you live, then?"

Without answering me, she turned around and walked into the complex. I waited there until she was no longer visible. She didn't look back.

After that day, I never saw her again. And I never told anyone about her.

"**YOUR FRIEND SOUNDS LIKE** a fun person," Seven Stars said.

I smiled. "Yeah, she was crazy."

"Your girlfriend?"

"Nope."

"Is she pretty?"

I tried to remember her features, but only vaguely recalled what she looked like.

"Did you like her, Mr. Ishida?" Seven Stars asked.

"Let's just say she captured my interest. It's not every day you find a girl who knows how to steal a car."

She rolled her eyes.

I cleared my throat. "How long are you planning to go on stealing gum?"

"Are you suggesting I upgrade to sports cars?" she asked. "I'll stop stealing if you ask politely."

"Please stop stealing, Miss Rio Nakajima."

"I wasn't finished. Having you say that is too easy."

I sighed. "What else do you want?"

"Buy me lunch."

She had to be kidding. "Why should I?"

"Because you're my teacher, and teachers should take care of their students."

"That doesn't make any sense."

"I need to change first, but let's meet at twelve sharp at the gazebo." She closed the drawer. "I'll wait there until you show up."

"Wait, I—"

Before I could raise any objection, she stood and walked out of the room. Not wanting to be there alone, I followed her out. Mr. Nakajima saw us, but he didn't say a word about me having been in his daughter's room. I thanked him for his hospitality and left.

Strolling around the neighborhood to pass the time, I thought about the Celica girl.

When the car had stopped at the traffic junction, a soft light had fallen onto her pale skin, highlighting her delicate features. My hand was on hers, but she didn't say a word, nor did she look at me. She didn't even flinch. Her body was there, but her mind wasn't.

That night, the two of us were lonely, isolated under Tokyo's dazzling lights.

1 5

All
I Ever
Wanted
Was
to Be
Happy

Seven Stars stood alone under the gazebo. She was in a white chiffon dress and espadrilles. Her hair was tied in a high ponytail, emphasizing her slender neck. This more feminine style suited her well. When she saw me, she smiled.

"What would've happened if I hadn't come?" I asked.

"That wouldn't've happened," she said. "You're not the type to break a promise."

"I didn't make any promises. You decided everything without asking," I said. "So, what do you want for lunch?"

"I'll leave it to you."

I'd known this would happen, so I'd called Honda from a public pay phone earlier to ask for a recommendation.

"A cozy place to have lunch . . . As in, for a date?" he asked.

"Not really," I said. The less he knew, the better. "She's just a friend."

"What kind of place do you have in mind?"

"Something casual? Preferably around Segayaki, and with good food."

He thought for a moment before he said, "I do know one you should consider."

WE ARRIVED AT A Western restaurant that, according to Honda, was, "Not too crowded and serves delicious steak." It was only a twenty-minute walk from the gazebo. Even on the weekend, the place was half-empty. Seven Stars chose a square table farthest from the other diners. We sat across from each other.

"Why do you want to sit in the corner?" I asked. It looked like we were trying to find a secluded spot. If anyone from Yotsuba saw us, they would misunderstand.

"I don't like to have other people sitting around me," she said. "It's too hard to have a proper conversation. Everyone stops and listens to what others are talking about. Anyway, why do you ask? Does it matter?"

"It's fine, as long as you're happy."

"I am," she said, glancing at the menu. "What's good here?"

"The pork rib isn't bad; the filet mignon, too. They both come with side dishes."

Seven Stars narrowed her eyes. "You've been here before?"

"No." I was only parroting Honda.

She clasped her hands. "I'm impressed, Mr. Ishida. You did your homework, for someone reluctant to go out to lunch."

"Just order your food," I said.

"Since you've gone to such great lengths to research, I'll let you decide."

"You might regret that."

"I doubt it."

I called the waiter over and ordered the pork rib for myself and filet mignon for Seven Stars.

"How about a drink?" he asked.

I glanced at her, but she simply shrugged.

"Two glasses of water, and that will be all."

The bespectacled waiter repeated the order back to us before disappearing into the kitchen.

Seven Stars leaned in toward me. "Mr. Ishida, why did you become a teacher at Yotsuba?"

"No particular reason," I lied, not wanting to mention my sister. "I have no plans for after graduation, and the pay is decent for the job they offered me, so why not?"

She tilted her head. "Wasn't there any other profession you wanted to pursue?"

I shook my head. "I wish there was."

"Which university are you graduating from?"

"Keio."

Her eyes widened. "You went to that prestigious of a university, and you have no plans after graduation? Not to be rude, but you're such a waste of space."

I laughed. "You're being rude."

"What did you study?"

"British and American Literature."

"Why?"

"I didn't know what to choose, so I went with the same majors as my sister, though she didn't continue on for a graduate degree."

She nodded. "So you have a sister complex."

"No, I don't," I protested. "I just wasn't drawn to any particular field of study."

"Being confused and not knowing what to do in the future, I thought that was exclusive to teenagers. But you're already old, and you're as clueless as I am."

I sighed. I didn't think being in my mid-twenties qualified me as old.

The waiter returned with two glasses of water and we stopped talking. Once he left, Seven Stars resumed the conversation.

"Last week, the school gave us a career survey," she said. "We're supposed to come up with three jobs we'd like to do, but I don't know what to write. It's still blank."

"Do you have anything you like to do? A hobby, perhaps?"

She shook her head.

"How about a childhood dream?" I asked.

"Didn't have any," she said. "All I ever wanted was to be happy."

"That's too vague."

"How about you? No childhood dreams?"

I regretted bringing up the subject. "I wanted to be a soccer player."

"And what happened to the dream?"

"I'm pretty good, but not good enough to play professionally."

"Too bad," she said. "I was hoping I'd figure out what I wanted to do sooner or later, and then I'd be set. Now I can see that it's not that simple."

"I had the same problem with the career survey when I was your age. I knew I wasn't going to make it in J-League, but there wasn't anything else I wanted to do. I ended up consulting my sister."

"What did she say?"

"She told me to submit some respectable professions so my teacher wouldn't call our parents."

"What did you write?"

"Doctor, lawyer, and engineer," I said.

Seven Stars laughed. "Maybe I should do the same. Accountant, secretary, and social worker. What do you think?"

"I couldn't imagine you working in an office, but I'm sure your teacher wouldn't complain."

She looked up at me. "What do you imagine me doing?"

"I think you'll take an unconventional path," I said. "Anyway, just move one step at a time. At least, that's what I'm doing."

She nodded, seemingly satisfied with my patchy advice. Changing the subject, she said, "I saw you with your girlfriend the other day."

That wasn't possible. "What?"

"You two were at a coffee shop near Yotsuba."

I shook my head. "That woman is just a friend."

"Is that so?" She raised her eyebrows. "You looked lovey-dovey."

"I'm telling you, that's not my girlfriend."

"Fine, fine," she said. "So you do have a girlfriend."

"Do I have to answer that?"

"Do you have a reason not to?"

"It's complicated right now."

She feigned sympathy. "Aww, you're on the verge of breaking up."

"We're not," I said. "But I'd appreciate it if you stopped asking about her."

Seven Stars looked unsatisfied with my answer. "Be honest, Mr. Ishida. How many girlfriends have you had?"

I did a quick mental calculation. "Eight, maybe."

"What do you mean, 'maybe'? And eight . . . that's a lot."

"What do you expect? I'm twenty-four."

She tilted her head. "How many boyfriends do you think I've had?"

"How would I know?"

"Just guess," she insisted.

"I don't know." I took a sip of the water. "You're young, but good-looking. Maybe four or five?"

She smiled, but didn't correct me. Instead, she continued to ask questions. "How long have you been dating your current girlfriend?"

"Around four years."

"And what do you like about her?"

Another complicated question.

Nae was always accommodating others' needs. She didn't demand much, and was easy to get along with. Above all, I knew she loved me. But was I only dating her because she was nice, and had feelings for me?

"Don't overthink it," Seven Stars said. "What do you find most attractive about her?"

I thought about it for a moment. "Maybe her sleeping face."

"What?"

"She has this peaceful expression when she sleeps. I feel at ease just watching her."

"So you have a fetish for sleeping girls."

"I doubt it," I said. "Someone I know never woke up from her sleep."

Her smile disappeared, and she went silent. I supposed she knew whom I was referring to. I glanced at the kitchen, wondering if our orders would be ready soon. If I'd been in Tokyo, I would have already finished my meal.

"Are you hungry, Mr. Ishida?"

"No, I'm fine."

"Then why do you keep looking at the kitchen instead of straight at me?"

"It's a bad habit of mine," I said. "I can't look into the eyes of the person I'm talking to."

"Why?"

I shrugged. "I just feel it's rude to stare."

"No, it's rude not to look at whoever you're talking to."

"It's not like it's obvious I'm looking elsewhere. I would look at your hair, or the scenery behind you. Most people don't know the difference. In fact, you're only the second person who's noticed."

"Your girlfriend was the first?"

"No, it was my sister."

A brief silence ensued before she asked, "Isn't it hard for you to be a teacher, then? How long have you been like this?"

"I don't know. I realized it when I was ten. Maybe it's always been that way, but I didn't know it before then."

This conversation made me uneasy. Luckily, our orders arrived. The same waiter laid everything on the table. The portions were huge, and the food looked scrumptious. I cut into my pork rib, but Seven Stars didn't touch her steak.

"Is something wrong with your dish?" I asked.

She shook her head and stared into my eyes. "Look at me. Is it that hard?"

I really didn't want to discuss this any more. "Can you please just eat your food?"

She didn't budge.

I had no idea what else to say, so I started cutting her steak into bite-sized pieces.

"What are you doing?" Seven Stars asked.

I didn't look up. "Helping you cut your food."

She laughed. "I'll let you off this time, because I like it when people cut my food for me."

"So you like having other people take care of you."

"I like *people* who care about me," she corrected. "Do you do this for your girlfriend?"

"Not really," I lied.

I usually did help Nae cut her food, since she wasn't good with

Western cutlery. "I'm a chopstick person," she had confessed. Yet for our dates, she always chose Western restaurants, because she thought they were more romantic.

"So this isn't normal, based on your dating history," Seven Stars said. "I must be special, then."

"This isn't a date," I said sternly.

She frowned, but finally took a bite. "Mr. Ishida, apart from my parents, you're the only person who has ever stepped into my room."

"Quite an honor," I joked.

"Yes, it is. You should feel proud."

"I'm sure you have invited one of your boyfriends over before," I said. "Or maybe not, since your father is always around."

"It's not because of him. My father is easygoing. It's just I've never had a boyfriend."

I couldn't tell if she was lying. She had no reason to make it up, really. She'd said it with a straight face, but for such a pretty girl, it was hard to believe.

"What about your friends? Surely, you've brought them over," I said, already knowing that wasn't true based on Mr. Nakajima's remark.

She shook her head. "I don't have any friends."

"But I always see you arriving and leaving with your classmates."

"Those are acquaintances, not friends."

"There's a difference?"

"Of course," she said. "Acquaintances are people you know, but friends are people you can count on. It's totally different."

"Do you want anything else?" I asked Seven Stars after we left the restaurant.

"No." She broke into a smile. "Thanks for the meal."

"With this, you'll stop stealing?"

"Yes, as promised," she said. "Not just bubble gum, but other things, too. I'll never, ever take anything that doesn't belong to me again."

"Good."

"You believe me?"

"I don't have a reason not to."

"Don't be so gullible," she said. "That's how people get hurt."

I furrowed my brow. "Why are you so cynical? Distrusting everyone is a sad way to live, isn't it?"

"Probably," she said before we parted ways.

I thought about what she had told me, that she had no boyfriend and no friends. Some people were too beautiful for their own good. Instead of working to her advantage, perhaps her looks attracted hostility.

I imagined her living alone in her bubble-gum-filled world. In that moment, I couldn't blame her for what she did. It might be the only way she knew how to go on, but no one could live that way forever. Not even her.

16

Miyuki
Katou

That evening, I finally called Nae, though we didn't end up talking.

It was her father who picked up the phone. I recognized his croaky voice and hung up straightaway. I had no idea why; it was instinctive.

I did miss Nae sometimes, but I wasn't ready to talk to her yet.

This was by far the longest relationship I'd been in. The previous ones had only lasted a couple of months. And Nae definitely cared about me. But I hadn't even begun to recover from my sister's death, and I'd started a new life here, at least for now. It wasn't a good time to reenter a relationship I wasn't sure about. I still didn't know how I felt about the future she wanted for us.

But I owed her news of some sort, after disappearing for weeks. I took a piece of paper from the desk drawer and wrote a letter.

Dear Nae,

How are you? Are you doing well? Or are you still angry?

I'm not sure if you're aware, but I'm no longer in Tokyo. I've been in Akakawa for over a month. If you remember, it's the town where my sister used to live. It's only a temporary arrangement, six months at most.

You might be wondering why I've come here. Well, a lot has happened. I should have let you know earlier, but I couldn't bring myself to call. The truth is

I stopped.

The truth is, my sister has died. The sentence replayed itself in my head, but there was no way I could write it down.

Crumpling the letter into a ball, I aimed it at the bin. I missed, and it rolled under the wardrobe. I crawled to retrieve it and saw the corner of a dust-covered paper peeking out. Hooking it out with my index finger, I shook it clean and smoothed it out.

It was a child's drawing, with *my family* written on top. A bespectacled man, a woman, and a girl with pigtails stood in front of a house. All three of them were smiling.

The artist's name was scribbled at the corner. Miyuki Katou.

MR. KATOU WAS READING a poetry book in the reading room. He did this every Sunday night without fail. Despite the overwhelming number of options, he only ever chose one book: *Silence.*

"Excuse me," I greeted him.

He put down the book and scowled at me. Anyone else would have thought he was displeased, but that was just the way he looked.

I passed him the drawing. "I'm sorry to interrupt, but I found this in my room."

He looked at it and remained silent.

"I thought it might be important," I continued.

"It's my daughter's, but she's no longer around." He tore the paper into tiny pieces and threw them away. "We've gotten rid of her belongings. It's easier to move on when you aren't constantly reminded of the past, but I guess we missed a thing or two."

"I understand," I said, and took my leave.

Returning to my room, I thought about the house. Based on the number of bedrooms, the one I was staying in had probably belonged to Miyuki Katou. After seeing the drawing, I wondered again if she was the little girl in my dreams.

THREE DAYS LATER, I met Seven Stars at the gazebo while on my jog. She was all by herself, smoking in her school uniform.

"Skipping class again?" I asked.

She turned to me. "Why do you ask the obvious?"

I said nothing and looked at the crushed cigarette butts scattered all over the ground.

"Are you going to tell me smoking is bad for my health?" she asked.

"Now you're asking the obvious," I said. "It's a contagious disease, you know—asking the obvious."

She clicked her tongue.

"Do you skip class often to smoke here?"

I didn't expect an answer, but she nodded.

"Why?"

She took a puff and exhaled slowly. "I don't see the point of going to school. I don't fit in. It's suffocating to be there and I'm tired of pretending." She turned to me. "Anyway, why am I telling you? It's none of your concern."

"Your father is worried that you don't get along with your classmates."

"What's wrong with having no friends? People are born alone, and they die alone. You can't take your friends to the grave," she said. "Don't mind my father. He tends to worry about insignificant things, but he doesn't care about what really matters."

"Like what?"

She didn't answer.

I thought about my own father, who didn't even turn up for my sister's funeral. This girl had no idea how blessed she was. "You shouldn't talk like that. He's your father; it's natural for him to be worried."

"Don't be patronizing." She dropped her cigarette and crushed it with her black loafer.

"There's a trash bin right over there."

"I like to litter," she said. "Got a problem with that?"

What a stubborn girl, and ill-mannered, too. I sighed, about to walk away.

"Are you going home now?" she asked.

"Yes, I need to get lunch."

She jumped down. "Let's go."

"Where?"

"Lunch, of course. Isn't that what you just said?"

Her eyes told me she would follow me no matter what.

"If anyone catches you skipping class, I'm not helping you out," I said.

Seven Stars smiled. "We have a deal."

"What do you feel like eating?"

"I want Hokkaido barbequed mutton."

"Did you bring enough money for that?"

"I was joking, don't be so serious. Let's have burgers."

She walked in front, and I followed a few feet behind. Every now and then, she turned around to make sure I was still there. We passed by a bustling market before arriving at a shopping complex. They had a MOS Burger in the basement.

Slipping some notes into my hand, Seven Stars said, "Order a fish burger with fries and a Pepsi for me. I'll get us a table."

She walked in before I could protest. When I left the counter with a tray full of food, she waved at me from a table in the far corner. I went over and sat down opposite her.

"Are you going to cut up my food again?" she asked.

"Don't be ridiculous," I said. "It's a burger."

She laughed and started eating.

"Good?" I asked.

Seven Stars nodded and made a peace sign with her fingers. I almost said she looked cute, but I stopped myself. It was inappropriate to say that to a student. Hell, I shouldn't be here, eating with her, when she was skipping class.

"I turned in the career survey yesterday, and followed your suggestions," she said.

"Was that good enough for your teacher?"

"I guess so, since she didn't say anything." She took a sip of her drink. "Mr. Ishida, do you miss your sister?"

I froze. "What do you mean?"

"Do you have any regrets? Things you wish you had done with her when she was still around."

I hadn't expected such direct questions from anyone, but that was the kind of girl she was. I knew she meant no harm. "Of course I miss her," I said. "And I do have some regrets. Anyone would feel the same when a person close to them passes away unexpectedly."

She tilted her head. "What kind of regrets?"

"Well, I wish I'd visited her more often. I wish I'd been more honest, told her I cared about her . . ." I paused, realizing I had said too much. "You know, that sort of thing."

She looked into my eyes with a wistful smile. "I'm so envious of her."

"What nonsense are you talking? There's nothing to be envious of." I looked down at my burger. "She's dead."

"When she was alive, she was so loved."

I stared at my burger, and we ate our lunch in silence. The place was soon filled with the incoming lunch crowd. It should have been too loud, but the hustle and bustle became white noise.

Or maybe it was this girl. She affected me in an odd way. She carried with her a profound sadness. And whenever we were close, it flew into me.

"Thanks for lunch," Seven Stars said, dabbing her lips with the paper napkin.

"You're welcome," I said. "I'll walk you home."

She shook her head. "Bad idea—my father is there. I don't want him to think you helped me skip class."

"That's surprisingly considerate of you," I joked.

I returned the tray and we walked out of the restaurant. Before we parted ways, I told her, "Don't skip class too often. You don't want to repeat the year with a bunch of underclassmen."

"I know."

She waved at me and left. From there, I went to the convenience store to buy a lunch box for Mrs. Katou. When I reached the house, I was surprised to see Mr. Katou in the entry hall. He looked as if he had been waiting for me.

"May I have a moment?" he asked.

"Sure," I said.

We went to the reading room and sat on the couch. He lowered his shoulders and laced his fingers, deep in thought. The tinkling of the wind chime echoed through the house.

Mr. Katou cleared his throat before speaking. "I have discussed my wife's condition with our family, and we believe a change of scenery might be good for her. The plan is to move her to Hakone where she can be looked after by our relatives. Her cousins run a pension there."

"Sounds like a good idea," I said, knowing this was a gentle dismissal.

"When she leaves, I'm moving into a smaller apartment. This house is too big for a man living by himself. And there are too many memories, some of which I'd rather forget."

"So you'll be selling the house?"

He nodded. "I know this is sudden."

"I'll look for a new place soon. Is there a date I should keep in mind?"

"If possible, I'd like to have the house ready for takeover by the end of the month. We've already found a buyer, but I told them I'd need some time to move out, so don't let it trouble you."

"It's no trouble at all."

"Thank you for your understanding," he said. "I appreciate what you have done for my wife and me. You've been a great help to us."

"I should be the one to thank you for letting me stay here."

THINKING BACK, I MIGHT have been too hasty to agree to the end of the month. It was presumptuous of me to think it would be easy to find a new place. In addition, I didn't have a large budget to work with.

"Cheap, fast, or good. Choose two out of three. You can't get them all." That was what my sister used to tell me. The priority was to move out fast. And cheap was a must, too. So based on her theory, the next place I was going to move into wouldn't be good.

But not everything was gloomy. The same day, I got my first paycheck. Hiroko personally handed out everyone's salary. One by one, we were called into the principal's office, and finally it was my turn.

"Thank you for your hard work," she said, handing me an envelope. "How was your first month?"

"I've gotten used to it," I said.

"That's great. In that case, how about joining our permanent staff?"

Once again, she'd caught me by surprise.

The edges of her lips curled upward. "I'm just teasing, but the offer is serious. I've gotten very positive feedback about your classes. You've got what it takes. Please consider it, and let me know if you decide to take the position."

"Thank you. I will," I said, before leaving the office.

I went to my desk and put the envelope in my bag. As I packed my teaching materials, I felt a tap on my shoulder.

"How does it feel, getting your first paycheck?" Honda asked, standing next to me.

I smiled. "Not bad. I could definitely get used to this."

"How are things at the politician's house?"

"About that . . ." I thought back to my predicament. "Do you happen to know any real estate agents who could recommend some short-term accommodations?"

He furrowed his brow. "Has a problem come up there?"

"No problem at all." I decided not to talk about the Katou family's circumstances. "I'd just prefer to live on my own, and the place is too fancy for my liking."

"Well, you're in luck. My cousin is a real estate agent."

Honda called his cousin, and by the next day, I had a list of apartments for rent. There were forty-plus options in the listing, but it wasn't difficult to narrow the field.

To begin with, I wanted a place that wouldn't require a long-term contract. That took out half of the options. Second, with my pay, I could only afford five out of twenty. Of the five, two of them were too far from Yotsuba. And so, I was left with three possible choices.

ON SUNDAY MORNING, I met Honda and his cousin. Mrs. Itano was short and plump. Her cropped hair was dyed auburn, but I could see the gray roots. She had thick makeup dominated by pink hues. Pink eye shadow, pink blush, and pink lipstick. Wearing a fuchsia skirt suit, she looked like a cartoon character.

"Trust me, she's capable," Honda whispered, seemingly aware of what was on my mind.

Still in doubt, I bowed to her. "I'm Ren Ishida. Thank you for helping me."

She giggled. "Don't worry, dear, I'll get the best apartment for you. I've been in this business for over forty years."

I mustered a smile.

"I know, it's hard to tell, isn't it? But I'm in my sixties. Working keeps me young." She flashed her porcelain-white teeth, which were probably fake. "Let's get moving, dear. We have plenty to do."

Honda drove us to the first apartment on the list. The building was shabby—in Mrs. Itano's words, "It looks like the roof is going to fall off at any time." I wouldn't mind an old building, but the place didn't look safe for human occupancy.

"Don't worry, dear. The next one should be better."

True, since I couldn't imagine much worse than the first.

The second apartment was near the train station. Its location was central and the building was new, but it was also next to an open market.

Mrs. Itano peered out the window. "It's a little noisy, but that shouldn't be a problem. Young people like you won't be home most of the time."

"Ishida works late," Honda said. "Cram school teachers tend to wake up late. The market is going to be noisy in the morning, I don't think we should settle for this one."

Mrs. Itano looked like she disagreed, so I quickly said, "Why don't we take a look at the third one?"

Since my budget was far below market rate, I had lowered my expectations. But luckily, the last apartment was perfect for me. Or at least, it was good enough. Quiet and rustic, it was located behind a park.

"It's an old building," Mrs. Itano explained as we climbed the staircase. "There's no elevator, and the only available rooms are on the fifth floor. But the rent is affordable. You only pay one month's deposit and the first month's rent. No key money needed."

Honda raised his eyebrows. "No key money? This is the first time I've heard of that."

"In recent years, some landlords have dropped it to attract more tenants, especially in more remote neighborhoods."

She led us to Room 503 and opened the door. It was a one-bedroom apartment with a separate dining and kitchen area. The bedroom had tatami flooring, while the rest of the unit, except the bathroom, had hardwood. The place was fully furnished, and even had kitchen equipment and a washing machine—everything I could possibly need.

Opening the living room windows, I felt the warm sunset on my face. It was breezy, and the apartment looked onto a scenic view of the park. It reminded me of the field where I used to play soccer when I was a child.

"This place is fine," I said. "I'll take it."

"Are you sure?" Honda asked. "There's no train station nearby, and the nearest bus stop is a long walk from here."

"I'm fine with that. It's good exercise."

"That settles it, then." Mrs. Itano clasped her hands. "Where are you staying now, dear? I'll bring the contract to you tomorrow. Once you've signed it and paid the deposit, you can move in within a week."

"I'm currently staying in Segayaki."

"Ishida is at that politician's house," Honda added. "Kosugi Katou."

"That's a beautiful place, dear. Why are you moving out?"

"Mr. Katou decided to sell the house."

Mrs. Itano's eyes lit up. "He'll get a good price for that. Has he found a buyer? Or is it still for sale?"

"I believe the deal has already gone through."

"Oh, that's a pity." She sighed. "By the way, how's his wife? I heard she was unwell."

"Do you know her?"

"I'm afraid not, but I helped her older sister to buy a plot of land. She's a strange woman, I tell you. The land was cursed. Nobody wanted it despite the ridiculously low price, and she was bent on acquiring it. Rich people have such weird taste. Anyway, who am I to complain? Business is business."

"What did she use the land for?" Honda asked.

"She built a hotel there. Remember the one I told you about? The Katsuragi Hotel."

1 7

The Origin
of the
Katsuragi
Hotel
(The Kimono
Lady's Story)

The hotel lobby was empty. The Katsuragi Hotel was always rather quiet, but that day, no one was around.

I went to the counter and called, "Excuse me, is anyone in?"

"I'm coming," said a voice from the back office.

The kimono lady hurried to the front and recognized me at once.

"Mr. Ishida, I'm sorry for keeping you waiting," she said. "I've been busy since last week. Mrs. Sakamoto is sick, and she has no relatives, so I have to look after her."

I assumed Mrs. Sakamoto was the cleaning lady, since I'd never seen a third employee around. "I hope she's feeling better."

"The doctor says she should be well in three, four days." She gave me a confused look. "No luggage this time?"

"I'm not here to book a room. There's something I'd like to discuss with you."

"With me?"

"Yes. It's about Miyuki Katou and her mother, Haruna Katou." I forced myself to look into her eyes. "I mean, Haruna Katsuragi."

Her expression changed. After a few moments, she told me to

follow her, leading me through the office behind the counter into a tea room.

We sat facing each other on the tatami floor, separated by a low table with a handcrafted tea set on top. The room was decorated with a calligraphy scroll and a simple flower arrangement. The kimono lady took out two ceramic cups and poured us green tea. Her technique was graceful, befitting the pale yellow kimono she wore.

Neither of us touched our cups. I didn't want to rush her, so I waited. But after several minutes had passed and she continued to look down in silence, I knew I had to say something.

"Mrs. Katsuragi?"

She looked at me. "First of all, how did you find out about Haruna?"

"I found her maiden name written inside a book in the Katou household," I lied, not wanting to implicate Mrs. Itano. "When I thought about the physical resemblance between the two of you, I figured you must be related."

She nodded. "Haruna was my younger sister. I know you're from Tokyo, so I'm not sure what your relationship with the Katou family is."

"I've been staying at their house."

"I see. Now I remember, there was talk of the late Miss Ishida having stayed there," she said. "But I'm no longer related to Haruna or the Katsuragi family, let alone the Katous. I'm afraid there's nothing to discuss."

I cleared my throat. This wouldn't be easy, but I had to try my best. "I believe you care about the well-being of your sister," I said. "And right now, she's harming herself."

The kimono lady drew in a sharp breath. "Is that true?"

"Yes. The Katou family is downplaying her condition to avoid scandal. My apologies for being so direct, but you should get in touch with your sister before it's too late. She needs help."

She shook her head. "I wish I could, but I can't. They've forbidden me from seeing her."

"But she's your sister."

"It's a long, complicated story."

"Why don't you tell me?" I said, sensing an opening. "I mean, if you don't mind. I've got the time, and I want to hear what you have to say."

She paused for a long while, before taking a deep breath and recounting the story of her life.

HER NAME WAS NATSUMI Katsuragi. She was the first daughter of the Katsuragi family, who owned Akakawa Hospital, the biggest hospital in town.

The family didn't have any male heirs. There were only two daughters, Natsumi and Haruna. Their mother could no longer conceive due to uterine cancer, which had forced her to undergo a hysterectomy.

The Katsuragi family had been running the hospital for generations, and figured a son-in-law would inherit the job. It was long decided that the successor would be Natsumi's future husband, who would be selected from the pool of young doctors working at the hospital.

As the daughters of a hospital director, Natsumi and Haruna had a privileged upbringing. They went to a prestigious girls' school, got good grades, and were well-behaved. Only three years apart, the two of them were inseparable.

At their father's suggestion, Natsumi attended Tokyo Medical University and became engaged to a promising surgeon at the hospital. Haruna studied at Waseda University, where she met and was proposed to by the eldest son of the Katou family. Everything was going according to plan until Natsumi's fiancé died of a heart attack. It came as a surprise, since he was young and had led a healthy lifestyle, but fate has a way of twisting one's direction in life.

Her father arranged a list of alternate suitors, but Natsumi turned them all down. Though her relationship with her late fiancé had begun as an arranged marriage, the two had fallen in love with each other. She wouldn't accept anyone else. The Katsuragi family was shocked, and what followed was a leadership crisis at the hospital. Getting Haruna to marry the next hospital director in her sister's place was impossible without offending the Katou family. Left with no choice, Dr. Katsuragi adopted one of the young doctors into the family to make him his successor. Needless to say, he was dismayed with his eldest daughter's disobedience and disowned her.

At age twenty-one, Natsumi Katsuragi had to leave the family home. Broken-hearted and depressed, she left with nothing but the family name and fond memories from before things had gone bad.

"THOSE DAYS WERE THE darkest days of my life," the kimono lady said.

I nodded in understanding.

"I hadn't graduated, and didn't have the money to continue paying rent or tuition," she continued. "Thinking back, perhaps my father thought I would agree to marry his adopted son once I learned how difficult it was to survive on my own. But he was wrong. I no longer cared about my life."

MOVING OUT OF HER luxurious apartment, Natsumi rented the cheapest place she could find, sharing it with illegal immigrants.

Most of them washed dishes in restaurants, earning low wages, and she took on the same job. Natsumi's mother couldn't bear to see her living in poverty. Without her husband's knowledge, she went every once in a while to visit Natsumi and give her some money. But a year later, Mrs. Katsuragi passed away.

"**AFTER THE UTERINE CANCER,** my mother was diagnosed with lung cancer," the kimono lady said. "But this time, the doctors couldn't save her."

She sipped her tea for the first time, and I followed suit.

"I'd always been close to my mother. Unbeknownst to me, before she passed away, she had instructed Haruna to discreetly support me. My sister became my source of strength until I met my husband three years later."

NATSUMI'S HUSBAND OWNED THE Japanese restaurant where she had been working. The man was by no means ideal husband material—he was a widower, and more than twice her age. His wife had been killed in a car accident, and he didn't get along with his grown-up children. Thin and sullen-looking, he was the opposite of Natsumi's late fiancé, but he had a sadness about him that attracted her.

It wasn't incorrect to say that what she felt for him was more compassion than love. The death of a loved one had bound them together, and they were soon married. Around the same time, Haruna entered the Katou family registry.

When Natsumi and her husband went to the Katsuragi house to ask for her father's blessing, Dr. Katsuragi didn't take the union well. A man who appreciated family background and high education, he was furious that Natsumi's husband possessed neither. And the fact that she was to become a second wife was an embarrassment for the Katsuragi family. Everyone was against the marriage, even Haruna. Natsumi and her husband were chased out of the house and told never to return.

In spite of that, Natsumi was content with her new life. Together with her new husband, she worked hard and made the restaurant flourish. Business was good. Though Natsumi didn't have the same level of financial comfort that she'd had growing up, the couple had all they needed. Unfortunately, this happiness was short-lived.

Some said it was bad luck, others said it was destiny when Natsumi's husband collapsed at work. They rushed him to Akakawa Hospital, but he fell into a coma. The doctor said he had a blood clot in his brain. Having once lost her fiancé, Natsumi was determined to make sure her husband survived. She spent all her time taking care of him. Despite all her efforts, his condition didn't improve.

Meanwhile, nobody watched over the restaurant, and its standards dropped. Regular customers stopped coming, and soon the business was running in the red. Eventually, the bank seized it. To make things worse, Natsumi had used up all of the couple's savings for her husband's treatments. Eventually, she had no choice but to ask her father for help.

"I SWALLOWED MY PRIDE and went to my family's house to ask to borrow money," the kimono lady recounted. "I lowered my head, begged my father. But since he had already declared that I was no longer his daughter and he disapproved of my marriage, he refused to get involved."

My chest felt heavy as I remembered my own parents disowning their daughter. "I'm sorry, did your husband . . ."

"He never woke up. After agonizing months with no progress, I made the decision to turn off his life support." She looked into her cup. Her eyes were empty, and the tea had turned cold. She lifted the cup and held it steady with two hands. Her wrinkled fingers traced the roughness of the pottery. "After the funeral, I had no desire to remain in Akakawa with all of its painful memories. But with my husband's passing, I somehow regained the will to live I'd lost after my fiancé's death. I wasn't about to waste it."

BEFORE HE'D PASSED AWAY, Natsumi's husband had promised to take her to Kyoto for their honeymoon, but the plan had to be postponed when the business started to flourish. Now that they no longer had the restaurant, Natsumi made it her mission to fulfill their dream. Armed with a single suitcase, she went to Kyoto and stayed at the traditional Japanese inn her late husband had chosen. As fate would have it, the establishment was looking for a new attendant. Natsumi saw it as a sign for her to remain in Kyoto.

"I DECIDED TO WORK there, never intending to return to Akakawa. But fifteen years later, I received a call from one of the Katsuragi family lawyers," the kimono lady said. "My father had passed away. In his will, he had left a sizeable inheritance for both my sister and me. I think it was his way of making amends." She looked at me. "He wasn't very honest with himself, was he?"

I mumbled in agreement.

"Behind the strong façade, my father was a softhearted person. He felt responsible for what had happened to my husband."

NATSUMI HAD ENDED UP with enough money to sustain herself without ever working again. Using part of the inheritance, she bought bonds and stocks of reputable companies. The dividends alone were enough to cover her expenses without touching the capital. Even then, a considerable amount remained, and she wanted to buy back the restaurant she had once been forced to sell.

After the bank had seized it, a restaurateur bought the place, but the business never took off, and eventually folded. A real estate company then took over the restaurant and tore down the building with the intention of turning it into shops, but the company ran into financial difficulties and the project went unfinished. Rumors began to circulate that the land was cursed.

"**I WANTED TO GET** it back by whatever means, and was prepared to pay above market rate," the kimono lady said. "Luckily for me, the real estate company was eager to get rid of it. I ended up paying close to nothing,"

I recalled what Mrs. Itano had told me about the property.

"As an abandoned plot of land, I wouldn't have much use for it. I had first thought of building another restaurant, but running that would have been too labor-intensive. I was getting on in years and wouldn't have the energy for it. Building a business hotel was a good alternative, since I had the experience of working at a traditional inn."

I nodded.

"Am I boring you, Mr. Ishida, with this old woman's story?" she asked.

"Of course not. Your life is fascinating," I said. "But there's one thing I don't understand; why did you name the hotel after your father's family instead of your late husband's?"

"In a way, the hotel is a tribute to my father. The inheritance he left allowed me to buy this plot of land and spend the rest of my life in peace, knowing I would have nothing to worry about financially."

I stole a glance at my watch. We had been talking for nearly an hour, but the question I had come to ask hadn't been touched on. "Based on what you've said," I began, "you've mended fences with the Katsuragi family. But why did you say earlier that you would have nothing to do with your sister and her family?"

She paused, taking the time to pick the right words. "By the time I returned to Akakawa for my father's funeral, fifteen years had passed. I hadn't been in contact with my sister since her opposition to my marriage—in fact, I still haven't."

"You don't know anything about her life here, then?"

"I heard she had a daughter who spent her entire life in and out of the hospital. I don't know much about Miyuki—I never met her." The kimono lady sighed. "The child passed away before I came back to Akakawa."

"Do you happen to know why Miyuki was hospitalized?" I asked.

"I heard she had a rare, incurable illness, but I don't know what it was. I assumed it eventually caused her death."

So she didn't know firsthand what had happened to her niece. "When was the last time you saw your sister?"

"The day I was exiled from the Katsuragi family," the kimono lady said. "Haruna didn't even attend our father's funeral. After her daughter's death, she went into a severe depression, refusing to leave the house or see anyone."

"Did you ever try to visit her?"

The kimono lady looked down. "I went to the residence a few times, but Kosugi Katou always asked me to leave. At first, he was civil about it, but eventually, he gave me a stern warning to stop coming."

I could very well imagine Mr. Katou doing such a thing.

"I ignored his words until a fire broke out at the hotel. Luckily, no one was hurt, and the damage was minimal. I filed a police report, but my intuition told me something was amiss. The authorities seemed reluctant to pursue any leads, even though it was a clear-cut case of arson."

NATSUMI HAD RECEIVED A call from Mr. Katou a day after the incident.

"I heard there was a fire at the hotel," he said.

"Thank you for your concern," she said. "I'm all right."

"I'm relieved to hear that. Now, listen. You're currently in a comfortable position that allows you to live in peace. Things like the fire wouldn't happen if you stopped meddling in others' private affairs. There's an old saying: Never wake a sleeping tiger. I hope for your sake that you'll take this to heart."

The brief call confirmed her suspicions, but she had no way to prove the incident was the work of the Katou family. Even if she did manage to find any incriminating evidence, the police would be reluctant to act on it. The politician's family held considerable influence in Akakawa.

"AFTER THAT, I STOPPED trying to reach Haruna," the kimono lady said.

"I can understand why," I said, "but your sister needs you."

She gave me a thin smile. "It was kind of you to come all the way here, Mr. Ishida. But after abandoning Haruna for so long, I have no right to step in as her sibling."

"That's not true. No matter what's happened, she's still your sister."

"I don't wish to go against Mr. Katou. He's a dangerous man. It's in your interest not to know too much about the family's personal affairs. My apologies, but I'm afraid I can't be of further help."

I sensed she was withholding important information, something I wouldn't be able to get to simply by asking the right questions. "I'll be taking my leave now," I said. "Thank you for your time."

"Not at all."

The kimono lady escorted me out. I deliberately slowed my pace, hoping she would say something else, but she didn't. I left the hotel and headed to the bus stop.

Halfway there, I heard her calling after me. I turned around and saw her walking hastily down the deserted street. I waited for her to catch her breath before she spoke.

"There's one last thing I should have told you, Mr. Ishida," she said. "I have the feeling Miyuki's death was unnatural."

I frowned. "What makes you think so?"

"At my father's funeral, I met his adopted son. According to him, Haruna had refused to send Miyuki to Akakawa Hospital."

"Maybe she thought the other hospital was better."

She shook her head. "Akakawa Hospital is the most advanced medical institution in the area. As granddaughter of the hospital's former director, Miyuki would've received nothing but the best treatment. Despite that, Haruna chose to send her daughter to a smaller clinic outside of town."

"When did Miyuki die?"

"Six years ago," she said. "In May."

"And how old was she?"

"If I'm not wrong, around six or seven."

Hearing that, I was almost sure Miyuki Katou was Pigtails.

"What are you planning to do, Mr. Ishida?" the kimono lady asked.

"Nothing yet. But please consider reaching out to your sister."

She sighed. "I've been marked by the Katous. It's too hard for me to get close to Haruna."

"Since I'm staying in the house, perhaps I could help in some way?" I neglected to mention the impending move.

"Mr. Ishida, I know you're a good person, but you're getting yourself into trouble. Please listen to this old woman. Try not to get too close to the Katou family."

"I'll keep it in mind," I said before we parted ways.

My plan had been to return to the Katous' house that afternoon and finish packing, but I decided to go elsewhere.

1 8

To
Load
and
Unload

Akakawa only had one public library, located on the other side of town from the Katou residence.

Upon entering the library, I walked over to the wooden cabinets where they kept archives of the local newspaper. I searched for the year 1989 and flipped through to the month of May. Removing the stack of newspapers, I carried it to an empty desk and went through the articles. It was a harder task than I'd imagined. After a while, I was dizzy from all the headlines. But I told myself this had to be done today, and continued to scan every single one.

An hour later, I'd only managed to get through half the stack. I was tired, and the tips of my fingers had turned gray. Exhausted, I stretched my neck until it cracked and forced myself to continue.

Halfway through, I finally found a short article about Miyuki Katou. The headline read: DAUGHTER OF KOSUGI KATOU PASSES AWAY. The piece, only six lines long, said she had died peacefully at the age of six due to terminal illness, but there was no specific information on exactly which illness it was.

In the same newspaper, I found her obituary. The column was small, listing her parents' and grandparents' names, and accompanied by a tiny black and white photograph.

The girl looked nothing like Pigtails—or rather, they were polar opposites. Unlike Pigtails, who was bright-eyed, Miyuki Katou appeared gloomy and thin. Her hair was cut like a boy's, and she wore glasses.

Looking closely, I found traces of Mr. Katou's features. His unapproachable air was reflected in Miyuki, who—like her father—appeared to be scowling.

So Pigtails wasn't Miyuki, after all. But her father was a famous politician. In a small town like Akakawa, there should have been more write-ups about her death. I continued to go through the newspapers.

Finally, I found a longer article about Miyuki's death in another local daily from a few days later. The news didn't mention names, but it was obviously referring to her.

THE MYSTERIOUS DEATH OF A POLITICIAN'S DAUGHTER:
A POSSIBLE CASE OF HOMICIDE

MK, the daughter of a politician in Akakawa, passed away three days ago in M Hospital at the age of six. The official cause of her death has been classified as multiple organ failures, but rumor has spread that the actual cause was inappropriate medical treatment requested by MK's mother, HK.

MK was a regular patient at M Hospital. According to the family's statement, she was born with poor health, which prevented her from attending school. Her symptoms have been described as resembling cancer. The diagnosis of her illness has never been made public.

S, a nurse at M Hospital, spoke to us on condition of

anonymity. According to her, Dr. H—who was in charge of MK—administered many invasive treatments, including several that haven't been approved by Japan's Ministry of Health. The treatment decision remains questionable, as the cause of the illness had not been determined.

Our attempt to reach Dr. H has been unsuccessful. After MK's death, he resigned from his post and left the town. Nobody we spoke to knew his current whereabouts.

We interviewed the patients at M Hospital, many of whom were familiar with HK, MK's mother. "That lady used to come every day. She's elegant and classy. It's not hard to spot her," said J, a patient who has been at M Hospital for a year and a half. But when we asked J about MK's father, politician KK, she told us she had never seen him. She was surprised to learn that KK was MK's father.

Our repeated calls to both KK and HK went unanswered. The white house where they reside in the upscale district of Segayaki has been shuttered. When we attempted to reach KK through his secretary, she told us the family was requesting privacy during their bereavement period and wouldn't be accepting any interview requests.

And thus, the cause of MK's death remains a mystery.

RETURNING TO THE KATOUS' house, I spent an hour packing my sister's belongings. I called to ask Honda if he wanted her cassettes, but he declined.

"They remind me too much of Keiko," he said.

I felt the same way. I'd planned to keep the jazz cassettes and stereo, but browsing through her collection, I was overwhelmed. Echoes of her were all over them. I could imagine my sister sitting next to me, picking up one of the cassettes.

"This album, I love the third song when it gets to the chorus.

It goes like this . . ." She would hum the melody while tapping her index fingers. After stopping, she would turn to me and ask, "You know which part, don't you?"

I would shake my head. Only you knew which part, but it doesn't matter any more since you're dead.

No, I couldn't keep the cassettes.

Mr. Katou's words replayed my mind. "It's easier to move on when you aren't constantly reminded of the past." This time, I agreed with him.

I sold the cassettes and stereo to a used music store. The shop hadn't offered a good price, but that wasn't important. I needed to get rid of my sister's stuff. I donated the rest of her belongings to a charity with pickup service.

Finally, the only thing left was the urn with my sister's ashes. I knew the moment I would have to part with it was getting closer.

I ENTERED MRS. KATOU'S room with Emily Brontë's *Wuthering Heights* in my hand. It was supposed to be my last day to read to her, and I hated leaving her alone in that condition, knowing no one else would come. She was alive, but her spirit was gone, ripped from her body. She needed someone to save her, anyone.

Putting the book down, I sat next to her on the bed. "Haruna," I called.

No reaction. I reached for her hands and held them. They were cold and lifeless. She looked in my direction, but her gaze was as empty as ever.

I took a deep breath before speaking. "Miyuki was six. She was old enough to know she wasn't sick, but she went along with it. For such a young girl, it must have been scary. Yet she put up with it."

Mrs. Katou still didn't move.

"I believe it was her way of saying she loves you, and she forgives you," I continued. "That's why you need to forgive yourself. For your sake, and hers."

I let go of her hands, picked up the book, and left the room. After closing the door, I heard faint, muffled sobs. In that moment, I knew she wouldn't need me or anyone else to read to her any longer.

After returning the book to its shelf, I took my belongings outside and waited for Honda on the porch. He had insisted on helping me move.

Passing time, I took one last look at the house. Silent as always, save for the tinkling sound of the wind chimes. The white curtains waved around, pulling me back to the first time I'd come to collect my sister's things. Two months had passed, but I still wasn't used to the place.

A black sedan pulled in front of the house. I opened the gate, and Honda came over to give me a hand. This time, I had a suitcase, a Boston bag, and a few large plastic shopping bags.

I loaded my belongings into the trunk of the car. "I don't know how I ended up with more things."

"That's always the case," Honda said with a laugh. "As time goes by, you get more and more baggage. It's why we do spring cleaning every year, isn't it?"

We got into the sedan and he drove me to my new apartment. It only took twenty minutes to get there, though, like he'd said, the building wasn't the most accessible without a car. Maybe I should get myself a bicycle. When was the last time I'd ridden one? In high school, if my memory served me right. Would I need to relearn how to ride? Or was it like tying shoelaces—once you got the hang of it, you knew it by instinct for the rest of your life?

The car made a sharp U-turn, and something on the rearview

mirror glistened. I stretched my neck to get a better view. A tiny white porcelain rabbit ornament was tucked behind the mirror; no wonder I hadn't seen it before.

For a grown man, Honda had surprising taste.

19

The House Behind the Flower Bushes

When I'd first seen the apartment, it had been late afternoon, and the sunset might have romanticized the atmosphere of the building. But in broad daylight, the apartment looked more run-down than I remembered. The faded pink walls were peeling and stained with watermarks. There was rust all over the metal railings, and the wooden staircase was chipped. At least the overall construction looked solid.

"I'm surprised they haven't torn this place down," Honda said, climbing the staircase. "It's been around since World War II and hasn't once been renovated. The landlord should have at least added an elevator."

"If they had, the rent wouldn't be so affordable," I said.

"Maybe the rentals are just a front, and some rooms store drugs or firearms."

"Don't be ridiculous."

Even if that were the case, I couldn't have cared less. The rent was within my budget, and they accepted month-to-month occupants. I wondered whether the landlord actually turned a profit here, charging so little.

Breathing heavily, we finally reached the fifth floor. I took out my keys and opened the door. After setting down my belongings, I surveyed the unit. There was a lingering musty odor. I opened all the windows to let the air circulate.

In one corner of the living room, I saw a television coated with a thick layer of dust. I tried turning it on, thinking Honda might want to watch something, but it was broken. After fiddling with it for a while, I gave up and went to the bathroom to wash my hands. To my dismay, there was no hot water. No wonder the place was so unpopular. I could always boil water like in period films, but I knew I was too lazy to do that. Well, I'd gotten what I'd paid for.

"Is everything okay?" Honda asked.

"Yes, yes," I answered, rinsing my hands under the tap.

The mirror in front of me was cloudy with dirt. It looked like my first task would be to clean the place thoroughly. I sighed. Not my favorite way to spend a day off.

THE APARTMENT WAS A five-story building, and each floor had eight units. A third were occupied, and several of the units weren't available for rent—not that I bought Honda's reasoning for that. In real life, things were seldom that interesting. Most likely, the units were damaged beyond repair.

As far as I knew, the first floor was fully rented out. The higher the floor, the fewer tenants there were. On my floor, there was only one renter apart from me.

The building's occupants were a mix of college students and young professionals. It wasn't hard to remember their faces, since there weren't many of them. They all lived alone, except for one young couple.

"The landlord wants to rent it out to single occupants only," the bespectacled building manager, Izumi, told me.

A week after my move, she called me to her apartment to pick up some documents. Room 304 doubled as her home and office. I paid rent each month through her. If there was any problem with the appliances, she was the person I should speak with. Though, in her words, "There's nothing much I can do about it, so try not to disturb me."

"There's a couple on the third floor," I pointed out to her.

"The girl is the only registered occupant, but her boyfriend comes every day. He's as good as living here. The landlord wouldn't be happy if he knew, but he won't find out if no one reports it."

I chuckled.

"What's so funny?" Izumi asked, crossing her arms.

"You look like a girl I knew in high school," I said. "She wore the same glasses as you, and she was a model student. Class representative, member of the student council, things like that. But unlike you, she would report us to the teacher whenever we misbehaved."

"Someone's holding a grudge."

"In a way."

"I'm not that serious, you know." She took off her glasses. "I just have not-so-good vision and not-so-good luck. I broke my usual pair, so I've got to use my old ones, which make me look like a dork."

Without her glasses, Izumi looked less like that girl I'd known.

"Okay, enough staring. I need to wear these all the time, or I'm literally blind." She put her glasses back on. "Before I forget, I have something in here to give you. Just a moment—my place is messy, so I don't normally invite people in."

"Don't worry, I'll wait here."

She left me standing at her door. I couldn't tell how chaotic the place was because a decorative curtain blocked my view, but I could hear Izumi rummaging around.

A couple of minutes later, she returned with a booklet. "Rules and regulations of the building, to read at your leisure," she said. "You're free to go now."

I tried hard not to look baffled. "Thank you, I'll definitely read it."

"Ah, one last thing. I've told you before, but I'll repeat it. Try not to bother me. Even if you tell me the washing machine isn't working, or the water isn't running, there's nothing I can do about it. You're better off knocking on someone else's door and asking if you can use theirs. I can only report to the landlord when his secretary comes once a month. Even then, his office is unresponsive."

"You sound like you hate managing this place," I couldn't help remarking. "Why did you volunteer in the first place?"

She looked surprised. "I didn't volunteer. You think I'd take on all that extra work for nothing? The landlord deducts half my rent for the trouble."

"Wow, that's a good deal. And if you smuggle someone else into your apartment, like that girl did, you could divide your rent even further."

I was teasing her, so I didn't expect a response.

"Brilliant idea, except I snore loudly. The only living being I've ever slept in the same room with is Midori, the cat I had in primary school."

"Good thing you know," I said. "Did Midori tell you that?"

Izumi smirked.

"Have you ever met our landlord?" I asked.

She shook her head. "I only communicate with his secretary."

"Then how did you become building manager?"

"I took over the position from a cousin. She moved out when she got married," Izumi said. "Anyway, enough about me. How about you? Have you managed to settle in and unpack?"

"I guess so," I said. "It's quiet here."

"Yeah, especially since you're on the fifth floor. There's only you and that skinny guy."

"Do you know him?"

She shrugged. "Not really. Have you talked to him?"

"Not yet."

Despite living a door away from him, I'd never spoken to my next-door neighbor and had seen him only twice.

The first occasion was when he returned to the apartment in the middle of the night, carrying two big plastic grocery bags. At the time, I was hanging the laundry I'd forgotten to take out of the washing machine.

My neighbor was tall and thin, with scruffy hair. He wore heavily layered clothes, as if he were in Hokkaido in the winter. But it wasn't even chilly that day. Even more peculiar was that, despite his thick clothing, on his feet he only wore zori, traditional straw sandals.

The second occasion I saw him, I was hanging around the common corridor because I couldn't sleep. It was around two in the morning. This time, too, he went off somewhere and returned with two plastic bags. His zori made a loud noise as he walked up the staircase. As he passed, I nodded at him and he nodded back.

The rest of the time, his door and windows were shut. I never heard a noise from his unit, and he didn't seem to hang any laundry outside. From the corridor, it looked as if nobody lived there.

"I speak to him, of course, when I collect the rent," Izumi said. "We never have any conversation beyond what is necessary. You could say I don't know him any better than you do. I heard he was a songwriter, but I've never heard any music coming from his unit, so that can't be true."

"Maybe he does it digitally," I said. "Connects his keyboard to headphones or something."

She shrugged. "Perhaps. He's an oddball. I remember seeing him at the park around midnight once. I greeted him, but he ignored me."

"Maybe he didn't hear you."

"I'm pretty sure I was loud enough. I practically shouted at him," she insisted. "Anyway, I'm going for my nap. Try not to—"

"Bother you unnecessarily."

"Good," she said before shutting the door.

I looked at the booklet in my hand. Fifty pages of photocopied documents held together by a ringed binding. The cover had an illustration of a house behind flower bushes, and WELCOME written in large letters.

Once I was in my apartment, I chucked it into a dresser drawer, where it would never see the light of day again.

MY ROUTINE HADN'T CHANGED much after my move. In the morning, I went to the nearby park to exercise. I jogged for an hour before returning to my apartment for a quick shower. Then, I headed to work.

The nearest bus stop was a twenty-minute walk away, served by one bus service, which came every fifteen minutes. Nine out of ten times, I had to wait a while.

On the way to the office, I bought my lunch and ate it before the first class. I usually had dinner with Honda, and he almost always gave me a lift home.

"I live near you, anyway," he had said. "And it's more fun to have someone to talk to when I'm driving."

After work, I was too tired to turn down his offer. I wanted to get home as soon as possible and throw myself on the bed. Honda, on the other hand, was full of energy during the nighttime drive. He seemed relaxed whenever he sat behind the steering wheel.

"I love driving at night with the windows down," he told me, smoothly shifting gears. "The sound of the engine and the wind blowing on my face always calms me down."

"Do you often drive at night to no particular destination?" I asked.

He didn't answer. We were approaching a traffic light. The car slowed before stopping on an upward slope.

"I used to, but not any more," he eventually said. "When I was still with my ex-girlfriend, we drove around at night. Ever since she left me, I try not to drive alone. Otherwise I'll start thinking about her."

The light turned green, and Honda released the hand brake. The engine roared when the car set off.

"How about you, Ishida? Do you have a girlfriend?"

"I do."

"In Tokyo?"

"Yes."

"Tell me about her."

I wasn't sure what to say, especially considering Nae and I hadn't talked for so long. "She's all right, I guess. We're at the same university."

"She's fine with you coming here?"

I forced myself to laugh. "To tell the truth, we had an argument and haven't made up."

"I see," he mumbled. "After my ex-girlfriend and I broke up, I realized something. If you love each other, anything can be solved with a simple word of apology. But if you don't, it's too difficult to sustain the relationship."

"I don't mind apologizing if I need to, but the thing is, I never live up to her expectations. Sooner or later, we'll have the same disagreement. She and I don't move at the same pace."

"Is that the reason you left Tokyo?"

I said nothing, and he didn't press further.

The black sedan moved through the quiet summer night. The streets were empty, illuminated by the streetlights. When I squinted, they blurred together, creating one continuous glowing line. I remembered seeing something like this before, but where?

20

A
Request
from
Tokyo

When I arrived at my apartment, I found a letter waiting for me. The white envelope was crumpled at the edges, and it had a purple butterfly stamp. My mother was the one who'd sent it. Tearing open the envelope, I removed a sheet of paper, folded twice. The letter said:

> *Dear Ren,*
> *Jin is looking for you. He says it's urgent. I told him you didn't leave a phone number and I didn't know when you'd be back in Tokyo, but he keeps on calling. Can you get in touch with him?*

Jin had been my friend since elementary school.

We were in the same class for many years, and both of us were on the soccer team, so we spent a lot of time together. But after high school, we went off to different universities. I followed in my sister's footsteps to Keio, while Jin got into Waseda. He called me every now and then when his team needed players, but we no longer saw each other as often. On the occasions we met off of the soccer field, we spent our time prowling the bars, looking for girls.

Jin wasn't good-looking. Well, I wouldn't say his appearance was off-putting. He just wasn't the kind of guy girls would glance at twice, but he had a way with words. Once he got a girl to stop and listen to him, he could pretty much find his way between her sheets. Yet, for some reason, he needed me to be his hunting partner.

"There's a secret formula," he had told me. "It has to be done in pairs. You and me, we make the best combination. We complement each other."

Why me? He wouldn't explain. But by following his dubious theory, I had hooked up with quite a few beautiful girls. It had always been a no-brainer to go along with his plans.

BEFORE I WENT TO work the next morning, I made a detour to the pay phone near the park. Even now, I remembered Jin's number off the top of my head.

Someone picked up. "Hello?"

I recognized Jin's distinctive low voice at once. "It's Ren," I said. "My mother isn't pleased that you keep on calling."

"Ah, that old hag. She slammed the phone down the other day." He laughed. "Where are you now?"

"I'm in Akakawa."

"What are you doing there?"

"Settling a family matter," I said. Jin knew my sister, but I doubted I'd ever mentioned she'd lived there, and I didn't feel like talking about her death. "So, why have you gone through so much trouble to reach me?"

"I need your help picking up a couple of girls."

I couldn't believe my ears. "Are you serious? That's why you kept calling?"

"Do you think I'm joking?"

I could sense from his tone that he was serious, but still, "What's the rush?"

"I'll tell you in person. When can you come over? Preferably for a week, and as soon as possible. You'll do it for me, won't you?"

It was the first time he'd ever pleaded for help. I couldn't turn him down, and anyway, summer break was coming.

"I'll be there next week," I said.

"Great." He sounded relieved. "I'll pay for the train ticket."

"Don't worry about it. Just don't let anyone know I'm coming to Tokyo, especially my mother."

"Got that. Who would want to talk to the hag anyway?"

So on the agreed date, I turned up at his house in Meguro.

JIN'S HOUSE WAS A three-story landed property with its own garage. His family had lived there for three generations.

The door swung open and Jin greeted me.

"Welcome to Tokyo, Mr. Ishida," he said, grinning. "We've been expecting you."

"What's the deal?" I asked, unable to contain my curiosity.

"The deal is . . ." He came out of his house with a Boston bag. "We're going to have fun."

Jin hailed a cab and gave the address of a hotel in Roppongi. On the way there, he pretended to be asleep, but I could tell he was faking it. When we got to his room, he threw his bag aside and jumped onto the queen-sized bed while I stood next to him. After a long silence, he began to talk.

"Would you believe me if I said I was getting married?" he asked.

My eyes widened. "Are you serious?"

Like me, Jin was twenty-four. It seemed early for a guy to settle down, especially one as commitment-phobic as him.

He replied flatly, "I wish I was only joking."

"What happened?"

"My girlfriend is pregnant," he said. "The wedding is next

month. It's a mad rush, but we have no choice since she's already seven weeks in. She'll start to show soon."

I didn't know what to say. I could imagine how devastating it was for him. Scratching my head, I asked, "Is this the short-haired girl you introduced me to last time? What was her name?"

"Sachiko," he said. "But it's not her. I broke up with her ages ago."

I knew Jin dated many girls, sometimes more than one at the same time, but the short-haired girl from Waseda was the last one I'd met. "So this is someone new."

"Yes," he said. "How about you? Still stuck with that Nae?"

"What do you mean, 'that Nae'? And yes, we're still together . . ." I scratched my head. "Sort of."

He looked at me and laughed. "So you finally broke up with her. About time, isn't it? I'll help you get over it."

"We didn't break up. And this isn't about me. It's about you and the girl you're marrying. How long were you dating before she got pregnant?"

"I don't know." He shrugged. "A year or two?"

"That can't be true. You were with Sachiko last year, unless you were seeing them at the same time."

"Fine, we only dated for a couple of months before she got pregnant. Are you happy now? Can we stop talking about it?"

"All right, all right," I said, sensing his agitation. "How did this happen? You've always been careful."

"I *am* careful," he said. "That's why I'm pissed. My girlfriend is happy, though. She's told the whole world about it. I don't have any other option but to take responsibility."

I pulled up a chair and sat. "This girlfriend of yours, do you love her?"

"I do like her, or I wouldn't be going out with her in the first place. I'm not crazy about her or anything, but I don't mind being with her," Jin said. "It's also an advantageous marriage. Her father's company is the main client of our family business. It's a difficult arrangement to say no to."

"So it's decided?"

"I guess so. It's just so sudden. The timing is off, you know what I mean? Honestly, I'm not ready yet, but I have no choice."

I sighed. "So what's the plan? Sleeping around for a week?"

"Something like that." He smirked. "If I can fool around enough to satisfy my whole life's desire, I might feel better about settling down so early."

"What a genius plan."

"Don't be sarcastic, Ren. I know it sounds shallow and foolish, but I'm a shallow, foolish man."

Jin was smiling, but I knew he was distraught. The guy had lost his mind. I empathized with him, but disagreed with how he'd chosen to handle this.

"Don't worry, I'll make sure you have fun, too," he continued.

"That's not the issue. I just doubt you'll feel any better after we do this."

"That's my problem, not yours. I'm taking a gamble, and I'll accept full responsibility for the outcome."

I knew he wasn't going to change his mind. Taking my shoes off, I asked, "So where are we heading tonight?"

"You'll find out soon enough." Jin took an extra hotel key from his pocket and threw it to me. "Don't take your shoes off here. Go to your room. You'd better rest up. I promise you, it's going to be a long night."

"Okay." I put my shoes back on, took my bag, and left.

JIN WAS AN ONLY child. His family had run a high-end traditional confectionary business for generations. It was labor-intensive work, but they'd built a good reputation and an elite customer base. Politicians, entertainers, and wealthy businessmen were their regulars. The factory was in Kanagawa, and Jin's parents had another house there. Jin was alone at the family home in Meguro most of the time. Being alone at home was something else we had in common, apart from our love for soccer.

When we were in high school, he often invited me to his house to watch adult videos. He had the largest collection I'd ever seen. After my sister left Tokyo, I often stayed over at his place.

Though his parents were almost never around, Jin didn't bring girls home. Instead, he fooled around with them at school—the infirmary, the storeroom, the bathroom, you name it. When we got older, he upgraded to love hotels. Money wasn't a problem, since he got a generous allowance.

I asked him once why he went through the trouble when his house was always empty.

Jin said, "I can't risk having my parents walk in on me with my pants down."

"Do they expect you to stay a virgin till you're married?" I joked.

"You know what I mean," he said. "They know I'm already having sex, but don't want to catch me doing it."

Because I went with him, I also became a love hotel regular.

Jin's method of picking up girls was simple. We would go to a nice bar in Roppongi, order a few drinks, and hang around until we spotted a pair of girls we liked. Not too young—more often than not university students or office ladies in their twenties— and attractive enough. Jin was always the one who went over and chatted them up. We would buy them drinks, listen to their stories, make them laugh. If we were lucky, we could have some fun afterwards. Jin made sure I had a good time; he would pick up the tab and let me choose which girl to bring to my room.

This time, too, we followed the same pattern as usual. The first three nights went as expected. Jin had always been good at picking up girls, but this time, he was especially smooth. I had no complaints, especially since I hadn't slept with anyone since I'd moved to Akakawa. But the fourth night was different.

Upon entering the bar, I spotted two younger girls having drinks by themselves. One was petite, with an infectious smile, and the other girl was willowy and fair-skinned. The taller girl looked glamorous in her black leather jacket and smoky makeup. Her chin-length bob revealed a long, slender neck.

I didn't think I had a chance with a girl like that, but Jin saw me eyeing the pair. Sensing I liked the modelesque girl, he insisted on giving it a shot. I was hesitant at first, but when the petite one made eye contact with us, I decided to let him try his magic. We went to the empty table next to them and ordered a pitcher of beer. After that, Jin made his move.

"How are you girls tonight?" he asked. "Would you like to join us?"

He posed the question in such a natural manner, as if he were asking whether the table was taken. It was something only Jin could pull off. It would've sounded forced if I'd used the same line.

The two girls looked at each other. After a brief silence, the taller girl nodded and the petite girl said, "Sure, why not."

"Do you come here often?" Jin asked, making space for the two of them.

The tall girl shrugged. "Once in a while."

As usual, he did the introductions. "This is Ren, and I'm Jin."

"She's Anzu, and I'm Kaori," the shorter girl said. "Are you students?"

Jin nodded. "We're law students at Tsukuba. We're here on holiday."

Creating a fake persona was part of Jin's secret formula.

University students—from anywhere but Keio and Waseda—were the scenarios we used most, but there were times he'd pulled off advertising executives, company employees, and civil servants. So far, no one had ever discovered we were lying. Not even when the girls we were talking to happened to study at the same university as the one he'd picked. Jin executed his lies with such conviction, it was like he believed everything he said was true.

On their part, Kaori did most of the talking. They were drama students at the same private art college.

"We're staging a play next summer, and I just got one of the leading roles," Kaori said. "If you're in Tokyo, you should come and see it."

"Really? That calls for a celebration," Jin said.

He led us in a toast and ordered more drinks. He continued talking with Kaori, which gave me a chance to get closer to Anzu. It worked well, since Kaori was all too happy to tell him about the production.

I turned to Anzu. In the dim light, she was captivating. But it wasn't just her striking good looks. The girl had a familiar aura I couldn't really explain. Even though we'd just met, I felt like I knew her.

"Why are you staring?" she asked.

"You look familiar," I said. "Have we met before?"

She swiped her long bangs off of her face, tucking it behind her ear. "Is that one of your pickup lines?"

"Maybe." I took a gulp of my beer. "What about you? Will you be in the play?"

"No," she said without a hint of disappointment. "I'm in charge of makeup and costumes."

"Is that what you're interested in?"

"Not really. I requested the job because I might not be around during the performance. We have a dozen other students doing the same job. It won't be a catastrophe, even if I don't turn up."

"Anzu is a famous model," Kaori chipped in. "She did a job for Comme des Garçons last week."

That must be why I thought I'd seen her before. "So we'll see your photograph on billboards?"

Anzu laughed. "No, not an advertising campaign. I was only involved in a small runway show. I'm not a famous model. Kaori was just teasing."

I glanced over at Kaori, but she was busy listening to Jin.

"I'm not that into theater, but I had to find something to study to please my parents," Anzu said. "They're particular about the need to have a degree."

"But any degree is fine?"

"Yes, any degree is fine," she repeated. "I thought drama was the closest to what I'm doing now, but it's turning out not to be the best choice. I'm bad at remembering lines, and I can't act at all. Fashion design might have been better."

"Why don't you transfer?"

"Half the time, I'm not around. If I moved into fashion, I wouldn't be able to cope with the schoolwork."

"Don't you already have problems meeting the minimum attendance requirement?"

"It's fine. My friends help me sign in," she said. "The lecturers know my circumstances, so they close one eye. It won't be hard to graduate. Ours is just a small private college, not Tsukuba University, and I'm not aiming to be the next big actress."

I finished my beer and refilled both our mugs. Jin and Kaori were in their own world. Kaori giggled as Jin slipped his arm around her waist.

"What about you?" Anzu asked. "Why did you choose law?"

I struggled for a moment to come up with an answer. "I didn't know what to study, so my parents suggested I follow in the footsteps of my older sister."

"Is she a practitioner?"

Clearing my throat, I nodded. "She is."

"Then you can ask for a recommendation. Your prospects are pretty much secured. You've made the right choice. Or at least, you've got your life planned well. A lot of people our age have no idea what they're planning to do after graduation."

"It's hard for twenty-somethings to decide what they want to do for the rest of their lives."

"True, but that's just how it is," she lamented. "The decisions you make in your twenties might be the biggest decisions of your life. The job you're planning to do, the kind of person you're going to marry, those sorts of things. But we're still young. Too naïve and foolish to make such important decisions."

I mumbled in agreement and finished my beer in a few gulps.

Jin put his arm around my shoulders. "Sorry to disturb your conversation, but I'm dead tired. I'm going back to the hotel."

Anzu lifted the sleeve of her jacket and checked her watch. She wore a chunky, vintage Seiko chronograph. "I didn't realize it was so late," she said.

"How are you getting back?" Jin asked.

"We'll have to get a taxi, since we already missed the last train," said Anzu.

"Our hotel is within walking distance from here. If you want, you can come over and rest until the train service resumes."

"Really?" Kaori clung to Anzu. "Let's just do that. I'm broke. I don't want to take a taxi."

Anzu didn't answer. Jin settled the bill and the four of us left the bar. Jin and I walked in front, while the girls followed a few steps behind.

I made sure they weren't listening to us before whispering to Jin, "Are you sure you're not interested in Anzu?"

"No, you saw her first. She's all yours," he said nonchalantly. "Plus, Kaori is cute. And who knows, one day she might become a famous actress—the highlight of my conquests."

"You wish."

As we entered the building, Jin took Kaori into his arms and whispered something to her. The two of them went straight into his room and closed the door without a word to me or Anzu.

I looked at her awkwardly. "Then . . ."

She shrugged. "I guess you're stuck with me."

"No objections here," I said.

I reached for her hand and took out my room key.

"ARE YOU ASLEEP?" ANZU asked, rolling closer to me under the blanket.

"Not yet," I answered. "It would be a waste for me to sleep when you're still awake."

"How sweet," she said, playing along.

She climbed on top of me, and we kissed. I brushed her bangs behind her ear. Somehow, she looked different from when we were at the bar, though not in a bad way. It took me a while to realize it was the color of her lips. Our friction had rubbed off her dark burgundy lipstick, making her look much younger.

"It's been a while since I've slept with anyone," she confessed.

I kissed her again. "Is that so?"

"My career is my priority. A relationship would only drag me down."

"But aren't you lonely?"

"Sometimes. I do eventually want a serious and loving

relationship. I've tried dating a few times, but they always call it quits because I don't give them enough attention."

"You haven't met the right person," I said. "How did you decide to go into modeling?"

Anzu lay down next to me. "It was my childhood dream." Her eyes were wide open; it didn't look like she was planning to sleep.

"Tell me more."

"Well, for as long as I can remember, I've loved poring through fashion magazines, admiring the models in their trendy clothes and perfect makeup. When I turned seventeen, I auditioned to be a reader model. I got in, and an agency offered me a contract."

"So it's a dream come true."

"Yup," she said, staring blankly at the ceiling before breaking into a laugh.

I stroked her hair. "What's so funny?"

"My parents didn't find out until a few years later. My father works in Manila and my mother accompanied him there. I live in Tokyo with my aunt." She turned to me. "Can you imagine their reaction to it? They thought I was just rebelling. Luckily, my aunt handled the situation well."

"Huh," I mumbled. "Is modeling what you expected it to be?"

She thought for a moment before answering. "Most of it, but not everything. I didn't know the competition would be so fierce. There are plenty of beautiful girls vying for every job. It's rejection after rejection, but I work hard. My agent recognizes my efforts, and she's been giving me more opportunities. When there's an emergency or a model falls sick, I'm at the top of the list as a possible substitute." She moved closer and laid her head on my arm. "For example, if I received a call from her right now, at this moment . . . I would leave you in a heartbeat."

"That's dedication," I said. Remembering Seven Stars' mother, I asked, "Are there any body parts models at your agency?"

"No, but from time to time we get odd requests like that. I was once asked to be a leg model for a stocking company, but it doesn't happen often. Why do you ask?"

"The wife of one of my acquaintances is a hand model."

"What's her name? Maybe I know her."

"I don't know her full name, but her family name is Nakajima. I hear she's famous."

"There are a few well-known hand models, since they're more marketable than any other body parts models, but I've never heard of a Nakajima," she said. "It's a tough job, though. The clients expect more than a pair of lovely hands. They're paying good money, so they demand flawless, hairless, poreless, veinless subjects."

"Those sound like high expectations."

"I worked with one before. A proper hand model, not someone who doubles as a body parts model like me. She wore gloves every day. And you wouldn't believe it, but she kept her hands at chest level at all times to improve the blood circulation. Pretty extreme, isn't it? I wouldn't want to—"

Two knocks on the door interrupted us. I put on my pants and answered it. Jin was outside, his crumpled shirt still unbuttoned.

"Sorry to disturb you, but Kaori isn't feeling well," he said. "She threw up in the bathroom, and she's crying now. I don't know what to do. I've tried talking to her, but she won't stop wailing."

"I'll check on her." Anzu got up and put her clothes on. "I'm sorry, Ren, but would you mind letting Jin stay in your room? I know what Kaori is like when she's drunk, and it would be best for me to stay with her."

"Not a problem," I said.

Anzu kissed me and left. Jin's eyes were glued to her the whole time.

"That girl is really thin, isn't she? You can practically see her bones," he commented. "Hey, sorry to barge in, but Kaori was really wasted."

"Don't worry about it, we were done anyway."

He took a pillow from the bed. "I'll sleep on the sofa. Don't argue. I've had enough for the night."

"Suit yourself."

I was too tired to disagree, anyhow. Climbing back onto the bed, I was about to fall asleep when I heard Jin's voice.

"Hey, Ren, thanks for sharing my last adventure as a free man."

I smiled. "Don't mention it. I had fun, too."

"Good." The sofa squeaked as Jin shifted uncomfortably. Punching the pillow, he said, "By the way, you haven't really told me what you're doing in Akakawa."

"Like I said, there's a family matter to settle." I still didn't want to talk about my sister. He would probably chide me for it when he eventually found out, but right now, I didn't care. "I should be back in Tokyo in a few months," I added.

Jin muttered something I didn't catch. I was expecting him to say more, but when I looked over at him, he was already sound asleep.

WHEN I WOKE UP, Jin was still sleeping. I opened the thick curtain and let the sun shine in. The sudden brightness roused him from his slumber.

"Good morning, sleeping beauty," I said.

He yawned. "What time is it?"

I glanced at the clock. "It's eleven. We need to check out soon."

After washing up and shaving, we went over to Jin's room. He knocked on the door, but no one answered.

"Weird," he mumbled, frowning. He must have feared the worst, since he'd left his belongings inside.

I reached for the door handle. It wasn't locked, but nobody was in the room.

"Guess they left already," Jin said. He scanned the place, picking up a piece of paper on top of the bedside table. "It's for you, from Anzu."

I took the note from him and read it.

Hi Ren,
Sorry for leaving early, but we have to attend a morning class.
Last night was fun, and I had a good time. Meeting you again
was unexpected, but I hope the future will continue to surprise me.
XOXO, Anzu

"Her handwriting is neat," Jin said. "But she didn't leave you her phone number. And what's this about? 'Meeting you again was unexpected.' Have you met her before?"

I was wondering the same thing, but I didn't want Jin to ask too many questions. "Not that I know of," I said. Crumpling the paper, I threw it into the rubbish bin. Was she actually someone I'd met before? Or was this a joke she was trying to pull off because I'd said she looked familiar?

We checked out of the hotel and took the subway back to Jin's house. I had to leave Tokyo later that day.

Standing at his door, Jin looked at me with a smug face. "So this is it."

"Yes, this is it," I said.

"Any parting words?"

"Take care, be a good husband and a good father," I said. "You know what, just have a good life. See you at your wedding."

"You too, Ren. Have a good life."

He gave me a firm handshake and hugged me before I left.

Back then, I wouldn't have guessed it would be the last time I saw him. Jin didn't invite me to his wedding.

When I left his house, I believed everything would work out for him. Though Jin was frivolous, he had his head planted firmly on his shoulders. So I was surprised when, a few years later, a mutual acquaintance told me he was going through a messy divorce.

"What a stupid guy," the friend told me. "Things were going so well for him. His wife is beautiful, and they have two kids. He even took over his father-in-law's company, but he was caught having an affair with the kids' drama teacher. It was a huge scandal, and the woman lost her job. I heard they went all the way to Bruges for their rendezvous, but just their luck, his brother-in-law was also there for a family getaway."

I wanted to tell Jin he should have stopped when he said he would, but we never bumped into each other.

21

Warm Pancakes on a Rainy Day

After the last class ended, I went to the office to tidy up my files and wait for Honda. He came shortly.

"Sorry, I can't give you a lift tonight," he said. "One of my students has a test tomorrow, and he still can't grasp the formulae. He'll fail the test if I don't give him some coaching. To be honest, I'm not sure when we'll finish."

"Don't worry, focus on that," I said. "I'll see you tomorrow, and try not to stay too late."

Putting on my parka, I grabbed my bag and walked down the stairs to the first floor. The reception area was dark, and the heat was already off.

When I came out of the building, a gust of cold wind blew into my face. The wet asphalt reflected the lights from the streetlamps. Puddles, dimpled by raindrops, lay beside the curb. I could have walked back inside for an umbrella, but it was only a drizzle, so I didn't bother. Tucking my hands into my pockets, I left the cram school complex.

Across the street, Seven Stars stood in the rain, wearing a red coat. When our eyes met, the corners of her lips curled a little. It was as if she'd been waiting for me.

I walked over, expecting her to say something, but she kept quiet. Her eyes moved between the puddles and me. The water droplets on her hair glistened.

"I don't have an umbrella," I said.

"I didn't say I needed one," she said.

"What are you doing here?"

She didn't answer.

"You're going to get sick if you keep standing out here," I said. "Do you want to walk to the train station together?"

Instead of answering, she fiddled with her fingers. She had painted her nails with beige polish, a breach of school rules.

"Say something, will you?" I said.

"I'm hungry," she said. "I want to eat something warm."

"Let's go to the convenience store and see what they have."

She shook her head. "I don't want convenience store food."

I was getting impatient. "Fine, what do you want, then?"

"I want fresh red bean pancakes."

"Brilliant, and where would we find that?" I glanced at my watch. "It's already ten-thirty."

"I know where to go."

Seven Stars led the way as I walked behind her. Every now and then, she would turn around to check on me. I didn't know if she was aware of it, but she was smiling to herself.

"Don't worry," I said. "I won't get lost."

She stopped. "Why don't you make it easier for both of us? Walk next to me."

Why had I been following her in the first place? I had no idea. I moved up and we walked side by side.

"I love walking in the rain," Seven Stars said. "It's fun, don't you think?"

This time, I was the one who said nothing.

She stomped into the puddles in front of us. The water splashed on my trousers. I glared at her and she laughed. Not long after, we reached a park I wasn't familiar with.

"It's over there." She pointed at a snack vendor near the entrance. "Wait for me here."

Before I answered, she ran over, leaving me alone. A few minutes later, she returned with two brown paper bags and handed me one.

"Thanks," I said.

Guiding me deeper into the park, Seven Stars said, "That pancake uncle is always here, no matter the weather. At all hours, rain or shine, he'll be at that spot. He's been around for as long as I can remember."

"Do you come here often?"

She nodded. "Since I was young."

"What are you talking about?" I patted her head. "You're still young."

She brushed my hand off. "Stop that. I'm not a kid."

We walked to an empty playground at the center of the park. There was a pair of swings, a slide, and a climbing structure. She sat on one of the swings while I sat on the other.

I opened the paper bag and warm steam escaped. The pancake was still piping hot. I waited for it to cool down before taking a bite. The skin was fluffy, and the red bean filling sweet and mushy.

"I used to come here all the time with my mother before she started working," Seven Stars said. "I only played on the swings. She tried to coax me into trying something else, but I wouldn't listen. Whenever we came, I would sit on this swing and she would push me. Somehow, I never got tired of it."

"Do you want me to push you?" I asked, laughing.

She pouted. "I outgrew that phase a long time ago."

Using her feet, she rocked the swing. The metal joints produced a few squeaky noises.

"Whenever I come here, I feel nostalgic," she continued. "After all these years, nothing has changed."

"Isn't it nice?"

She nodded. "How about you, Mr. Ishida? Did you go to the playground when you were young? Or are Tokyo kids too serious for that?"

"Serious? Not that I remember," I said. "There was a playground near my house, slightly bigger than this, but I rarely went there."

"Where did you go, then?"

"There was a grassy field near my school where I used to play soccer with my friends. We had to be careful, because the field was next to a canal. If we kicked the ball too hard, it would roll into the water and be impossible to fish out. It still happened though, a couple of times."

Her eyes lit up. "I remember you telling me about your dream of becoming a pro soccer player. Quite good, but not good enough."

"Stop mocking me."

I tried to nudge her, but she dodged me.

"Don't be upset," she said. "At least you were quite good."

"I'll take it as a compliment, then."

"It *is* a compliment," she said. "So this grassy field, is it still around?"

"No, it's been developed."

After I'd said farewell to Jin, I'd had a few hours to kill before boarding the train back to Akakawa. On a whim, I went to visit the field. Spending time with Jin made me feel sentimental. I kind of missed those childhood days, when we played soccer together every day and my sister was still in Tokyo.

A lot had changed since my sister had left our hometown, including that field. The area had been paved over and converted to a parking lot. The only thing that remained the same was the cement staircase leading to the field. Yet, standing at the top of the staircase and looking at the rows of parked cars, I knew I'd lost my connection with the place. The once-familiar area now felt distant. I felt as if I'd imagined the time I'd spent there.

"Mr. Ishida, how's the pancake? Is it good?" Seven Stars asked, still rocking on the swing.

"Warm food on a rainy day is usually good," I answered, looking at the puddles. They were still; the rain had stopped. Turning to her, I said, "You haven't told me why you've brought me here."

"I said I was hungry."

"If you want to talk to me about something, now's a good time to speak up."

She gave me a puzzled look.

"That's why you brought me here, isn't it?" I continued. "To discuss something. What is it?"

"Nothing. I was just craving a pancake."

Right. She had dragged me all the way here just to play on the swings and eat pancakes together.

The leaves on the trees around us made loud rustling noises.

"Even though I've eaten, I still feel cold," she said, changing the subject. She rubbed her palms together. "Mr. Ishida, have you given up exercising? I haven't seen you on your morning jog."

"I moved to a new place a few weeks ago."

"No wonder," she murmured and blew hot air into her hands.

I stood up. "Let's go back, or we'll miss the last train."

Seven Stars followed, and we walked side by side. The wind was getting stronger. Her hair kept blowing into her face, and she had to tuck it behind her ears. Her hands must have been frozen. I felt like grabbing those hands to warm them up.

What are you thinking? I told myself. She's just a kid.

"Mr. Ishida," Seven Stars said, kicking a piece of gravel. "What did your first love look like?"

I looked at her. "Why do you ask?"

"No particular reason, I'm just curious."

"People don't normally ask about those kinds of things."

She tilted her head. "Why can't you just answer me?"

"If you insist . . ." I sighed, trying to recall the characteristics of the first girl I'd fallen in love with. She was unremarkable. "She was a quiet girl, nothing special."

"Your classmate?"

"No, but we went to the same school. She used to sit on the staircase leading to the green field I told you about, watching me and my friends play soccer."

"What did she do there? Toss errant balls back to the field?"

"Sometimes." I rubbed my nose. "Kind of cliché, isn't it?"

"So you asked her out? And let me guess, she turned you down."

I sighed. The nerve of her. "I never asked her out. But you aren't wrong, either. She would've turned me down if I'd ever asked."

"Why would you say that?"

"She preferred the goalkeeper to the team's ace."

"Hang on, hang on. The team's ace . . ." Seven Stars feigned a surprised look. "That can't be you, can it?"

"You . . ."

My words trailed off, and we both laughed. I was surprised that she'd gotten me to talk about my personal life.

Actually, it was Jin who had gone out with that girl. She was his first date, and she was the one who had asked him out. He wasn't as serious about her as she was about him. Not that I bore a grudge against Jin. I never asked the girl out, not even after they broke up. Maybe I hadn't actually liked her that much.

Jin was the first one in our grade to have a girlfriend. The rest of the boys looked up to him. From time to time, they came during recess to ask for relationship advice. Apparently, he was good at it. He had helped a few of our classmates get girlfriends.

At the time, I was more interested in soccer than the opposite sex. I did like that girl, but I'd never thought of dating her. I wasn't at the stage where I wanted a romantic relationship.

Once, though, I did ask Jin, "Do you love your girlfriend?"

He nodded. "More or less."

"Do you even know what love is?"

I had no idea why I was being so patronizing. Perhaps I couldn't believe true love existed at our age. Our classmates who claimed to be in love were mistaking excitement and fuzzy feelings for love.

"It's simple once you know the basics," Jin said. He opened his notebook and drew a Venn diagram of two overlapping circles. He wrote L, L, L inside the three sections. Pointing at his drawing, he explained, "'Like,' over here, is when you want to spend time with that person. 'Lust,' on the other side here, is when you want to sleep with that person. Or, 'I want to touch her boobs,'—that's lust." Finally, he pointed to the L in the overlapping area. "This section in the middle is what we call love. It's an intersection between 'like' and 'lust.' Do you get it now?"

"I think so."

We stopped our discussion there, but his words rang in my mind long afterward. I found myself curious about girls' breasts. How would it feel to touch them?

So when a girl asked me out, I said yes. She happened to have well-developed breasts. Unfortunately, after touching them, my initial enthusiasm was gone.

"Mr. Ishida, it creeps me out when you stop talking so suddenly," Seven Stars said.

"What do you want me to say, then?" I said. "Do you have any other questions?"

"You're not going to ask about my first love?"

"You'll tell me if you want me to know."

"True."

But Seven Stars didn't say another word. She remained silent on our entire walk to the train station, even when I bid her farewell at the platform.

I was taking a different train from her, and mine came first. As I boarded the carriage, she continued to look at me. Once the doors were shut, her mouth moved. She was saying something to me, but I couldn't make out the words. Then the train departed and she blended into the sea of people.

When I got to my station, the last bus running to my apartment had already gone. I'd known it was late, but hadn't realized we'd been out so long. I pulled up the collar of my parka to protect my neck from the cold wind and left the train station. The scent of rain was still thick in the air.

It took almost an hour to walk to my apartment. Half running, I climbed the stairs to the fifth floor. When I reached my unit, I found an envelope in front of the door.

2 2

Searching
for
the
Kobayashi
Women's
Clinic

I picked up the thick brown document envelope. My name and address were written on it in black marker, but the sender's name was missing, and there was no stamp. The sender must have had it delivered in person.

But I hadn't given anyone my new address. The only people who knew it were Honda and Mrs. Itano. It wouldn't be Honda since I'd seen him earlier, so the letter must have come from Mrs. Itano or Izumi. Perhaps there were some remaining tenant documents for me to sign.

I unlocked the door and went inside. Sitting on the floor, I tore open the envelope and pulled out a stack of letter-sized papers. They were photocopies of medical records from the Kobayashi Women's Clinic. I'd never heard of the place. I looked at the patient's name and my breath caught.

Keiko Ishida.

I studied the charts carefully. The harder I tried to interpret them, the more jumbled they became. Soon, the lists broke down into words, and the words lost their essence. I read them, but couldn't grasp their meaning. My consciousness faded and my soul seeped from my body.

Soon, I found myself standing in front of another me, the physical me, who had lost his spirit. The man sitting on the floor holding the photocopies had empty eyes. The shell of me was disturbed by the content of the medical documents, yet he remained in a daze. He read the photocopies again and again, without even a hint of expression.

I shook him. "You need to show these to the police."

He stared at me.

"Call the police and tell them you've found a clue!" I shouted.

He averted his eyes and kept quiet. Folding his knees, he buried his face between them. Crouching like this, he looked much smaller. No, he didn't just look smaller. He actually shrank into an eight-year-old boy.

The boy looked up. His eyes told me he was about to cry. I sat next to him and patted his shoulder, trying to console him.

"I understand you're in shock, but tomorrow you'll feel better," I said. "Trust me, you'll be fine."

For a moment, I was taken aback, realizing those words were what my sister would've said.

The little boy started to sob, and I continued to pat his shoulder. He cried silently until he fell asleep, exhausted. And then I dozed off, too.

WHEN I WOKE UP, I found myself lying on the floor. What a weird dream.

I'd been curled up in an awkward position, and now my whole body felt stiff. Stretching, I yawned and looked at my watch. Three o'clock in the morning. I took the watch off and changed from my work clothes into a sweatshirt and drawstring pants. I returned to the living room to turn off the light, but I stopped myself before flicking the switch.

What was that? A thick brown envelope peeked out from beneath the low table. I bent down to retrieve it. It was already torn open. I didn't need to remove the contents to know what was inside.

Then it wasn't a dream, after all. My sister really had been pregnant five years ago.

I TOOK AN URGENT leave of absence the next day to find the Kobayashi Women's Clinic.

I knew I could have handed the documents to the police. They would definitely do a better job investigating the lead than I could, but my sister wouldn't have wanted anyone to find out about what had happened, and I felt obligated to respect her decision.

According to the address on the letterhead, the clinic was located in a suburb of Kuromachi. It was an hour train ride from Akakawa, followed by another bus ride.

When I arrived at Kuromachi central train station, the place was half asleep. There were only seven commuters, including me. Once I stepped down from the train, time seemed to slow. The people walked without hurrying, the ticket collector took his time, and the man standing next to me breathed heavily.

I went to the information center and showed the man behind the counter the address I was looking for. He directed me to the bus stop outside the station.

"Which bus should I take?" I asked.

"Any bus is fine," he answered. "There's only one bus service."

I waited twenty minutes before the bus arrived. It was almost empty. The only other riders were an elderly couple and a house-wife with groceries. I showed the clinic's address to the bus driver. He nodded and I took a seat in the second row.

The journey was strenuous, the path taking the bus along curvy roads. The stops were far apart and the bus didn't stop often since no one was waiting to board. I kept eating mints to fight my motion sickness.

About half an hour later, the bus driver shouted, "Young man, it's your stop."

"Thank you." I got off quickly.

A dizzy spell struck me. It was midday, and the sun was at its peak. I should have brought a cap, but I hadn't expected it to be scorching hot in September. Not knowing which way to go, I crossed to the other side of the street, where there was a row of shops.

An old man was selling canned drinks in front of a sundries store. They were chilled inside a Styrofoam box filled with ice cubes. I bought a can of Pocari Sweat and asked for directions.

"You got off at the wrong stop," he said. "You can either walk or wait for the next bus, but it won't come so fast."

I decided to walk. Big mistake—the next stop turned out to be over a mile away. By the time I reached it, my T-shirt was drenched in sweat. Now in a residential area, I looked around for a road sign. At least I'd found the right street. The clinic should be somewhere nearby. I finished my drink and resumed my search.

The address was a cordoned-off construction site. I explored the location to confirm it. I wasn't mistaken. The clinic should have been there. I peered through the half-open gate, but no one was there.

I wandered around the neighborhood, looking for someone I could speak with. Finally, I saw an elderly lady sweeping her porch. I watched her for a while before approaching the house. She was hunched over. Twice, she stopped to hit her back. The sound of her hemp broom brushing against the tiles reminded me of home.

"Good morning," I greeted her. "I'm looking for the Kobayashi Women's Clinic. Do you know where it is?"

She looked at me with narrowed eyes.

"I'm looking for the Kobayashi Women's Clinic," I repeated, slower and louder this time.

"The clinic . . ." She nodded. "No more . . . no more . . . gone . . ." She pointed in the direction of the construction site. "No more."

"Have they moved elsewhere?"

She looked down and continued sweeping, as if I were no longer there. Shortly after, a girl in a middle-school uniform came out of the house. She wore a stack of colorful plastic bangles on her wrist and had a lollipop in her hand.

"My grandma's hearing isn't good," the girl said. "But like she said, the clinic moved away."

"When was that?"

"Two, three years ago, maybe? The developer was planning to build a shopping complex, but there was some trouble with funding, so the project is suspended."

"Do you know where the clinic moved to?"

"No idea." She licked her candy.

I thanked her for the information and left. The elderly lady was still sweeping when the young girl went back into the house.

On the corner of the block, I saw a convenience store. I went in to buy a bottle of water and used the opportunity to ask about the clinic, but the shop attendant told me he had just moved to the town a few days ago.

"I've heard the construction site has been abandoned for a while now," he said.

I went around the area and asked a few more people. A housewife on her way home from the supermarket, a group of children playing hide-and-seek, and a postman walking a bicycle with a flat tire. None of them knew what had happened to the clinic—it was as if the institution had vanished into thin air one day.

Completely spent, I took the bus back to the train station. I tried to sleep on the train ride to Akakawa, but I couldn't. The brown envelope inside my bag made me uneasy. I had too many unanswered questions.

23

Autumn Moon and Half Moon

I needed sleep badly that night, but my mind wouldn't shut down. I found myself tossing around on the bed after midnight, eyes wide open. It was a long, bizarre night; the darkness seemed oppressive.

Moonlight found its way through the gaps of the thick brocade curtains. It spread across the white ceiling and illuminated a patch where the paint had peeled. How long would it take for that paint to fall? A month, a year, a decade?

On nights like these, time stretched and my senses became heightened. The sound of the occasional vehicle passing in the distance became piercingly clear. If I concentrated, I could even pick out the ticking of my alarm clock's second hand. Though I'd left Kuromachi, everything was still moving slowly. Hopefully tomorrow, time would go back to normal.

I got up and went to the kitchen to grab a beer. Just my luck—I'd run out when I really needed a drink.

IF I CUT ACROSS the park, the nearest 24-hour convenience store was two kilometers away. The night wasn't windy, but it was cold. I quickened my pace to try to keep warm.

The bright lights and colorful advertisements on the store's glass panels provided a stark contrast to the dimly lit park. I pushed the door open and the bell tinkled. Even though I'd come at an odd hour, another customer was inside. It was my mysterious neighbor, the zori man. I should have expected to bump into him one of these days.

His black hoodie covered his unruly hair. Underneath, I caught a glimpse of gray sweater. And of course, he had on his signature zori. His toes must have been freezing.

I picked up a pack of Asahi Super Dry and took it to the cashier. The zori man stood directly in front of me. He loaded his items from the basket onto the counter one by one—instant noodles in various flavors and a pack of canned Diet Coke. After paying, he walked off without glancing in my direction. Was he too preoccupied with his own thoughts? Didn't he recognize me at all? I purchased my beer and left.

Naturally, we walked in the same direction. His pace was slower than mine, probably because he was wearing those zori. The sandals made loud scraping sounds against the asphalt with every step he took.

Soon, I caught up with him. He stopped and turned to me.

"I'm your neighbor," I said, thinking it was better to identify myself in case he mistook me for someone suspicious. "We live on the same floor."

"Sorry, I didn't catch that," he replied in an unfamiliar accent. "Would you mind repeating yourself?"

"I'm your neighbor."

He nodded. "I've seen you before."

"I should have introduced myself when I moved in."

"It doesn't matter."

He turned around and we walked back alongside each other.

"I've noticed that you only come out at night," I said.

The zori man maintained a long silence, as if he hadn't heard me. Feeling awkward, I pretended I hadn't said anything. The scraping sounds marked the quiet night.

Suddenly, he turned to me and said, "If you're saying something and I'm not responding, it's not because I'm ignoring you. I'm actually deaf. But don't worry, I can read your lips, though it's a bit hard now since it's dark out."

"I said I've only seen you come out at night," I repeated slowly.

"Yes, I try not to go out during the day. Too many people talking at the same time, it's confusing."

I nodded and didn't follow up. It would be hard for him to read my lips while we were walking. Exiting the park, we climbed the five flights before reaching our common corridor.

"Good night," he said.

I bowed. "Good night."

Entering my apartment, I went to the kitchen. I tore open the box of beer and put all the cans except one inside the refrigerator. I put that single can in the freezer before going to the bathroom. By the time I returned, it was already chilled. I pulled up the ring and took a big gulp. Not as cold as I'd have liked it to be, but I could live with that. I went out to the corridor with my beer to enjoy the quiet of the night.

I wasn't the only one with the idea. The zori man was already standing in the corridor, leaning against the railing. He was looking at the park, seemingly absorbed in his own thoughts. His thick clothing was gone, and now a loose white T-shirt hung on his skinny frame. Just looking at him made me feel cold.

Coming over, I tapped his shoulder gently. "Would you like a beer? I bought a pack."

He looked surprised at first, but then he gave me a polite smile.

"I don't drink alcohol—my tolerance is too low. But thanks for offering."

I stood next to him. "Can't sleep?"

"I don't usually sleep at night."

I took another sip of my beer, looking idly at the scenery. They ought to put on more lights in the park. The place was so dark. Then again, hardly anyone went there at this time. I counted two joggers and a man walking his dog.

"Pretty, isn't it? The moon in autumn," the zori man said.

"Yes." I turned to face him. "It feels peaceful."

He nodded in agreement. After a few moments, he said, "I've been curious. What kind of work do you do? I often see you return late at night."

"I'm a cram school teacher. I only leave the school after nine-thirty."

"I see," he murmured. "What do you teach?"

"English."

"Is it fun?"

"I have no complaints. It pays the rent," I said. "How about you? I've heard you're a songwriter."

He laughed. "What makes you think I could be a songwriter with my condition?"

My cheeks burned in embarrassment. "Sorry, that was inconsiderate. I didn't think much about it; it was just something another resident told me."

"It's close enough, actually," he said. "I write poems."

"You're a poet?"

He nodded. "Not a famous one, though."

"What are your poems about?"

"Anything that piques my interest, even this apartment." He grinned. "Maybe that's why I'm not famous."

"You mean, not famous *yet*."

He laughed again. "That's a good one."

"So you work from home," I said.

"Yes. Easier for me, isn't it?" He tilted his head. "I don't resent my condition. I've been deaf for so long that I've grown accustomed to it. It feels natural, like everyone was born deaf. Some people outgrow it, while others don't. Do you understand what I'm trying to say?"

I didn't, but I couldn't bring myself to say so. "Were you born deaf?" I asked.

"No, I wasn't," he said. "It's a long story; I doubt you want to hear it."

"I have the time. You can tell me, if you want."

He tapped his fingers on the railing before talking. "When I was in primary school, my teacher realized I had bad hearing and advised my parents to take me for a checkup. We went to see an ENT, who diagnosed me with failing hearing. Eventually I would lose it altogether, though he couldn't identify the exact cause. We could choose to do therapy, but it would be painful and only slow the process, not stop it."

"Did you do it?"

"I did, for a while. Then I told my parents there was no point in suffering since I would eventually be deaf anyway. The procedure was costly, too. They were upset, but they saw the logic so we stopped the therapy. As expected, my condition deteriorated rapidly. One day, I woke up and realized I couldn't hear anything. Just like that, my hearing was gone." He stopped to catch his breath. It looked like he wasn't used to talking so much.

I waited a while before asking. "What does it feel like to lose your hearing?"

"Not as scary as I imagined," he said. "Most of the noises around us are unnecessary. My ears block that noise, but in the process, they also shut out everything else. The main problem is, it's harder to socialize. I learned lip-reading, but it's not easy when people talk too fast, or several of them talk at the same time. I feel embarrassed asking people to repeat what they're saying. And if they purposely talk slowly, I feel bad for making them put in the extra effort. Other than that, I guess I'm doing fine."

I downed the rest of my beer.

"You're not from this town, are you?" the zori man asked. "Did you move here for work?"

"I came to settle some personal affairs, but since I knew I was going to be here a while, I got a job to cover my expenses."

"Do you like teaching?"

"I guess so." I crushed the empty can. "Like I said, I have no complaints."

"Is this your first job?"

"Yes. First full-time job, anyway."

"This is my first job, too."

I yawned involuntarily. Despite my insomnia an hour ago, now I felt sleepy.

"I'm sorry, I must have bored you with my talk," the zori man said. "You should get some sleep."

"It's not you. Cold weather and beer make me sleepy. But you're right. I do need to go to bed soon, since I'm working tomorrow."

"I need to finish some work, too. Thanks for keeping me company."

"It's my pleasure. Let's hang out again sometime."

He nodded before going into his apartment. I should have asked him why he always wore those zori, but I didn't want to pry.

After he left, I stayed out there for a while. The sky was vast and black, devoid of moon or stars. I thought it looked so lonely up there.

IN MY DREAM, I sat on a bench in front of a lake with Pigtails. The dark water sparkled, reflecting the moonlight. The wind blew and rustled the leaves.

I looked at the half-moon. "Pretty, isn't it?"

She was quiet.

"Can you see the moon?" I asked.

The girl nodded twice. "Someone cut the moon into two and took half of it. See?" she said.

I smiled, not bothering to correct her.

"Finally, I can talk to you," she said. "There were too many noises before, but now, some of them have been blocked, so you can hear me clearly. Makes things much easier, doesn't it?"

"Yes. Can you finally tell me who you are?"

Pigtails shook her head. "I can't. You have to work it out yourself."

"Why?"

She smiled. "Once you figure out who I am, everything will become clear."

"So my mission is to figure out your identity?"

"Correct."

"Why me? What has this got to do with me?"

She shook her head again. "Sorry, I can't say."

"Can I guess?" I didn't wait for her to answer. "Are you Miyuki Katou? Or—"

"The fact that you're asking me this means you haven't figured it out yet. When you find the answer, you'll know."

"How am I supposed to recognize it when I see it?"

"Think. Think properly. And look around you. Look harder." When Pigtails spoke, she sounded older than she looked. "Once you pinpoint the key, everything will become clear."

That again. I sighed.

"It's actually simple, and you're very close," she said.

"What will happen after that?"

She looked at the moon. After a while, she answered, "I'll disappear."

24

A
Lazy
Sunday
Morning

I woke up early, but lazed around in bed since it was Sunday and I didn't feel like going for a jog. I finally got up around ten, and when I opened the curtains, the sunshine flooded in, blinding me. I squinted until my eyes adjusted to the brightness. At least the weather was good. It didn't look like it was going to rain.

I took a quick shower, brushed my teeth, and shaved. Thrusting my wallet and keys into my pockets, I left the apartment. It was my sister who'd originally gotten me into the habit of going out of the house every single day, without fail.

"If you stay at home doing nothing, that's as good as wasting a day of your life," she would say in the morning. "Imagine today is your last day on earth. Won't you regret not doing anything?"

I would pull the blanket higher. "Get lost."

"Don't be stubborn," she would say, trying to grab the blanket away.

We ended up fighting over it, but somehow, she always won. I used to think she was such a bother sometimes, but now I wished I could return to those days.

I stopped at the magazine vendor and bought the local

newspaper. While waiting for the bus, I flipped through the pages and scanned the headlines. The town had constructed a new bicycle path, and an actress who I'd never heard of had graced the grand opening of a new shopping mall. The advertorial sections covered some local businesses. Nothing significant.

Closing the paper, I checked my watch. It was eleven. Since I'd skipped breakfast, I was starving. As I debated between going to the convenience store for a snack first and continuing to wait at the bus stop, my bus arrived, rendering the decision irrelevant. I boarded and sat in the last row. The vehicle passed through the park, an empty field, and a residential area before stopping at the train station.

While taking the train to the center of town, I ran through a checklist in my head. Did I need to buy anything? Shampoo, shower gel, toothpaste or toilet paper? How about beer and coffee? No, I'd stocked up on everything. I could just go for a quick lunch and visit the bookshop for a few paperbacks.

Exiting the train station, I walked to the McDonald's across the street. After ordering a teriyaki burger and a coffee, I went to a table in the corner of the restaurant. This had to be Seven Stars' influence.

Seven Stars. Why was I thinking about her?

I opened the coffee lid to let the beverage cool down. They always served coffee boiling hot in fast-food joints. Why couldn't it be the right temperature?

"May I join you?"

Startled, I looked up and saw Seven Stars in front of me with a tray. Before I could answer, she plopped down opposite me. She had a Croquette Burger and a cup of Coke.

"What are you doing here?" I asked.

"The same thing as everyone else," she said. "Having lunch,

of course. What's the matter? You don't want me to sit here, Mr. Ishida?"

"I didn't say that. Are you by yourself?"

"How could I be by myself? You're here with me, aren't you?"

I said nothing and ate my burger. Teriyaki sauce oozed out and dripped onto my hand. Seven Stars took a paper napkin and wiped the sauce off.

"Are you clumsy, Mr. Ishida? Or are you *that* hungry?"

"I'm starving." I took the paper napkin from her hand, embarrassed. "I didn't have breakfast."

"It's almost lunchtime. You can skip a meal and save some money."

"Guess so," I said. "This is the second time I've seen you eating a burger. Do you like burgers that much?"

"I like most foods that are soft and warm." She opened her burger and used her open ketchup packet to draw a smiley face on the croquette.

"Seems like you're having fun," I said.

"I *am* having fun," she said. "What about you, Mr. Ishida? What's your favorite food?"

"Curry rice," I answered without thinking.

"But they serve that everywhere."

"Perhaps. It's a long story, but it's not just about the food."

"Let me guess, your girlfriend used to make it?"

"Not my girlfriend," I said. "My sister."

I thought she would ask more questions, as usual, but this time she said nothing. I guessed bringing up a dead person had ruined the atmosphere.

"My parents were seldom around," I said, trying to ease the tension. "When I was young, my sister and I used to eat convenience store box lunches every day. It got boring after a while, so she started to cook for me. The first dish she ever made was curry rice."

"I didn't mean to bring her up and upset you," Seven Stars said. "Now I feel bad for asking."

"I'm not upset, so there's no need to feel bad. My sister was a big part of my life. She's someone who was—and still is—dear to me." I bit my lip, realizing I sounded overly sentimental. Why had I told her that?

Seven Stars was quiet. She looked calm, almost sweet. If she didn't talk, most people wouldn't guess she was so feisty.

"You think I look better when I shut my mouth," she said, reading my thoughts.

I laughed. "I didn't say that."

"I hear it all the time." She shook her cup, making the ice cubes clink against each other. "Young lady, you need to change your attitude."

"Hey, I wouldn't say that. It's one of your charming points."

She said nothing, but when I glanced at her, a slight smile graced her face. We ate our food in silence. The restaurant was empty. Not many people went to McDonald's for an early lunch on Sunday.

"Mr. Ishida, you really do have a sister complex, don't you?"

I was taken aback by her bluntness.

"You don't even bother denying it," she continued. "How boring."

I took a sip of my coffee. It still burned my tongue, even though I'd left it to cool for so long. I looked at Seven Stars, but her gaze was elsewhere.

"Maybe you're right," I said. "Maybe I do have a sister complex. At one time, she was the only person I had."

Still looking away, she asked, "And your sister? Did she have a brother complex too?"

I shrugged. "Probably. She was always overprotective."

"But you still managed to have eight girlfriends."

"She didn't know about most of them. The ones she knew of, she didn't like. But to be fair, none of them liked her, either," I said. "It's kind of weird, since they'd never even met."

"Really." She clicked her tongue, as if to say she wasn't surprised.

"Except for my current girlfriend," I added. "My sister was very enthusiastic about her."

"What did your girlfriend do to melt her heart?"

I hesitated. "She stopped me from taking sleeping pills. I used to have insomnia, and I guess I took more than I needed a number of times."

Seven Stars looked surprised, but offered no opinion. "What did she do to stop you, Mr. Ishida?"

"She simply told me to stop harming myself. To be honest, I was surprised I listened to her. Well, I guess she was sincere. She cared about me, and I felt it."

Once the words were out, I regretted them. Why couldn't I keep my mouth shut around her? This was unprofessional. I shouldn't be sharing details of my personal life with a student.

"Mr. Ishida, let's take some sleeping pills together," Seven Stars said.

I frowned. "Are you crazy? Why?"

"Because your girlfriend would be upset, and maybe you two would break up."

"And what good would that do you?"

"Both of us would be single."

"There are enough single people in Japan to form a colony. There's no need to involve me."

She burst into laughter. "You're so dense, do you know that? But never mind, I guess it's one of your . . . What was the term you used just now? Charming points? Yes, that's it. One of your charming points."

This girl was so frustrating.

"What about you, Mr. Ishida? Did you like any of your sister's boyfriends?"

"She never had a boyfriend," I said.

Seven Stars broke into a mocking smile. "You don't know women at all, do you? I'm sure she had one. She just didn't want you to know."

"Possibly, but why would she hide that? She wasn't a child. And it wasn't like I was against her dating."

She shrugged. "I don't know, maybe she thought you wouldn't approve of the relationship."

"I doubt that was the case. I'm a reasonable person. I didn't have extraordinary expectations about what kind of guy she should be with. As long as they loved each other, that would've been good enough."

"Some kinds of guys you would never want as your brother-in-law, no matter how easygoing you are," Seven Stars said. "Like a married man with kids, or one with a contagious terminal illness, or . . . I don't know, maybe she was into women and didn't want you to find out."

I shook my head. "You have a wild imagination, young lady."

"I know, I've been told. But at least I make you laugh. That's generous of me, isn't it? Accompanying you to lunch, and on top of that, entertaining you."

"Yes, yes. Thank you."

She smiled. "Where are you going after this?"

"Maybe the bookstore."

"May I accompany you?"

"To the bookstore?"

She rolled her eyes. "Where else?"

"I don't mind, but won't you be bored?"

"I won't," she said, before adding, "I love books, you know."

I knew that was an afterthought.

She pretended to be angry. "Hey, what's that look? Why wouldn't you believe me?"

"I do believe you," I teased her. "You love books."

"I'm done," she said, pulling a paper napkin from the dispenser. I stared at her fingers as she dabbed her soft, pink lips.

Her eyes widened. "What are you looking at?"

"Nothing," I said. "Don't be conceited."

I finished my coffee and returned both of our trays. We left the restaurant and headed to a bookshop near the train station. Seven Stars went past me and walked backward.

"Mr. Ishida, what are you going to buy?" she asked.

"I don't know. Any book that catches my interest." I took her by the shoulders and turned her around. "Don't walk like that. You're going to run into a pole."

She looked at me over her shoulder. "What kind of books do you like?"

"Good ones." I sighed. "Can you please look where you're going when you're walking?"

Seven Stars ignored me, continuing to walk with her head turned over her shoulder. "You didn't even name a genre. You need to be more specific."

"I just know it when I see it. Now, can you please walk properly?"

She giggled and let me catch up with her. We entered the bookshop side by side. A young man with an olive green apron welcomed us. I nodded at him and looked around, Seven Stars trailing behind me. When I spotted the fiction shelves, I went straight to the new arrivals and scanned the covers.

"Ishida, is that you?" a familiar voice greeted me.

I looked up and saw Izumi, my building manager. She wore an olive-green apron, and her hair was tied in a high ponytail. She looked sharper than the first time I'd seen her in her casual clothes.

How odd that we'd run into each other—second coincidence of the day, I supposed. Or maybe the town really was that small. I was too used to Tokyo, where the probability of meeting even one acquaintance in the course of daily events was slim.

"So you work here," I said. "The uniform suits you."

Izumi smiled and blushed. It was the first time I'd seen her do that.

"Stop teasing," she said. "Is it your first time here?"

"I've come in a couple of times now."

"I bet that was on the weekend. I don't usually work on Saturdays and Sundays, but I'm covering for a sick colleague today. Is there a book you're looking for?"

"Nothing in particular. Do you have any recommendations?"

"Enough to make you go bankrupt. I've worked here close to four years already." Izumi looked over at Seven Stars, who stood next to me. "Hey, Ishida, you brought a cute girl with you. Why don't you introduce us?"

"It's not what you think," I said. "She's my student, and we happened to bump into each other."

"How disappointing. I thought you'd gotten yourself a local girlfriend."

"Mr. Ishida," Seven Stars said, "I'm leaving now. It looks like I'm getting in the way of you and your friend."

"I didn't say that," I said, but she had already walked off. "See you on Monday," I called after her.

It wasn't clear if she'd heard me, because she walked off without turning back. Teenagers were so rude these days.

"Are you going to let her go?" Izumi whispered.

I looked at her.

"It's obvious, isn't it? That student of yours has a crush on you," she said. "What are you going to do? Will you chase after her? She's quite a pretty girl, don't you think?"

"What are you talking about?" I brushed her off. "That girl is only seventeen. She's practically a child, and my student."

She shrugged. "If you insist."

"Even if what you said was true, it would be better not to go after her. I don't want to give her false hope."

"True," she murmured. "But if it's love, isn't it already too late? Or are you one of those people who don't take teenage love seriously?"

I said nothing.

"So, you're a teacher," she said.

I nodded. "I teach English at a cram school."

"That makes sense. I was wondering what kind of work you did. You leave the apartment around noon, and return pretty late. I thought you were in retail, like me."

"That would have made sense, too."

"Hey, Izumi." The young man who greeted me earlier approached us. "Sorry to cut in, but your shift is over."

"Already?" She checked her watch. Her wrist was slim and bony. "You're right. Thanks for letting me know."

"No problem," the young man said before leaving us.

Izumi took down her ponytail and combed through her hair with her fingers. "What are you doing this afternoon, Ishida?"

"Not sure yet, I don't really have any plans."

"In that case, could you help me run some errands?"

"What do you need to do?"

"I'll let you know in a second. Wait here, I'll be right back," she said over her shoulder as she walked off.

Left alone, I grabbed a few novels and turned them around to read the summaries. None caught my interest, but I felt I should buy something, since I'd come all the way here.

"I'm done," Izumi said. She had taken off her apron and was carrying a canvas tote bag. "Found anything you like?"

"Not yet."

"Maybe you're not meant to buy anything today." She dragged me out of the store. "Let's go. We've got plenty to do."

"Wait, you haven't told me what's happening."

"Don't be impatient, you'll find out soon enough. Let's get out of here."

Of course, her words only fueled my curiosity.

25

Strange
Fruits

After leaving the bookstore, we walked to the main road, following the pedestrian walkway. Izumi was humming. Seeing her so cheerful, I relented, deciding to play along with whatever scheme she had in mind.

Soon, she led me into a flower shop. Unlike the one I'd gone to, the shop had a building of its own and offered a wide selection, but it was unattended. I felt overwhelmed by the sea of colorful flowers. There were roses, lilies, tulips, and many more I couldn't recognize. And then, I saw a bunch of baby's breath inside one of the buckets.

"You like that flower?" Izumi asked. "A little plain, isn't it?"

"It has a beautiful meaning," I said.

"Really?"

"It symbolizes everlasting love."

"How romantic. That settles it, then." She called loudly, "Excuse me, can anyone help us?"

A lady emerged from the back of the shop. "My apologies, I didn't notice you come in. May I help you with anything?"

"Yes." Izumi pointed to the baby's breath. "Can you make these flowers into a bouquet? Or will that be too white?"

"If it's too white, how about mixing them with blue hydrangea?" The lady walked to the other side of the shop and returned with a bunch of fresh flowers. She held them against the baby's breath. "What do you think?"

"Looks good," Izumi answered.

She paid for the flowers and we left the shop. Outside, she passed the bouquet to me.

"Who is this for?" I asked.

She gave me a playful smile. "You'll find out soon."

We boarded a bus and chose seats in the middle. I'd never taken this particular line, so I had no idea where we were headed. Izumi seemed to enjoy being the only one aware of what was going on.

When the bus took off, she turned to me and asked, "Are you sure this is okay? We're sitting together and you're holding flowers. Anyone who sees us will think we're going out."

"Are you scared your boyfriend will catch us red-handed?"

She shook her head. "I don't have a boyfriend. How about you?"

"I don't have a boyfriend either," I joked.

"Be serious."

"I am being serious," I said. "I don't have a boyfriend."

Izumi sighed. "Fine. What about a girlfriend?"

"We won't bump into her. She's in Tokyo."

I hadn't thought of Nae in a while, or our argument. Had she wondered why I hadn't called? Maybe she thought we were over. I didn't want our relationship to end like this, but why couldn't I muster the resolve to talk to her? How long would I avoid her? Our problems weren't going to solve themselves.

"Ishida," Izumi whispered. "Since your girlfriend is all the way in Tokyo, how about being my boyfriend for two hours?"

I leaned away from her. "What are you planning?"

"I'm planning to be in your debt." She pressed the button on the pole near her seat. "Get ready, we're off at the next stop."

We got down in front of a park. It was the one I'd been to with Seven Stars in the rain.

"It's another twenty-minute walk from here," Izumi said. "You can manage, right?"

"That's fine, but I'd still appreciate if you told me your plan."

She pretended not to hear me. We cut across the park, passed a bridge, and entered a quiet residential area. The houses in this neighborhood were almost as large as those in Segayaki, but they looked more run-down, their gardens filled with overgrown shrubs.

Izumi walked in front of me without slowing down. She knew exactly where to go, as if she'd taken the route a thousand times. Finally, we arrived in front of an old folks' home.

"Who are we visiting?" I asked.

"My grandmother," she said. "She's been living here for six years. I always visit her on my day off."

We entered the compound and walked into the lobby. The receptionist nodded at Izumi, who nodded back. Izumi led me down a long hallway to Room 108 and knocked.

"Who is it?" called a soft voice from inside.

"It's me, Grandma," Izumi said, opening the door.

She gestured for me to follow her. I came in and saw a frail woman sitting on the bed. Her hair was completely white.

"Who's this handsome young man?" Izumi's grandmother asked.

"I told you I was going to bring my boyfriend, didn't I? This is Ishida. He's a teacher." Izumi pulled up a chair and sat next to her. "Look, he brought you a lovely bouquet. He wants to be in your good graces."

The woman smiled.

"Good afternoon, I'm Ren Ishida," I said. Seeing an empty vase on her bedside table, I asked, "Shall I put the bouquet here?"

"Yes, please," she said. "Ishida, you don't need to trouble yourself by bringing me gifts. I know any man my granddaughter chooses must be someone worthy of her affection. She's the pickiest girl I have ever known."

"Stop that, you're embarrassing me," Izumi protested.

I kept quiet while arranging the flowers.

"How are you feeling, Grandma? Did the doctor visit you this week?"

The elderly woman nodded. "He said everything is good."

"Have you taken your medicine?"

"Yes, stop fussing over me."

Izumi turned to me and saw the fruit basket next to the vase. "Did Uncle come?"

"About an hour ago."

Izumi stood and inspected the basket's contents. "Look, Grandma, it's your favorite, cantaloupe."

She opened the drawer and took out a fruit knife. I stood at the corner of the room, watching her work the knife. Underneath the pale green skin, the flesh of the cantaloupe was orange. Fruit juice dripped onto her fingers. She had painted her nails with clear polish. They glistened, reflecting the sunlight that came through the thin white curtains.

Izumi cut a small section and took a bite. "Yum," she said, before cutting two bigger sections and passing them to her grandmother and me.

I sunk my teeth into the fruit. The flesh was hard but succulent, bursting with sweet flavor.

"Trust Uncle to pick up such a fancy fruit," she said.

As the three of us ate cantaloupe together in Room 108, the curtains flapped around as the wind blew. Thin white curtains now reminded me of Mrs. Katou. I wondered how she was doing right now—better, I hoped.

Izumi continued to chat with her grandmother. A tiny dimple appeared on her left cheek whenever she smiled.

After a while, their voices started to fade. They were smiling and laughing. Little by little, I felt as if I were leaving the scene, watching them from afar. It was like I was sitting in front of the television, with the happy granddaughter and grandmother onscreen, part of a different reality.

I crossed my arms and rested my head against the wall. Before long, I fell away into the past.

I had been sitting on the sofa in the living room with my sister. We were watching a man in a black tuxedo on television. He was playing a jazz piece on a Yamaha grand piano in front of a large audience.

"He's doing an improvisation of 'Strange Fruit,'" my sister said, reading the subtitle.

"Is he good?" I asked.

"I think so, or they wouldn't be showing his performance on TV."

My eyes were glued to him. He played well, producing beautiful music. But what piqued my interest were his fingers. They were long and slender, with wide nail beds in a healthy pinkish color. They moved gracefully on top of the monochrome keys like a group of synchronized dancers.

The pianist sent his audience into raptures and received a standing ovation. He bowed to the audience amidst thundering applause. Wearing a confident smile, he waved with his beautiful fingers.

"ISHIDA, DID YOU HEAR me?" Izumi startled me.

We were walking back to the bus stop.

"Sorry," I said. "Can you repeat that?"

"I said, I appreciated your help. It meant a lot to me," she said with a smile. "Grandma is the most important person in my life. I lived with her from a young age until I was seventeen."

"What about your parents? Why didn't you live with them?"

"They passed away when I was two," Izumi said. "It was a car accident. My father was speeding. I don't have any siblings, so I was left alone."

"You must have missed your parents a lot."

She shook her head. "How can you miss someone you barely remember? I know their faces from the photographs, but I have no personal recollections of them. To me, they're just two names written on my family register."

I was quiet.

"Do you think I'm a cold person, Ishida?"

I didn't answer. It sounded to me like more of a statement than a question.

"Even though Grandma always had health issues, she was the only one who offered to take me in," she continued. "But as Grandma got older, her condition became much worse. She had a couple of mild heart attacks, but I couldn't watch her all the time since I had to go to school. The family decided it was better for her to live in a nice old folks' home where she would get professional help around the clock."

We were silent for a moment before I said, "It must be hard on you."

"Nah, I'm all right," Izumi said. "Thankfully, I have a rich uncle who takes care of my Grandma financially. He also paid my expenses until I graduated from high school. I'm slowly paying him back. I don't earn a lot at the bookstore, but I should be able to return the full sum by sometime next year. I'm also saving up for university."

I mumbled in agreement. No wonder she was so adamant on keeping her rent low.

"By the way, what did Grandma tell you when I went to the restroom?" Izumi asked. "Did she ask you to propose to me or something?"

I grinned. "Nothing so specific. She told me to take good care of you."

"And what did you say?"

"What else? Anyone in that situation would have to say yes. I couldn't just tell her, 'No, madam. I'm only a temporary boyfriend. My contract expires in two hours,' especially since she's such a nice old lady."

"Really?" Her eyes widened. "You'll take good care of me from now on, Ishida?"

"I was playing the part of a perfect boyfriend. You can't hold me accountable for that."

"I was joking, don't be so serious." She put her hand on the crook of my elbow. "It would be nice to have a boyfriend."

"Why don't you have one?"

"A boyfriend?"

I nodded.

"Not now, I don't want to get involved with anyone yet."

I kept quiet. Her grip was getting tighter. Her palm was warm, and its heat flowed into me.

We strolled side by side through the park by the river. Izumi hadn't let go of my arm. A group of children passed us. They laughed and chased after one another. Behind them, two young mothers pushed their baby strollers. Six middle-aged men were exercising by the river.

"Do you know how the name Akakawa came about?" Izumi asked.

"No," I said. "Why don't you tell me?"

"I know two versions of the story," she said. "The first, I heard from Grandma. She said this place used to be a farming village. A group of farmers arrived in autumn and set up a colony around this river. At that time, countless Japanese maple trees lined both sides of the river. The red leaves fell into the water, painting the river red, so the farmers named the town Akakawa. It's 'aka' from red, and 'kawa' from river."

"What about the second version?"

"Two groups of farmers were fighting over the land. In a moment of rage, they attacked each other with their farming tools. One of the groups was completely wiped out. The other farmers threw the corpses into the river, and the blood turned the water red."

How gory. "So, which one do you believe?"

Shrugging, she said, "I have the feeling both are true."

We passed a few joggers with towels around their necks. After a while, I realized we had done a large circuit, but I pretended not to notice.

"We've walked enough for today," Izumi said. "Shall we go back now?"

I nodded. "How much longer are you going to hold my arm?"

She looked at her watch. "Twelve more minutes, until our contract ends."

"We're sticking to it that closely?"

Izumi smiled and patted my arm. "Since you're well-behaved, I'll give you an early release."

She pulled her hand away and walked in front of me. The sunlight shone on her hair, revealing a reddish tint I hadn't noticed before. She looked radiant in the afternoon sun.

Whenever I saw a girl's long hair glinting in the sun, I remembered my sister. She had naturally dark brown hair, unlike the rest of the Ishida family. I'd always liked the color of her hair.

Once, I'd even tried to dye my hair chestnut brown. But when it grew out, I hated the black roots and was too lazy to touch them up. A couple of months later, I dyed it back to black. That was the first and last time I changed my hair color.

"Walk faster, will you?" Izumi shouted, a few steps ahead of me.

I picked up my pace to catch up with her. We had to change buses twice to return to our apartment building. I walked her to her door. Before going in, Izumi took a plastic bag from her tote and gave it to me.

"What is this?" I asked.

"Payment for being my boyfriend for two hours," she said, closing the door before I could thank her.

Walking up to the fifth floor, I went into my apartment and opened the bag. Inside was an English edition of *Ulysses* by James Joyce. What a choice. I assumed a comfortable sitting position and began reading. After a while, I closed the book and put it away.

At times like this, I missed the days I'd spent with Mrs. Katou in her windy room at the corner of the house. She should be in Hakone by now. Was she still sinking in her guilt? Or had she managed to forgive herself? I hoped she felt much better now. If anything, the fresh mountain air in Hakone would do her good.

I opened a drawer and put the book inside, next to the medical documents from the Kobayashi Women's Clinic. For some reason, I felt a sudden urge to take them out again.

Ever since I'd returned from Kuromachi, I hadn't touched the documents. It was too hard to read them. It pained me to think about what my sister had had to go through alone, pretending everything was okay during our calls. Looking at every column, every word, every letter, I asked myself, *How could you not have realized anything was wrong?*

And then I noticed something odd. Her blood type was listed as *A*.

It had to be a mistake. Didn't our whole family have blood type *O*? I flipped through the other pages. Over and over, her blood type was listed as *A*. Had the clinic really recorded the wrong blood type? No, they wouldn't have made that kind of mistake. And that could only mean one thing. Keiko and I weren't biologically related. So that was why she had lovely dark brown hair, and I didn't.

"Mother always picks on me unfairly," my sister had told me, but I'd dismissed her as being too sensitive. And then there was my mother's coldness when my sister left the family home. Now everything made sense.

Considering my mother's age, she had probably given up on having a child of her own when she took my sister in. But nine years later, I came into her life, and she no longer needed the adopted child.

What a trick of fate. My parents had adopted my sister, but in turn, she ended up adopting me, trying her best to fulfill their roles. Yet, deep down, we knew something was missing. There was a void within us. We were both lonely.

I lay on the floor with the medical documents strewn all around me. When I looked up at the windows, the sky was dark. The moon hung high. It was past my dinnertime, but I didn't feel hungry. I focused my eyes on the orange moon. Staring at it, I felt like the world was spinning too fast. Or was it the clouds that were speeding by? One moment I could see the moon, and the next I only caught a faint glow.

Staring at the sky, I slipped into a dream.

MY SISTER PUT A blanket over me and accidentally woke me up. The moon had illuminated the room, highlighting her long, flowing dark brown hair.

"Is this a dream?" I asked her.

Smiling, she brushed her hair behind her ear. She slipped under the blanket and lay down next to me. "If it is, why wake up now?"

We were so close that I could smell her perfume. She wore a sheer, clean scent that reminded me of freshly ironed linen.

I looked into her eyes, and without thinking, I said, "Keiko, I really miss you."

She was silent. It was the first time I'd called her by her first name, which must have affected her. Then, the edges of her lips curved up into a smile.

"I miss you too, Ren."

I closed my eyes. A warm and familiar feeling enveloped me. I wasn't sure what it was, exactly. Something beyond grief, or even comfort at seeing her again . . .

I opened my eyes and whispered, "I think I was in love with you."

She looked at me in surprise, but regained her composure. "It's okay, Ren. It's all in the past. Don't think about it now."

I nodded, and we both drifted off to sleep.

26

A
String
of
Previous
Existences

I went to the police station to collect my sister's belongings. The day before, Detective Oda had called me at Yotsuba.

"We have clearance to return most of Miss Ishida's personal belongings. There aren't many, but I thought you might want them back. We'll have them ready for pickup tomorrow, if that's convenient."

"Tomorrow is fine," I said. "I'll come before noon."

But when I arrived, the detective was nowhere to be seen. A skinny female officer with a sharp chin manned the counter. After checking my identity card, she handed me a release form to sign.

"Detective Oda had to attend to another case," she said, apologizing on his behalf.

I was taken aback. I'd assumed he would see to this personally, and provide me with an update on the murder investigation. This gave me the impression that he no longer cared about her case. Was it because the media interest in it had cooled?

After I filled out the form, the female officer took the items out and matched them aloud against her list. Everything fit inside a document envelope, which I thrust in my bag before heading to work. It felt inappropriate bringing the envelope into the office, but if I returned home first, I would be late for class. Pressed for time, I boarded the bus to Yotsuba.

"ISHIDA, YOU LOOK SPACED-OUT," an older colleague whose name I couldn't remember told me. "Are you all right?"

"I'm fine, just a little tired," I said.

He nodded before leaving me alone. I closed my eyes and took a deep breath. Stop thinking about the case, I told myself. I had a job to do.

Opening my eyes, I scanned the attendance file. Seven Stars was in my first class of the day. I had forgotten about her storming out of the bookstore. But now, I remembered what Izumi had told me: *It's obvious, isn't it? That student of yours has a crush on you.*

Stupid Izumi. Now I couldn't shake the thought from my mind.

I gathered my teaching materials and went into the classroom. Half of the students were already there, including Seven Stars. When she saw me, she averted her eyes.

The bell rang and I started roll call. Once I finished taking attendance, I explained a few points of grammar, answered some questions, and handed out the worksheets. Seven Stars kept her distance. Whenever our eyes met, she took care to look elsewhere. She didn't smile during the entire class. After the lesson ended, she packed her bag and walked out in a hurry. I ran after her. There were students all around us, but I reacted before I could think about it.

I grabbed her hand. "Why are you angry?"

"Who says I'm angry?" she asked, glaring at me.

"Look, do you have something you want to say?" I forced myself to look straight into her eyes. "I'll listen to whatever is on your mind."

She pulled her hand away. "It's nothing, Mr. Ishida. And why would I want to talk to you, anyway?"

I knew better than to listen to her. When a girl said it was nothing, it meant there were plenty of things I'd missed. I didn't want to leave things like this, but I could feel the students staring at us.

Not wanting to attract more attention, I returned to the classroom. Maybe this wasn't all that bad. I'd gotten too close to her, and it was better for us to keep a safe distance. She was still my student. Any more involvement was dangerous.

I REACHED MY APARTMENT around eleven. Taking the envelope from my bag, I poured its contents onto the living room table. There was a passport, a photo album, and some notebooks. I checked the travel document. It was empty, but had been marked so it couldn't be used any more. Keiko Ishida, why did you have a passport? She'd never gone overseas even once. Or had she planned to go away one day?

I wasn't sure what to do with the items, but I knew no good would come of hanging on to sentimental things. I put them back into the envelope and grabbed a lighter before heading out.

It had been raining earlier that day. The fresh scent lingered, and the foliage had fine mist on its surface. Some of the leaves, having been scattered by the rain, coated the black asphalt.

I found a discarded metal pail in the empty lot behind the building. Crouching down with my back to the wind, I took the items out of the envelope, lit it on fire, and threw it into the pail. Smoke rose, giving off a thick, pungent smell.

One by one, I burned my sister's belongings, starting with the passport.

I flipped through her notebooks. Lesson notes. Her handwriting was neat, as always. No wonder she used to comment on how messy mine was. After going through each notebook, I tossed it into the fire. The papers curled up before turning into ashes.

The last notebook at the bottom of the pile had a Japanese fabric cover with a geometric pattern. The blank pages were yellowing, and I found five 10,000-yen notes slipped in among them. I contemplated keeping the money, but decided to leave it there.

Throwing the last notebook into the fire, I could feel my sister's presence start to vanish. Her death was finally sinking in.

Next was the photo album. It was filled with photographs from a Yotsuba teachers' outing. I spotted Maeda in a few of the pictures. She always wore a serious face at work, but on her day off, she knew how to let her hair down. When she smiled, her eyes disappeared into two tiny lines.

Honda was in a lot of the photographs. He looked jovial as usual, and there was a photograph of him asleep with his mouth open. I was tempted to keep it and use it to make fun of him, but my sister was also in the photograph, making a peace sign. No, I shouldn't hold on to it.

There were other familiar faces, too. The principal, Hiroko, Abe, and many more staff members. They looked so different when they weren't in their work clothes. I was used to defining them by their specialties—the Japanese language teacher, the mathematics teacher, the social studies teacher. But outside the classroom, their personalities shone through. The social studies teacher wore a Hanshin Tigers jersey. The Japanese language teacher was in a colorful jumpsuit. And among them was my sister. She was in a white blouse and navy pencil skirt. Her smile was gentle. She was full of life.

I looked at the photograph in my hand, a solo shot of her.

Standing in front of a row of Jizo statues, my sister looked lovely. She carried a beige handbag on her arm, the same one she'd had with her when she was murdered. That bag transported me back to my first time inside the police station.

Detective Oda had shown me the photographs of the blood-spattered handbag and its contents: wallet, a red scarf, keys, a pack of birth control pills, an organizer, and pens.

The keys were held together by a metal ring with a porcelain rabbit ornament dangling from it. Wait. I had seen that ornament before. It hung behind the rearview mirror and caught the sunlight when the car made a sharp U-turn, blinding me.

His name flashed into my mind.

Honda.

27

I
Have
Something
to
Say

As we had instant noodles for dinner again in the teachers' lounge, I asked Honda if he could come over to my place that night.

"Is something wrong?" he said.

I shook my head. "I just wanted to hang out."

"You're lonely," he joked. "Well, you're in luck, because I'm feeling lonely too. Let's have a party then, just the two of us."

"Great." I finished my noodles. "See you later."

I threw the Styrofoam cup away and returned to my desk. I didn't want to prolong the conversation and make him suspect something was amiss, but he must have sensed it. Usually, we would chat all the way until the next class.

STARTING THE CAR, HONDA asked me, "What do you want for supper?"

"Are you still hungry?" I asked.

"Not really, but I never pass up the opportunity to have supper."

"How about we order some takeout sushi? It's my treat, but I don't know any good shops."

"Leave it to me."

The car exited the underground parking lot and went to the main road. In just a couple of minutes, we'd stopped in front of a sushi joint. The place was just around the corner, yet I'd never noticed it. I went into the shop while Honda waited in the car.

The sushi shop was quiet, save for two salarymen who looked drunk. It was probably almost closing time.

"Welcome," the serious-looking chef behind the counter greeted. "What would you like to order?"

I glanced at the menu. There were a few different sushi platters. Pointing to one, I said, "One set to go."

The chef nodded and prepared my order. He molded the sushi with a practiced perfection and fit it carefully into a black plastic tray. He added sliced ginger, wasabi, and shredded white radish. His movements were smooth and efficient. I paid for the items and returned to the car.

Honda peeked inside the plastic bag. "You don't think this is too much for two people?"

"Better too much than not enough," I said.

He laughed, and we drove off to my apartment.

As the journey progressed, I felt increasingly nervous. I didn't know how to bring up the topic. I'd tried to think about various ways to approach it, but none of them seemed right. I began to wish I'd gone to the police instead.

I LISTENED TO HONDA'S stories while eating sushi in my tiny living room. I didn't talk much, nodding at appropriate times as he told me a few interesting things that had happened at work.

"Two days ago, I gave my class a practice test," he said. "A multiple-choice exam with four options per question. Even if you don't study at all, chances are that some of your guesses will turn out to be correct. It's practically impossible to end up with a zero unless you hand in a blank answer sheet."

I mumbled in agreement.

"But I had to give one of my students a zero," he continued. "He was obviously cheating. The answer for number two was supposed to be for number one, the answer for number three was the right one for number two, and so on."

"He didn't even cheat properly."

"Indeed," Honda said, looking at me. "Anyway, enough of me talking. What's on your mind, Ishida? There's something you want to discuss, isn't there?"

I nodded, but I didn't feel ready. I gestured to him to take more of the food. "Let's finish the sushi first, before it goes bad."

After we polished off everything, I cleaned the table and asked him what he wanted to drink.

"I'm making coffee for myself," I said.

"I'll have that too, then," he said.

I went into the kitchen and returned with two cups of hot coffee, a teaspoon, and a packet of sugar. I put one of the cups in front of him together with the spoon and sugar.

"You don't take sugar?" he asked.

I shook my head. "I don't like sweet things."

He nodded and tore open the paper packet, pouring the white powder into his cup. As he stirred the coffee, its aroma escaped. The rich scent of roasted beans filled the room, but neither of us touched our drinks. After what felt like a long time, Honda finally spoke.

"How long are you going to keep quiet, Ishida? We're not getting anywhere."

"Uh-huh." I took my first sip of coffee before putting it back on the table. "The ex-girlfriend you mentioned to me—was she my sister?"

Honda looked at me in surprise before averting his eyes.

Since the words were out, I no longer saw the need to hold back my thoughts. "It's true, isn't it?"

He remained quiet and stared at the wall.

"Were you the one who killed her?" I asked quietly.

Honda took a deep breath. "So basically, you have two questions. First, did I date your sister? The answer is yes. Keiko and I were together for a little while. Unfortunately, things didn't work out for us."

It was my turn to say nothing. As I'd suspected, Honda and my sister had bought the rabbit trinkets together as a couple.

"As for the second question, was I the one who killed her? No, it wasn't me. I was upset about what happened between us. To be honest, I felt some resentment, but I learned to accept her decision."

I nodded, still undecided on whether I believed him.

"When I first met her, I was thirty-four. She was the textbook image of a teacher. Well-educated, prim and proper, and she genuinely cared about her students. I had nothing but respect for her." He reached for his coffee. "Though she certainly did leave an impression."

"What kind of impression?"

He gave a thin smile. "Not a good one, I'm afraid. You probably can't tell now, but I used to be a quiet person. I don't like to stand out in a crowd, and my name isn't easy to remember."

"Honda?"

"That's a nickname that was given to me by your sister. My real name is Shinosagawa, and most people don't remember it. One day, Keiko saw me cleaning my car with distilled water. She made a huge fuss about it. Weird girl, wasn't she? Isn't it a common practice?"

I wanted to say it wasn't, or at least I'd never heard of it, but I kept my opinion to myself.

"If you use tap water to wash your car, it leaves residue. My car is black. It wouldn't look good with white water streaks."

"Uh-huh."

"Keiko told everyone about it, making it sound like I had OCD. Ever since then, they've called me Honda."

"You fell in love with her because of that?"

He laughed awkwardly. "You think that's what happened? No, I was pissed off back then. But I admit, the nickname sort of grew on me. We actually got closer during a period when she kept falling sick, unlike her usual self. I felt the strong urge to take care of her, and I figured that meant she was more than a colleague to me."

"And she was."

"Only for a while." He sighed. "I wasn't the one who killed her, Ishida. I was angry and disappointed, but I loved her. I should have told you earlier, but I didn't know how to bring it up."

"It's all right. There was a lot going on."

He nodded. "To tell you the truth, I didn't have an alibi. The night she was murdered, I was out in the street, driving alone. I don't have anything to prove myself innocent."

"Don't worry, I trust you. And it's not like I have anything to implicate you, either."

I couldn't explain it, but I believed Honda was telling the truth. He wasn't someone who knew how to lie.

"I have one last question, but I'm not sure if it's one I should be asking you."

"Just go for it." He took a sip of his coffee. "We're already this far in."

I cleared my throat. "This might be rude to ask, but I need to know. Were you the one who got my sister pregnant?"

Honda kept quiet, but his hands clenched the coffee cup tighter. He didn't drink any, nor did he put it down.

"I'm sorry if I've offended you," I said.

"No, I'm not offended. I just . . ." he mumbled. "It definitely wasn't me. She dumped me, actually, for another man."

I couldn't believe there were two men in her life—not just one—whom I hadn't known about.

"Even before I asked her out, I knew there was someone," he continued. "But she told me the relationship was over, and she had moved on. I trusted her. I guess I made a mistake. Keiko never got over him. That person was like a part of her."

"Who is this man?"

"I don't know, Ishida, or I would've told the police already. Keiko was secretive about him, and I didn't want to press her about it because she said he was in the past, and I didn't want to be the jealous boyfriend. But if she was pregnant, I'm certain that it was by this man." He drank his coffee. "There's no way it's my child. We never, well, you know . . . did it."

I was at a loss for words.

"She never felt comfortable with it, and I didn't want to pressure her," he said. "I knew something must be wrong. But she hurt my pride when she left me, so I pretended not to care. After we broke up, I kept my distance from her."

Having heard what had happened, I couldn't blame him.

"I regret it now. I should have been more honest. If I had, perhaps she would still be around. I hate myself for that. I could've helped her if I hadn't given up so easily. In a way, I do feel responsible for her death."

"You shouldn't blame yourself," I said. "You know as well as I do that she wouldn't have listened to any of us. If you're to blame, then I'm as guilty as you. I was indifferent toward her, too preoccupied with my own problems. I knew something wasn't right, but I turned a blind eye. You could've said it was me who killed her."

Silence descended upon us. I looked at my coffee. The steam had disappeared, and the dark liquid was still. Tiny bubbles settled around the rim of the cup.

"If I'd been more persistent, do you think she would have chosen me?" Honda eventually asked.

I shrugged. "But you couldn't do that, could you?"

"You know me well, Ishida. I needed her to choose me because she wanted to, not out of guilt or pity. Otherwise, there would be no meaning to it. Call me naïve, but that's how I feel."

"I would've done the same thing in your position."

He nodded. "Did it surprise you?"

"You and my sister?"

"Yes."

"Not really, I mean—" I stopped halfway. It didn't seem right to tell him I'd always known she had a thing for teachers.

"Keiko never said that she loved me. Not even once," Honda said. "She only told me that she liked me. Silly girl, she didn't make any attempt to hide it. I wish she'd lied to me instead. I would've believed her."

I reached for my coffee and gave it a gentle swirl.

"When Keiko and I dated, she lived in an apartment a lot like this one," Honda said, assessing the room. "That was a few years ago. The place has been redeveloped now. I knew she would have to move out, but I never guessed it would be to the Katous' house."

I took a sip from my cup. "It was an unusual arrangement."

"When we were together, she used to talk a lot about you."

"What did she say?"

"That you were a good-looking kid, but you changed girl-friends more frequently than hairstyles." He smiled, seemingly back at ease. "According to her, you had dated over fifty different girls."

"She was joking," I said. "That's an exaggeration."

"What's the real number?"

"I don't know. Twenty, thirty maybe? Definitely not fifty."

"That's a lot."

"You must have a bad impression of me."

"Not really," he said. "Underneath that carefree attitude, she said you were sensible. And that once you found the right woman, you would cherish her forever."

I forced a smile.

Honda patted my shoulder. "You're still young. Don't be too hard on yourself. Most relationships simply don't work out, no matter how hard you try."

I knew he was speaking from experience, but our situations weren't the same. "In my case, it was all my fault," I confessed.

"What do you mean?"

My sister, smiling gently, flashed through my mind.

"I was infatuated with someone," I said. "Or rather, it was more of a fantasy. I created an idealized image of her and compared everyone I dated against it. Because of that, nothing would ever have worked out."

I thought of Nae, and the countless arguments we'd had before I'd left Tokyo. Not just her, but also the other girls I'd gone out with.

"It took me too long to realize my mistake, and in the process, I ended up hurting a lot of people who cared about me," I went on. "Maybe that was why my sister left me."

"That's not true," Honda said. "Keiko's coming to Akakawa had nothing to do with you. She was fond of you, Ishida. You know that, don't you?"

"I do," I said, nodding slowly. "But she always thought of me as her eight-year-old brother who needed his big sister to constantly keep an eye out for him."

"That's because she cared about you," Honda said. "She spoke so highly of you that sometimes I felt jealous, even though I was her boyfriend. But after meeting you, I agree with her. I do think you're a good guy."

I looked away to hide my embarrassment.

"Her protectiveness must have rubbed off on me. I don't know how it started, but I feel like I have to watch over you on her behalf, playing the role of big brother."

So that was why he'd been so helpful with everything.

"Keiko was actually worried that she was bothering you."

"Really?" I hadn't known she'd felt that way.

"I know she used to call every week," Honda said.

I looked down. "I kind of miss those calls."

"It's common for people to realize what's important after it's gone."

"Uh-huh," I mumbled, stretching my legs. "Do you want a beer? It's a good way to wash away the sentiment."

"I have to pass this time, since I'm driving back." He checked his watch and stood up. "It's almost midnight. I've got to get moving. Thank you for being honest with me—it feels so much better to have finally gotten things out in the open."

I nodded, still trying to digest everything he'd told me.

"See you tomorrow, Ishida," he said.

I walked him to the door. After he left, I went to the kitchen and looked at the beer in the fridge. There were five cans of Asahi Super Dry left. I carried them all to the living room. After everything that had happened, I needed a drink.

Before I could open the first can, someone knocked on the door. Had Honda left something behind? Putting down the beer, I went to see who the late-night visitor was.

2 8

Birthday
Girl

Standing alone in the corridor, Seven Stars was still in her school uniform. She held a white plastic bag in her right hand. When our eyes met, she asked, "Can I come in?"

Before I recovered from the shock of seeing her, she slipped past me into the apartment. She put down her backpack and sat in front of the low table.

I reluctantly closed the door. "What are you doing here?"

"Just visiting," she answered casually, scanning the table. "You drink a lot, don't you?"

I ignored her. "I thought we weren't talking to each other."

She glared at me.

"How did you find out where I live?" I asked.

"I followed you in a cab. I know Mr. Honda usually drives you home, and I figured I could come over after he dropped you off. But he followed you in today, so I had to wait. The two of you took so long, I nearly froze outside." She glanced at the beer. "I thought you were discussing important work-related issues. Who would have guessed it was a drinking party?"

"That's none of your business." I walked over to her. "Didn't you tell me you had severe motion sickness?"

"I also told you I can manage it, if I want. My mother used to drive me around before she got busy with work. It's only recently that I more or less stopped riding in cars. My father can't drive."

I turned to her. "Since you came all the way here, I take it that you're no longer mad?"

Seven Stars nodded.

"So everything is good now?"

Smiling, she nodded again and made a peace sign. "Yup, everything is good."

"All right." I stood up. "Since we've made up, you need to get going now. It's late, and this is a single man's apartment. You shouldn't be here."

She gave me a cold stare, not moving from her spot.

"Does your father know where you are? It's past midnight." I remembered that her parents had a high-ranking friend in the police force. "For all we know, he might have filed a missing persons report."

"Trust me, he hasn't. This isn't the first time I've come home late, and it won't be the last, either. I do it often, so relax, okay? Just sit down." Seven Stars moved the beer to create space on the table. Opening the plastic bag, she took out a white cake box. Inside was a round cheesecake. "Look, Mr. Ishida, I brought you a bribe."

"I appreciate the thought, but you really need to leave now."

She ignored me and continued talking. "This is the best soufflé cheesecake in the world. You should try it. It's so light and fluffy, even cheesecake-haters would love it."

I scratched my head. This looked really, really bad.

"Plus today is my birthday," she said. "You're not going to chase me out on my birthday, are you?"

I took a deep breath. "Only today," I said. "And only because it's your birthday."

She looked pleased. "It's a deal."

I sat at the other end of the table.

Seven Stars took out a few colorful candles and arranged them on the cake. After putting on the last one, she looked at me and asked, "Can I borrow a lighter?"

"Aren't you the one who smokes?" I said.

She shook her head. "I've quit."

I thought she was joking, but her expression was serious.

"Since when?"

"Today."

"What's the occasion?"

"It's my birthday," she said. "Isn't that a big enough occasion to stop smoking?"

"Of course it is. Good for you."

I went to the kitchen to look for the lighter—the same one I'd used to burn my sister's belongings. The fluid was still three-quarters full. Well, I'd hardly used it, after all. I returned to the living room and lit the candles one by one as Seven Stars watched me in excitement.

"Do you want to sing the happy birthday song?" I asked.

She laughed and sang aloud. I joined her midway. After the song ended, Seven Stars clasped her hands together. A few seconds passed in silence before she blew out the candles.

"Happy birthday," I said.

She grinned. "Aren't you going to ask what I wished for?"

I shook my head. "It's supposed to be a secret."

"I'll tell you if you ask."

I laughed. "I don't need to know."

"If you say so," she said, shrugging.

I helped her take the candles off the cake. She took out a plastic cutting knife that had come in the box while I returned to the kitchen to retrieve plates and spoons.

When I got back, she had tied her hair up. She bent down to plate the cake slices and I got a clear view of the back of her slender neck. My heart raced. I looked away, hoping she hadn't noticed me staring.

"Mr. Ishida," she called, handing me the first plate. "Give it a try."

I took the plate from her. The tips of her fingers grazed mine, and I felt tense. Seven Stars started on her slice. I watched her dig her spoon into the cake and bring it to her rosy lips, then set the plate down.

"Perfect," she said, chewing happily. "Mr. Ishida, you should eat your cake instead of staring at me."

Flustered, I put down my plate and dug my spoon into the cheese-cake. What was wrong with me? I took my first bite. The cake was delicious. Smooth and airy, it was the perfect balance of sweet and creamy. "It's really good," I said.

She nodded in agreement and took another bite. Tilting her head, she asked, "Mr. Ishida, do you think I'm pretty?"

"Yes," I answered without thinking.

Her lips curled into a little smile. "Would you believe me if I said I liked you?"

This girl was messing with me. "I don't know. Maybe?"

Seven Stars put her hand on top of mine and looked into my eyes. "I like you, Mr. Ishida."

I pulled my hand away. "Don't joke about things like that. It's not funny."

"I'm serious," she said. Her voice was soft, almost pleading. "I really, really like you."

At a loss for words, I said nothing. I should never have let her in.

"The least you can do is answer me," she said.

I put down my plate and hardened my expression. I had to stop her before things went too far. "What do you want?"

"I want you to stop seeing me as a child and denying my feelings. I've said it already, and I'll say it again. I like you, and I'm serious about you. Can't you see me as a woman?"

I hadn't been prepared for this. "You want me to treat you like a woman?"

She glared at me. "I *am* a woman."

Not thinking clearly, I decided to try scaring her off. I grabbed her wrists and pinned her down. The spoon fell from her hand and clattered to the floor.

"Do you know what a grown man does to a woman when he's alone with her?" I asked.

She freed her wrists, but didn't try to get away.

Circling her arms around my neck, she whispered, "We can do that, if you want."

"Aren't you scared?" I asked, my body still on top of hers. "Have you done it before?"

She shook her head. "No, but I'm not scared, because it's you."

Hearing that, I felt a lump in my throat. No, I couldn't do this. I got off of her and sat down. "You should go now."

A moment of silence passed before she sat up and faced me.

"What's wrong with you?" she shouted. "Am I not pretty enough?"

I sighed. "Of course not. You're attractive, you already know that. But you're too young."

"Didn't you say age was only a number?"

"You're my student. I feel like I'm taking advantage of you."

Her eyes narrowed. "Mr. Ishida, just because you're older than me, that doesn't mean you get to decide what's right and wrong."

Her tone was cutting, almost hostile. I had to find a way to calm her down.

I took a deep breath. "You're confused. Your feelings for me are just because I happen to be around, and acting hastily on them will ruin your life. Trust me, this isn't the real thing, and you'll get over it."

"Why don't you teach me what the real thing is?"

"Stop it, this has gone too far," I told her sternly. I had to cut this off before we hurt each other further. "No more. End of discussion."

Seven Stars bit her lower lip and stared at the wall. I wondered if she was about to cry. I hadn't meant to be so harsh, but lenience would create an opening, and I couldn't afford that. Now, all that was left was to ask her to leave. I could call her a taxi, just to make sure she would get home safe.

The next thing I knew, she leaned toward me, and our lips touched. Surprised by her spontaneity, I froze for a moment, but my desire soon took over. I let her tongue slip into my mouth and touched her hair as she gave a sensual murmur.

Hadn't she told me she'd never had a boyfriend? But she was such a good kisser, I felt as if I was being dragged into a raging sea storm, with no chance of escape. I let the waves pull me down, deeper and deeper into pleasure.

Seven Stars opened her jacket, pulling off her vest and dropping it on the floor. She climbed on top of me, and I felt myself getting hard. I couldn't believe this was happening.

I turned away from her, hoping she hadn't noticed. "Stop it, this is—"

"Just relax," she whispered into my ear.

She silenced me with a kiss and unbuttoned my pants. I knew we were headed to damnation, but I couldn't stop. Some of her hair had fallen into her face. I tucked it behind her ear. She smiled at me and blushed. Looking at her, I couldn't control myself. I knew I wanted her. I pushed her down to the floor and rolled on top of her.

"Are you sure about this?" I asked. "It's still not too late."

She nodded. "Never been more sure."

Hearing that, I gave in to my urges. I reached for her necktie and loosened it, sliding it from her collar before undoing her buttons. She looked away. I felt my heart beat faster. I tried my best to be gentle.

Suddenly, I heard a loud bang. I looked up and saw that one of the windows hadn't been closed properly. I turned to Seven Stars. Three of her shirt buttons were undone, revealing a glimpse of her white lingerie. She looked at me with innocent eyes.

An unbearable heaviness surged in my chest. What was wrong with me? She was only eighteen—around the same age my sister had been when Mr. Tsuda crushed her.

I moved away from Seven Stars. "I'm sorry. We shouldn't be doing this."

She came to me, unconcerned with her gaping blouse. "What are you talking about, Mr. Ishida?"

"We need to stop," I said. I couldn't look at her. "This isn't right."

"Are you afraid to admit your feelings?"

"Neither of us has real feelings for each other. It's just lust. A universal biological need." I said those words knowing well that they weren't true, and that I would probably regret them one day, but I had to drive her away. I let out a sigh. "Get out. I'm not in the mood to play with you."

"I'm not playing. Tell me what I have to do to make you understand that I'm serious."

I looked away from her. I wanted to say something, but my mind was clouded.

She moved in front of me. "Look at me, Mr. Ishida. Which part of me isn't grown-up enough? You're scared of losing someone else—just admit it. But I would never leave you. I'll stay with you forever, unlike your sister."

The mention of my sister made me angry. I stared coldly at her. "What do you want me to do? Be your boyfriend? I already have a girlfriend. Or are you hoping to be my lover? Someone for me to casually have sex with whenever I get the urge?"

Seven Stars looked at me with blazing eyes. She raised her hand to hit me, but I quickly caught it.

"Don't," I said sternly.

She tried to yank her hand back, but I held on tight.

"Let me go," she said. "You're hurting me."

I loosened my grip and she pulled away. I was afraid I'd used too much force, but I really had to get her to leave before things got out of hand again.

"You can see yourself out," I said before walking into my bedroom.

Once I'd locked the door to my room, I dropped onto the floor. I couldn't believe what had happened. I'd never lost control like this before. I was angry and ashamed. How could I nearly repeat the mistake Mr. Tsuda had made, knowing well how badly my sister had suffered because of it?

I closed my eyes and waited for the sound of the front door opening. I heard nothing. How long was she planning to stay? But I wouldn't leave the room until she was gone. I wouldn't be able to walk away from her again if I did.

After a long stillness, I heard a muffled noise. It was soft at first, but gradually became louder. I tensed up and opened my eyes. It brought me back to the night I'd found my sister crouching in the kitchen.

I remembered staring at her, unable to move. Even now, I still didn't know what to do when faced with a crying girl. Was I supposed go out and console her? Wrap my arms around her, tell her it would all be okay? That was probably what Mr. Tsuda had thought back then.

If it hadn't been for that night, I might have done it with Seven Stars. No, there was no doubt. I would have stepped out from my room and pulled her into my arms. I would have kissed her and taken her to my bed. But I couldn't. I had to stop myself from destroying this brilliant young girl. I couldn't do to her what had been done to my sister.

Seven Stars' stifled sobs were audible. She sat there for a long time. She cried and cried until she couldn't any more.

A brief silence followed, before I heard someone open and close the front door. Finally. I took a deep breath. My palms were sweaty. I thrust them into my pockets to wipe them.

Leaving my bedroom to lock the front door, I passed through the space where she had been. Her presence still lingered. She had left the remaining cake inside the box, which sat closed on the table.

I sat down and opened a beer, taking a few gulps. What a mess this had all been. At least it was over. I stared at the table and counted the cans. One was missing. Oh well, let her have it. It had been a long night, and it was her birthday. I took another gulp. I pictured Seven Stars walking alone in the cold, cradling a can of beer with her frozen hands. Her steps were heavy, occasionally crushing the dried leaves scattered on the ground.

Just when I'd thought the hurricane had passed, there was another knock on my front door. I sat up with a jolt. I hadn't thought she would return. Or could it be somebody else? But who would come over at this hour?

The person knocked on the door again, louder this time.

I stayed where I was, conflicted. I wouldn't know who was standing outside unless I opened the door. But if it was her, then answering it would be a grave mistake. I would start acting on impulse again if I saw her crying.

"Ishida, I know you're inside," said a familiar voice. "Open the door, please."

"**WHAT ARE YOU DOING** here?" I asked Honda. "I thought you left hours ago."

"How could I?" He entered the apartment. "Just as I was about to drive off, I saw that girl at your door. I couldn't believe you let her in."

I couldn't respond. Honda was right.

"She's the student who caught your interest, isn't she?" He sighed. "You really put me in a difficult situation, Ishida. It would have been awkward for me to storm into your apartment with her here, but I couldn't just leave."

"You worry too much. Nothing happened, trust me."

He seemed unconvinced. "Why was she here?"

"She happened to be passing through and saw you leaving the apartment, so she dropped by." I pointed to the cake box. "She brought cheesecake."

"Is that so?" Honda sighed again, still looking uncomfortable.

I waited for him to say something, but he didn't. He probably realized that, even if something had happened, we were both consenting adults and it was a private matter.

"But you're right. I shouldn't have let her in." I sat down and offered him a lukewarm beer. "Why don't you drink with me?"

He sat next to me. "Okay, I'll have one."

I handed him a can. Pulling the tab up, he drank it slowly

while gazing at the wall. I used the opportunity to finish my own drink.

"That girl is pretty," Honda said, "but there's something about her that makes her unapproachable."

"I hadn't noticed."

"What's her name? Nakajima?"

"Yes."

"She's an only child, isn't she?"

I nodded. "Do you know her?"

"Not really, but I like cars, and her mother drives a red Mazda Miata. It's one of my favorites, a rear-wheel-drive beauty. Once, when I was stopped at an intersection, her car was next to mine."

"What does her mother look like?"

"To be fair, I didn't get a proper look. It was only for a couple of seconds, and all I saw was her profile. At a glance, she was beautiful."

So it was true, then, that Seven Stars took after her mother. "When was this?"

"A while back, at the beginning of the year."

"You have a good memory."

"There was something odd about her, that's why I remember," he said. "She was wearing elbow-length white gloves. I don't know what they were, but they definitely weren't driving gloves."

"She wears those to protect her hands. She's a hand model."

"A what?"

"A professional hand model," I repeated. "You know those advertisements where they show a hand holding a product? Someone needs to do the job."

"Huh." Honda looked into my eyes. "Hey, Ishida, when you mentioned being infatuated with a woman, you weren't talking about Nakajima, were you?"

I forced myself to laugh. "Of course not. How would that be possible? We only met a few months ago. And she's still just a girl." I looked away. "The person I told you about was someone from my past."

"If that's the case, don't let it continue to haunt you."

I nodded. "I'll keep that in mind."

We stopped talking and drank in silence. I listened to the occasional sounds of the two of us sipping beer. Honda had a lot on his mind, and so did I. That night, I really needed to get drunk.

"Do you mind if I lie down?" Honda asked.

"Go ahead," I said.

He lowered his body to the floor and folded his arms behind his head. Closing his eyes, he remained in that position. I opened another can of beer. Before long, I heard him snoring. There were gaps under his eyelids that revealed the white part of his eyes. They made him look like he was pretending to sleep. But from the rhythm of his movements, I could tell he was sinking into a deep slumber.

The silence slowly thickened, engulfing the living room. It crept through the gaps between the windows and under the doors. The air solidified, forming a blanket of dense translucent mist.

I am breathing the silence.

It went inside me and turned me into silence.

I am the silence.

I FOUND MYSELF SURROUNDED by white mist.

"Hello?" I shouted. "Anybody here?"

All I could hear was the echo of my own voice.

I knew I had to move, but which direction should I go in? Everywhere I looked was masked in the thick fog. I felt as if I'd been here before.

Arms in front of me, I walked forward, hoping to reach the end of the fog. But no matter how far I went, it seemed infinite. I walked faster and faster, and finally I ran. I ran until I was about to collapse in exhaustion, but I was still trapped in this vast whiteness. I stopped to catch my breath. At this rate, I would never get away. The thought sent shivers down to my spine. Was I trapped here forever? Walking aimlessly with no end in sight?

When I started to despair, I heard footsteps approach. I stared in the direction they were coming from, but I couldn't see anything. The mist sealed my field of vision.

The sounds stopped. It was back to stillness, but I could tell someone was standing a few steps from me.

I shouted, "Keiko? Is that you?"

No answer.

"Pigtails?"

Again, it was quiet. The silence was suffocating me.

"Ren, over here," someone shouted from the opposite direction. It was Nae's voice.

WHEN I WOKE UP, Honda had gone.

I had a terrible headache. I got up and went to the bathroom to wash my face, but ended up vomiting into the toilet bowl. Crouching down, I expelled everything, then flushed the toilet twice. I must have emptied the entire contents of my stomach. Goodbye, soufflé cheesecake. Still dizzy, I brushed my teeth, taking my time to gargle the water. After that, I popped a mint into my mouth.

My apartment was a mess, but I wasn't planning to clean it yet. Leave it for tomorrow. Right now, all I wanted was to sleep.

2 9

Chance, Decision, and Phone Calls

"Ishida," Maeda called me when I arrived at the school. "The principal is looking for you. Can you go to his office?"

My palms went clammy. Was it something to do with Seven Stars' visit? Perhaps someone else had seen her, or her father found out where she'd been and reported me. Calm down, I told myself. Nothing happened.

When I entered the principal's office, he was watering the peculiar-looking potted plant on his desk with a water bottle.

"Ishida, please take a seat," he said. "What do you think of our school so far? Have you adjusted to the job?"

"Yes, I find teaching enjoyable," I said.

"Good, good." He nodded slowly. "Are you still thinking of going back to Tokyo?"

I wasn't sure where the conversation was headed.

"Looks like you haven't made up your mind," he went on.

"Yes," I answered, taking the easy way out.

"All right, I'll get straight to the point. I called you here because your contract with us is ending soon, and I'd like to offer you a permanent position. I'm sure you've heard about it from Hiroko, but are you leaning one way or the other?"

So that was what this was about. I breathed a sigh of relief. "My apologies, but I need more time to consider it."

He nodded. "Of course, I don't expect you to answer right away. I know there are many factors to consider, especially since your family is in Tokyo. Do give it some thought. Let me know your decision before your contract is up."

"I will," I said. "Thank you for the offer."

"I shouldn't keep you any longer. Your first class is going to start soon."

I bowed and left the office. Returning to my desk, I was still packing up my materials when Maeda came over.

"Will you be joining us, Ishida?" she asked.

I turned to her. "How did you know?"

"I overheard Hiroko discussing it with the principal the other day." She looked at me with anticipation. "So, did you take the offer? You're doing well here, aren't you? Just a few weeks ago, a parent called to say good things about you."

"Who was it?"

Maeda covered her mouth. "You didn't know? Maybe he wants to remain anonymous. Then I shouldn't have told you, silly me."

"It's not like I'm going to tell anyone I heard it from you."

She dropped her voice. "It was Rio Nakajima's father."

"I see." All because of the one time I'd stopped her from stealing bubble gum?

"Ishida, you haven't answered my question," Maeda said.

She was so persistent. "To tell you the truth, I'm not sure," I said. "I like teaching, but my original plan was to return to Tokyo. I feel obligated to take care of my parents, especially since I'm now the only child."

"That's true. You could also always choose to teach in Tokyo. I'm sure there are more cram schools there. Or you could try to become a public school teacher. I've heard the examination isn't easy, but the public sector has better benefits."

That sounded like a good idea.

"You should consider it, Ishida," Maeda said.

I smiled. "I'll think about it."

She looked pleased and returned to her desk. A few minutes later, all of us dispersed to our assigned classrooms.

As I walked down the stairs, I thought about what Maeda had suggested. Becoming a teacher sounded much better than working for a corporation. I was nervous about it after what had happened the night before, but I knew I would never make the same mistake again.

The bell rang as I opened the classroom door. I put down my materials and looked at the young faces greeting me. They were so lively, full of vivacity and innocence. Being close to them, their youthful energy flowed into me, too.

It might not be a bad idea after all, I thought as I opened the attendance book.

HONDA AND I HEADED out for dinner and saw an unfamiliar face behind the reception counter.

"Where's Abe?" Honda asked the woman.

"She's taking three days' leave to attend a relative's funeral in Osaka," the woman said. "I'm Iwaya, and I'll be covering for her until she's back."

"Nice to meet you. I'm Honda, and this is Ishida."

She turned to me. "Mr. Ishida?"

"Yes," I said.

"A woman called just now and asked for you, but I told her you were still teaching."

I furrowed my brow. Could it be about my sister? "What's her name?"

"She hung up before I could ask, but told me she would call again after the class was over."

I thanked Iwaya for passing along the message and left the school with Honda.

"Were you expecting a call?" he asked.

"Not really," I answered.

"Should we have instant noodles instead? So you can wait here for the person to call back."

"It's all right. I don't think we'll miss much by having a quick dinner."

"Let's go to the ramen stall then, since it's nearby."

But when we returned half an hour later, Iwaya told me I'd missed the call by a couple of minutes.

"Did you get the name of the person?" I asked.

"I'm afraid not. When I asked what her name was, she hung up quite suddenly." Iwaya lowered her voice. "Actually, I think she did it on purpose."

That was strange. A police officer would have clearly identified herself. In this case, who would be calling me?

Honda inched toward me and whispered, "Could it have something to do with that student of yours?"

"Impossible. Like I said, nothing happened." I turned to Iwaya. "Please let me know when she calls."

"She mentioned she'd try again after your last class."

I nodded and walked upstairs with Honda.

The next class soon started, but the entire lesson, I kept thinking about the phone call. I doubted it had to do with Seven Stars. She was too proud. The fact that I'd pushed her away should have been enough to stop her from approaching me. Could it be my mother?

No, she didn't have my number. I recalled the envelope containing my sister's photocopied medical documents. Could it be the work of the same person? I glanced at the wall clock for probably the tenth time. I hoped my students hadn't noticed. If they had, no one said anything.

Finally, the bell rang. After dismissing the class, I rushed to the office to grab my bag and went down to reception.

"Did anyone call?" I asked Iwaya.

She smiled politely. "Not yet, Mr. Ishida."

"May I wait here?"

"Of course."

I pulled out a chair and sat in front of her.

Students and faculty started to leave the building. Honda came and asked if I needed a lift, but I said I wanted to wait for the call. He offered to stay with me, but not wanting to keep him any longer, I told him to go ahead. He looked reluctant, but he had been planning to watch a new episode of one of his favorite television shows that night, so he relented.

A couple of minutes later, Iwaya told me she had to leave. I nodded and continued to wait. It looked like most people had gone home. The heat was off, and the place was quiet.

I grew bored and inspected the phone from every angle. The device was black and seemed like a newer model than the one in Mr. Katou's house. I turned it around to let its shiny surface catch the light. The paint on the receiver had faded a little, and some of the numbers were completely unreadable.

I felt a touch on my shoulder. Looking up, I saw the janitor.

"I'm sorry, but I need to lock up," the old man said.

I looked at my watch. How time flew—I'd been waiting for my anonymous caller for close to two hours. "I'm sorry for holding you up," I said, picking up my bag.

"Don't worry about it," he said. "Have a good night."

I helped him shutter the front door before walking to the bus stop. In the end, I'd waited there for nothing. If I'd left with Honda earlier, I would've been in bed by now. But what was done was done.

THE CALL I'D ANTICIPATED came the next day. I was in the reception area, waiting for Honda so we could leave together.

"Mr. Ishida, it's for you," Iwaya said, covering the receiver with her hand.

"Thanks." I took the phone from her and cleared my throat. "This is Ren Ishida. May I know who is this on the line?"

"It's me," said a husky voice I didn't recognize.

"Sorry, who?"

"Anzu."

"Anzu?"

A pause. "Have you forgotten about me already?"

"Of course not," I said. Luckily, I'd just managed to recall who she was. "You were with Kaori in Roppongi."

"Yes, I'm glad you remember this time."

"It's just that . . ." My voice trailed off. She had said "this time"; had I met her before that night? "I didn't recognize your voice, that's all," I stalled. "You sound different over the phone."

"It's been a few weeks. Maybe you've forgotten how my voice sounds."

I hadn't realized it had been that long. "Was it you who called me yesterday?"

"Yes, but you were still teaching. When I called again, you were out for dinner. It's not easy to get hold of you." She paused, then sighed. "So you're a teacher."

It took me a while to realize that someone had finally called Jin's bluff. Damn, she'd gotten us. *This is bad.* I fumbled for the right words. Even though Jin had been the one who'd started it, I was guilty, too, since I'd played along that night.

Next to me, Iwaya whispered that she needed to leave.

"I'm sorry for making things up," I said after she was gone.

"No, you're not sorry for lying. You're sorry for getting caught," Anzu said. "And your chatty friend? Is he your coworker?"

"He's a student, but not in law school." I vaguely recalled that Jin had majored in business, but I wasn't sure.

"Anything else?"

"We're from Tokyo." At this point, I figured I might as well show all my cards. "Jin is at Waseda, and I used to be at Keio. I'm teaching at a cram school in Akakawa right now, but you already know that."

"Interesting," she said flatly.

A long, awkward silence followed.

I knew she was waiting for something, perhaps an explanation, but I couldn't think of a real justification for our deception. I cleared my throat. "We're terrible, aren't we?"

Anzu burst into laughter. "Good that you know."

I breathed a sigh of relief, knowing she'd taken things in good humor.

"I promised to phone a third time after your class was over, but I ended up being called in for an urgent casting. You didn't wait, did you?"

"No, don't worry about that," I lied. "But how did you manage to get this number?"

She laughed. "It's a secret. Anyway, that's not the point. I called because I heard something that might interest you. It's about the hand model you told me about."

Seven Stars' mother. "What about her?"

"She's someone I know," Anzu said. "We're not terribly close, but we have worked together a couple of times. She uses her maiden name for work, so I didn't recognize the one you gave me earlier. I know her as Maria Saeki."

"I see." It wasn't common, but I'd heard of some women choosing to keep their maiden names professionally.

"The thing is, she went missing a few months ago."

"What happened?"

"Nobody knows. She never turned up for one of her shoots. Her agent didn't know anything. No calls, no letters, nothing. Poof. Just like that. But Saeki is known to be reliable. She wouldn't miss work for no reason."

"Right."

"Her sudden disappearance caused a lot of problems. Her agent needed to find a replacement for her, but hand models aren't common, let alone one as experienced as Saeki. He even went to Akakawa to look for her, but her husband told him she no longer lived there."

I thought of what Rio said, about her mother abandoning her and Mr. Nakajima. "Surely he knows where she is."

"According to him, she had gone back to her parents' house in Hokkaido, but something wasn't right. You wouldn't go on leave without telling anyone at the office, would you? Not to mention, she had several prior work engagements. No one commits to a job if they know they're going away soon."

"Probably not," I agreed.

"Her agent said Saeki didn't even collect her pay. I feel like something bad happened, though I don't know what."

"Do you know when she disappeared?" I asked.

She paused to think it over. "If my memory serves me right, it was around the beginning of June this year."

My heart skipped a beat. It couldn't be . . . but there was no way that timing was mere coincidence. Could Maria Saeki's disappearance have had something to do with my sister?

"Ren, are you still there?" Anzu asked.

I tightened my grip on the phone. "Yes, please go on."

"There's nothing else. That's all I wanted to tell you."

"I see," I mumbled, gathering my thoughts. I needed more time to digest this information. In the meantime, I asked Anzu, "Did you send me something in the mail?"

"No, I didn't. What makes you think so?"

"I received something recently, but the sender didn't write their name."

She giggled. "A love letter?"

"No, but it was something important, so I want to thank the person."

"It could be anyone, really," she said. "You know, Ren, I wouldn't have guessed anyone from Keio would move to a small town like Akakawa to become a teacher."

I didn't respond.

"Let me guess," she continued. "You quit school, broke up with your girlfriend, and had nothing to do, so you went there for a change of scene."

"Hey, I didn't break up with my girlfriend."

She was quiet for a moment, then said, "So you do have a girl-friend."

I cleared my throat. "Yes."

"And you still went to Roppongi to fool around."

"I was drunk."

"That's no excuse."

"And you?" I asked, changing the subject. "Do you have a boy-friend now?"

A few seconds passed before she answered, "It doesn't matter."

She hung up on me without another word. I gave her a pass, considering the falsehoods I hadn't bothered to correct.

"Are you done, Ishida?" Honda asked. He was standing near the door.

I put down the phone, wondering how long he had been there. "Yes, sorry to keep you waiting."

"Who was it?"

"An acquaintance."

He nodded, taking the hint that I didn't want to talk about it. Exiting the building, we walked over to his car and promptly drove off.

The streets, as usual, were quiet at night. Unlike Tokyo, Akakawa went to sleep early. Honda drove his black sedan in the highest gear. He only needed to slow down when we approached traffic lights.

When the car stopped at the intersection, I felt I'd forgotten something important. But what was it? It had something to do with traffic lights. But when? And where? Was it in Tokyo, or in Akakawa?

The light turned green, and Honda pulled the hand brake. He shifted the gear swiftly while the car picked up speed. And then I remembered something I should have recalled much, much earlier.

It had happened on my birthday. I'd saved up from my part-time job to take my girlfriend somewhere fancy, but we'd broken up a few days before. She learned that I'd slept with another girl. Because of that, instead of going for a romantic date, I found myself wearing a scratchy pizza delivery uniform, in a flashy yellow Toyota Celica, next to a peculiar girl.

I reached for her hand, which rested on the hand brake. She didn't say anything. Her hand was cold. I let it go when the light turned green. The engine roared as the car moved off.

The streetlights blurred together, creating one continuous glowing line.

Before we parted ways, she told me, "You're a good guy, Ren. If we meet again, I'll let you know my name."

I ASKED HONDA TO drop me off at the public pay phone near the bus stop by the park.

"Have to call home," I said.

He nodded and stopped the car in front of the phone booth. I got out and went inside, rubbing my hands together to keep them warm as he drove off. I inserted some coins into the slot, pressed the familiar numbers, and waited for someone to pick up.

"Hello?"

I cleared my throat. "Mother, it's me."

"Oh." No hint of surprise in her voice.

"How are you and Father?"

"We're fine."

"That's good," I said. "I'm coming home in a few weeks' time."

An awkward silence ensued.

"I'll see you when I'm back," I continued.

I was about to hang up when she said, "Wait, Ren."

"Yes?"

"About Keiko . . . Did the police manage to . . ."

My chest went tight. My mother's voice was small. It was the first time in years that she'd said my sister's name.

"Unfortunately, there's no update yet," I said. "I assume there's been no progress in the investigation."

"I see," she replied vaguely.

I took a deep breath. "Actually, there's something I've been meaning to ask."

"Yes?"

"Was Keiko adopted?"

My mother was quiet for a minute before asking, "How did you know?"

I thought of the clinic's records, my sister's pregnancy. "It's not important."

"To be honest, I didn't ever want you to learn about this. But since you've already found out, it's probably best to tell you the whole story," she said. "Your father had an affair with a woman from Akakawa."

I was taken aback that she'd admitted this so straightforwardly. So she *was* my sister. My half-sister.

"I'd never expected him to betray me, let alone ask my consent to adopt his love child. Back then, we'd been married for four years, but I hadn't gotten pregnant. I couldn't say no to his request, especially in front of my in-laws. It's the one decision I've regretted until now."

My throat was dry.

"That child. I always hated her. It wasn't her fault, but I couldn't help directing my anger at her."

Her voice became shaky, and she stopped talking. Even though I wasn't with her, I could picture my mother wiping at her tears with her inner wrist.

"I'm so thankful I finally got you, Ren. You were the child I'd been waiting for. I shouldn't say this, but I'm glad you're a boy. You won't have to experience the same things I did."

Hearing that, I felt sorry for my mother.

"When you were born, I asked your father to send Keiko away. He wouldn't agree, no matter what I said."

So this was why they'd always argued. It had been me, in a way, but also my sister.

My mother continued, "I told him Keiko would be better off

somewhere else, raised by a woman capable of loving her. I was the one who chased her out that day. I know you were close to her. You must be upset with me."

I sighed. "I am, but I understand how much you've suffered."

She didn't respond.

"Please take care," I said, "and send my regards to Father."

Her silence continued until I hung up.

Walking back to my apartment, I thought about what my mother had said. So much had happened during my childhood, and I hadn't had a clue. If I'd stayed in Tokyo, I would never have learned any of this. But I'd made up my mind to pursue the truth. Was I better off knowing, or not?

I closed my eyes and felt the cold wind blow into my face. Tomorrow wasn't going to be easy.

3 0

Cold
Coffee

The next day, I applied for urgent leave. I wanted to visit Mr. Nakajima while Seven Stars was in class at Yotsuba. If, for any reason, she were around, I would leave right away. Thankfully, as expected, Mr. Nakajima answered the door.

"Mr. Ishida." He greeted me with a smile. "So pleased to have another visit from you, but Rio isn't at home."

"I know," I said. "I'm here to speak with you."

He shook his head. "She hasn't given you more trouble, has she?"

Not wanting to create a scene outside the house, I didn't bother to answer him.

"Please, come in," he said.

I followed him into the house and we sat on the sofa. The living room hadn't changed since the last time I'd been there. Photographs of Mrs. Nakajima's hands still graced the wall.

"Can I get you a drink?" Mr. Nakajima asked. "Coffee, perhaps?"

"Don't trouble yourself—I won't be long." I paused, trying to keep calm. "There's something I need to ask you. Did you know Keiko Ishida?"

He looked surprised for a second, but quickly regained his composure. "Yes, of course I knew her. She was Rio's teacher."

Despite how he'd played it off, I could tell he was uneasy. The way he concealed his emotions was quite similar to Seven Stars, though she was better at it.

"To be more specific, were you in a relationship with her?" I asked.

Mr. Nakajima hid his flustered expression by adjusting his glasses. His clumsy action confirmed my suspicion. "I'm not sure if I understand what you're trying to say," he said.

"We both know what I'm trying to say," I insisted. "You were having an affair with my sister."

He went pale.

"And five years ago, you got her pregnant."

"How—"

I continued to press him. "But you forced her to terminate the pregnancy."

"Wait a min—"

"Do us both a favor and stop pretending," I said evenly, forcing myself to look him in the eye. I'd expected to lose my temper, but I had to keep my emotions under control to get any answers.

Mr. Nakajima averted his gaze. "Please, just let me get you something to drink, all right? After that, I'll tell you what happened."

I took a deep breath. "Coffee is fine, if you insist."

He nodded and adjusted his glasses again before going to the kitchen. If I was really in the home of a cold-blooded killer, I probably shouldn't have left him alone to make me coffee, but I needed his cooperation to uncover the truth.

Left alone, I stared at the images of Mrs. Nakajima's hands. They were truly beautiful subjects—smooth and slim in elegant poses—but looking at them now made me sick.

Mr. Nakajima returned with two cups of coffee. Neither of us touched them. He fidgeted with his fingers and stared at the wall of photographs. Without looking at me, he asked, "Does Rio know?"

"She has no idea, and I don't plan to involve her," I said.

He turned to me. "How did you find out?"

"That's not important."

Mr. Nakajima nodded and returned his gaze to the wall. He shifted his coffee cup on the table before speaking. "You're right, I was in a relationship with Keiko."

I clenched my fists. I'd expected him to confess, but hearing it with my own ears made my anger surge. "So you're the one who killed her."

He turned to me, eyes wide. "No, you're mistaken. I mean . . ." He looked down and shook his head. "Why would I—" His voice cracked. "I had no reason to do that."

"I can think of a thousand reasons for you to have murdered her."

"Let's get this straight. I didn't kill your sister. I was in Kyoto that night."

I hesitated. If this was a lie, it would be the easiest kind to expose. But if he was telling the truth, the next likeliest person was . . .

"Was it your wife?"

He didn't answer.

"Is that why she disappeared?"

Mr. Nakajima laced his fingers together on his lap. "Since we've come to this, it might be better for me to give you the full account of what happened."

I couldn't believe he was so composed about it. "Go on," I said.

"First of all, I never asked Keiko to terminate the pregnancy. From the beginning, I made it clear to her that I would support whatever decision she made, and she chose to keep the child.

Unfortunately, though, she lost the baby due to health complications in her second trimester."

A miscarriage? I wondered how my sister could have suffered through this without saying anything.

"I know I wasn't entirely blameless," he continued. "The stress from hiding the pregnancy and the numerous confrontations with my wife might have been contributing factors."

"She fought with your wife?"

He nodded. "We were trying to discuss our options."

I dug my fingernails into my palms. Had he just said "options"? "What kind of *options* could a married man possibly give his pregnant lover?"

"I wanted to marry Keiko," he continued. "I'd proposed an amicable separation with my wife a number of times, but she wouldn't agree to it."

I stared at him. "That's why your wife killed my sister, isn't it?"

"What makes you think it was my wife? It could have been anyone."

"Like who?" I scoffed. "Your daughter?"

It was an absurd accusation. We both knew Seven Stars would never do something so vicious, but his placid tone infuriated me.

Mr. Nakajima put his hands on his knees. "Who killed Keiko, and why, to be completely honest, I don't know for sure. But I've come to share the same conclusion as you. My wife went missing on the day Keiko was murdered."

"I don't see that as mere coincidence."

"Neither do I," he said. "I even thought of taking the blame, so my wife could return to a normal life with Rio. After all, I was the one who started this mess. But I was at a friend's wedding that night. A lot of people saw me there."

I wondered how much I could trust this man, who had already

told so many lies. He could simply have killed his wife to cover his tracks and pretended she'd disappeared.

"Your sister was wonderful. I loved watching her cook. She told me she used to cook for her younger brother. Who would've thought that one day I would get to meet you?"

I felt a sharp pain in my chest, hearing him talk about my sister that way.

"What happened to Keiko was a nightmare—something I never would've expected. She didn't deserve it. Everything was my fault. I was the one who pursued her, and she was the one who ended up suffering the most. The hurt I've caused you and your family . . . there's no way I can ever atone for it. I will carry this burden for the rest of my life."

Since he'd given up his attempts to hide anything, I was at a loss as to what to say next. I ended up asking him, "Did you love my sister?"

He looked straight at me. "Yes, I did. Of course I did."

"Is that why you don't have any photographs of your wife's face?"

"No, that has nothing to do with Keiko. My wife never liked to be photographed. She had an accident when she was young that left her with a scar on her face. It was just a tiny scar above her left eye, but she was self-conscious about it." He looked down. "Sorry for blabbing—this probably isn't what you want to hear."

"You speak as if you love your wife," I said.

He nodded. "I do love her."

"Are you trying to tell me that you were in love with two women at the same time?"

Mr. Nakajima paused for a moment, choosing his words carefully. "If you were to ask me long ago, before I'd met Keiko, I would've said it was impossible. Even now, I'd like to think the feelings I had for Keiko were different from the feelings I had for my wife. It would be easier to dismiss what happened with your sister as a momentary lapse in judgment, rather than to admit that my marriage was the mistake. But I can't say that. I did love Keiko, and I still do, and probably always will. Does that make sense to you, Mr. Ishida?"

"My opinion isn't important," I said.

He sighed. "In the beginning, I thought I could carry on without hurting anyone. Now that I think about it properly, even though she didn't say anything, Keiko was probably hurting badly."

He looked at me as if expecting a response, but I maintained my silence and kept my eyes fixed on him.

"Eventually, my wife found out," he continued. "It was a huge blow to her. She was always emotionally fragile. Please understand, she's a victim too, and I should be the one to blame. What my wife did, or at least what I think she did, is unforgivable, but she's not a monster. She—"

"Please, stop these excuses." I cut in. I didn't want to hear any more of this nonsense. "My sister is dead, and that makes your wife a murderer. That's the truth."

My words shut him up. Keeping his head low, he tapped his fingers on the edge of the table. I thought about Seven Stars and her erratic behavior—skipping class, stealing, staying out at night. Did he notice that she was affected by her mother's disappearance? Did he know how he had harmed his daughter?

"Other than what you've told me, is there anything else I need to know?" I asked.

"Mr. Ishida, if you're planning to report this to the police, I'm afraid nobody knows her whereabouts. I have told some people my wife returned to her parents' house, but she's actually an orphan."

"That's not my intention," I said. "Even if the police managed to find your wife and throw her in jail, that wouldn't bring my sister back." And it would be disrespectful to make known the affair and the pregnancy she had gone to such pains to keep to herself.

Mr. Nakajima kept his head down.

"Do you have anything else to say?" I asked, standing up.

He looked up at me. "This entire time, I've wanted to tell you all of this. Ever since the first time you came to this house . . . No, even before that. When I first saw you from afar at Keiko's funeral, I wanted to walk up to you and tell you the truth. But you were sitting next to her coffin with empty eyes, and knowing how much she meant to you, I just couldn't—"

"Enough!" I shouted. "Don't you dare talk about my relationship with my sister." I took a deep breath to calm myself. "You know nothing about us."

He hung his head again.

There was a long pause before I finally said, "I'll be taking my leave."

"Hold on a moment." He stood up too. "May I apologize to you on behalf of my wife?"

"No. You can only apologize for yourself."

He climbed down onto his knees and bowed. "I'm sorry. I'm so sorry for what I did, for what happened to Keiko, and for causing your family such grief."

I clenched my jaw. I had no forgiveness for this man. Even if he was truly sorry, what good did it do now? The dead would remain dead. If anything, he was sorry for himself, hoping to find closure. He wouldn't get that from me.

"You've got the wrong person," I said. "You should be apologizing to the women you have hurt, not me. But if what you've said is true, both of them are gone."

Mr. Nakajima didn't respond. He didn't budge from his position, and I left the house without touching the coffee.

To be honest, I hated the man. I wanted to beat him senseless, but it would only disgrace my sister's memory and offer him atonement. I didn't want him to think he could pay for his mistakes by taking punishment. Let him drown in guilt instead.

As much as I wanted his wife to be caught, I couldn't bring myself to go to the police. I still felt the instinct to protect Seven Stars, who'd done nothing wrong and had now lost her mother. Her parents' actions going public could ruin her life, and Mr. Nakajima's involvement in everything could remove her father, her only remaining family. I knew how hard it had been to grow up alone, eating alone at a table for four, going without parents to school ceremonies, having no one to share osechi with on New Year's . . . The last thing I wanted was to subject Seven Stars to that same loneliness.

And, deep down, I knew I would go to any lengths to protect my sister's honor, even though I would hate myself for it forever.

I STOOD AT THE spot where my sister had been murdered. I had no idea how I'd gotten there. It was as if I'd simply closed my eyes and reopened them on the side of that road.

I was in daze until I heard children chattering behind me. Turning around, I saw two children playing across the street. One was a skinny boy wearing a black leather backpack, and the other was a little girl with pigtails in a dark-blue pinafore.

The little girl looked in my direction, and our eyes met. She smiled before running down the road. The boy called after the girl. I couldn't make out what he shouted, but I was sure it was her name. The boy was about to run after the girl, but he hesitated and turned to me. We looked at each other. No words were needed. A few seconds later, he ran after the girl. I watched them disappear around the bend.

I took a deep breath and looked one last time at the site.

Keiko Ishida, do you remember the black leather backpack you bought me when I started primary school?

"An acceptance gift?" I asked my sister when she called me into her bedroom and showed me the backpack.

"Yes." Her eyes gleamed. "You need a new schoolbag."

"You don't need to spend your pocket money on me. The bag is expensive. It's not worth it. Mrs. Kawano said I could have her son's old backpack."

"What are you talking about? You can't start school with an old bag. I won't allow it." My sister helped me put on the backpack before leading me to the mirror. "A good bag completes an outfit. Don't you agree?"

I grinned and muttered a thank-you.

She messed up my hair, and we both laughed.

31

Getting
Sucked
into
a
Tornado

When I told the principal about my intention to return to Tokyo, he didn't seem surprised. He gave me a pat on the shoulder and said, "If that's your decision, then I wish you all the best. We're going to miss you. You've been a great help to us these past few months."

"Thank you," I said. "Do let me know if there's anything I can do to help with finding my replacement."

The principal rearranged his potted plant. "To be honest, I'm a little relieved that you turned us down. It's better for you to leave this place. Call me superstitious, but the old folks in Akakawa believe the town only accepts those who were born here."

I had no idea what had driven him to say that, so I simply nodded before taking my leave.

A WEEK BEFORE THE semester ended, the principal announced that I would be leaving Yotsuba. A few colleagues gave me a handshake and a few others passed me their contact numbers, promising to keep in touch. The vast majority seemed unconcerned.

"It happens pretty often," Honda said. "Turnover is high for contract staff. People come and go. No one cares, except those who'll be getting a heavier workload."

"I hope it's not you," I said.

He laughed. "I doubt it. I can't teach English."

I hadn't told anyone I was planning to teach in Tokyo, but somehow it became known that I was going to apply to be a public school teacher.

"When are you leaving?" Honda asked.

I made a mental calculation. "In two weeks."

"Do you need any help?"

I shook my head, but then I remembered something. "By the way, did you and my sister ever go to an Italian restaurant on the mountain?"

"Yes, we did. It's a charming little restaurant, about a two-hour drive from here. Are you planning to go? The view is great, but the area's too windy. Not many people go there."

Strong wind . . . I could make use of that. "Could you give me directions?" I asked. "I'm thinking of scattering my sister's ashes there, if the wind is strong enough."

Honda nodded. "It should be fine. If you're planning to go this Sunday, I can drive you."

"Don't trouble yourself, I can get there on my own." I didn't want to burden him with the past.

"Oh, it's no trouble at all. It might be the last thing I can do for Keiko," he said. "So, this coming Sunday? I'll pick you up at ten if that's okay."

"Of course," I answered, secretly glad that someone would be with me when I scattered her ashes. I couldn't imagine saying goodbye to my sister alone.

AFTER WORK, I STOPPED by Izumi's place. She came out with her hair in a towel, skin still damp from the shower. She had her old-fashioned glasses on.

"Is this a bad time?" I asked.

She grinned. "That depends. What do you want? If you're going to complain about the water heater, any time is a bad time."

"It's nothing like that," I said, smiling. "I came to bid you fare-well. I'm going to be moving out at the end of the month."

Her eyebrows rose. "That's next week, isn't it? Are you going back to Tokyo?"

I nodded.

"I'll let the landlord know—or rather, his secretary."

"Thanks a lot, Izumi."

"No problem," she said. "Since you're moving out, too, the fifth floor will be tenantless again."

"What about the other guy?"

"The songwriter?" She tilted her head. "Didn't you know he was gone? I guess he moved out when you were at work."

"I see." I hadn't seen that coming. "I only spoke to him once."

"Trust me, that's more than most residents here," she said. "Hey, want to come in and have a drink? I have some beer."

"I have to pass. I've got so many things to pack up."

Izumi shrugged and closed her door, and I returned to my unit.

Thinking about it, this was the first time I'd rejected a girl's invitation to drink. It was probably that Izumi still reminded me of my high school's class rep.

I actually slept with the class rep once. The episode had caused some discord. I could still remember Jin marching over to me during lunch break.

"Is it true?" he asked. "Did you sleep with the class rep?"

The question startled me. I hadn't told anyone about it, so the news must have disseminated from her. To be fair, I hadn't asked her to keep it to herself, but I hadn't thought she would go around talking about it.

"I thought she didn't like us," Jin said.

I flipped open my textbook, ignoring him. I knew Jin didn't like the girl. A few months prior, she'd caught us smoking and ratted us out to the teacher. Or rather, ratted Jin out as the one who was smoking and me as a bystander. The teacher wouldn't buy that, so I was punished too.

"Why would you sleep with her, Ren? Did you lose a bet or something?"

"I don't know," I said. "I was curious."

Jin put his arm around my shoulders. "That doesn't sound like you, my friend."

I shoved him away. "Well, you can decide whether you want to believe me or not."

"There's something wrong in your head."

I kept quiet, and Jin left me alone. But it was the truth. I had been curious. I'd wanted to see what she looked like without her glasses on.

The class rep and I lived in the same neighborhood; her house was only a few blocks from mine. She had walked up to me when I was looking at the comics display at the local bookstore.

"My parents are at a family event in Izu," she said. "They won't be back until tomorrow. Want to come over to my place, Ishida?"

I was speechless for a moment. At first, I thought it was a joke, but her expression was serious. I didn't know what had prompted her to ask me. Maybe something to do with raging teenage hormones.

I scratched my head. "Sonoda . . ."

"It's Sumida," she corrected. "My name is Miwako Sumida."

"Well, Sumida . . ." I leaned toward her. "You know that if I come over, we're not going to be doing much studying, right?"

The class rep nodded, still unsmiling. After saying that, it would have been weird for me to back down, so I followed her to her house. I remembered feeling nervous as we climbed the wooden stairs, which creaked with each step I took.

She opened her bedroom door. "Please come in."

"Excuse me," I said, a little too politely. It sounded awkward.

Her room was neat, just the way I'd imagined it. She walked in and sat on her bed, and I followed suit. Neither of us said anything. She clutched her pillow and I stared at my knees. Her sheets had roses embroidered on them.

The long silence was unbearable. Before that day, we'd never really talked to each other. Just as I was about to attempt small talk, the tips of our fingers touched. I turned to her reflexively. She looked at me too. I could hear her breathing deepen.

I reached for her hair and kissed her. She didn't respond. She didn't move when I unbuttoned her blouse. Before long, I was inside her, but her silence worried me.

"Are you okay?" I asked.

She nodded, but didn't say a word. Maybe she was the quiet kind. Not knowing what else to do, I continued to thrust myself into her. I would've preferred someone more responsive, but it was still good. I wasn't picky.

Thankfully, despite her seriousness, it hadn't been her first time. Otherwise I might have felt bad about it.

She fell asleep after we were done, and I slowly lifted her glasses off. Without them, she looked different—she was actually quite pretty. I kissed her on her forehead before getting dressed and walking back home.

At the time when we were full of raging hormones and sex was a novelty, sleeping with a girl was considered an accomplishment. The boys came and gave me a pat on the back.

"You're good, Ishida. How did you manage to get her?" they jokingly asked.

Somehow, I'd ended up with more friends.

What I'd lost was my girlfriend, who had heard the rumor and confronted me. When I told her all of it was true, she slapped me in front of our classmates and ran away sobbing.

Jin peered over my shoulder. "You screwed up, Ren. It's one thing to cheat on your girlfriend, but were you actually stupid enough to admit it? Even worse, it was with that glasses girl." He gave a dry laugh. "What's wrong with your eyes, my friend? Have some standards."

I glared at him.

"Hey, don't get mad," he said. "But seriously, you should make better use of that face. If you want, I can introduce you to my girl-friend's best friend. She has huge jugs, I kid you not."

I'd never told anyone, but I was glad it turned out that way. Back then, I'd been tired of my girlfriend, but couldn't find a reason to dump her. I didn't have the courage to break up with someone who'd done nothing wrong. Plus, my birthday was coming up, and I'd already saved up enough from my pizza delivery job for a fancy dinner. The timing hadn't been great, as I would've preferred to break up after we'd made some better memories on that date, but the class rep had still done me a favor.

As for Sumida, I never spoke to her again beyond what was necessary. Even if she'd asked, I wouldn't have slept with her again, though I was curious as to what had prompted her to approach me in the first place.

I stopped for a moment outside the zori man's old unit. The door and windows were shut, as usual. No sign of anyone ever living there. Even when he'd been around, no one noticed him—he seemed more like a ghost than a person. Well, wherever he was, I bet he was still wearing his zori.

I went to my apartment and took a quick shower. I had some long overdue housekeeping to do. First on my list was laundry, which had been piling up from weeks of procrastination.

As I finished loading dirty clothes into the washing machine, it occurred to me that among them were the pants with the phone number of the girl with the mole on her neck in one of the pockets. I could have fished out the pants and saved the piece of paper. But instead, I pressed the start button and watched the water fill the compartment. The machine made a loud gurgling sound, revolving its contents. Shades of gray and white swirled around, and bubbles formed.

The piece of paper would have been soaked, the ink bleeding and the whirling forces tearing it to pieces. By the time I took out my pants, it would be a mushy clump.

I closed my eyes and imagined being inside the washing machine, immersed in its rolling movements. Washed along with a bunch of dirty clothes. Circling, tumbling, sloshing, submerged in the water and suspended among the bubbles. When the noise stopped, I emerged damp but clean.

If only the soul could be cleansed that way.

I had almost fallen sleep when someone knocked on my door. I rubbed my eyes and glanced at the clock. It was past midnight. One thing I'd learned was anyone visiting so late was probably someone I didn't want to see. I ignored the knocking and continued to sit there, watching the washing machine.

But my guest was persistent and had started pounding on the door. I grunted. At this rate, the neighbors downstairs would complain. Left with no choice, I got up to answer the door.

It was Seven Stars. This time, too, she was still in her school uniform.

"Don't." She held the door with her hand before I could shut it. "I just want to talk. I promise I won't cause any problems."

Again, she walked into my apartment without my consent. I closed the door but didn't move from where I was standing.

"Well," I said, "what do you want to talk about?"

She turned to look at me. "I've heard you're quitting."

"I was only supposed to teach until winter break."

"They offered you a permanent position, but you turned them down."

"You're well-informed, young miss."

She didn't react to my condescension. "Are you going back to Tokyo?"

"Yes," I said. "I've finished what I wanted to do here."

"Finding your sister's murderer?"

I froze. This girl really knew how to catch me off guard.

"My father isn't lying when he says he doesn't know where my mother is. She completely disappeared from our lives." She looked into my eyes, unfazed. "What are you planning to do now? Are you going to track her down?"

I shrugged. "What for?"

"Revenge."

"That's not going to fix anything."

"Aren't you angry that I didn't tell you?"

I shook my head. "I wouldn't have believed you, anyway. I needed to find the answers myself."

Seven Stars crossed her arms. "Miss Ishida and my father . . . They went on for years, you know. I bet you didn't have a clue. I found out about it even before my mother did."

"Is that why you started stealing bubble gum?"

She shrugged and muttered, "Probably."

"Did you learn anything from it?"

"Not really—the difference is huge. I was stealing bubble gum, not someone's husband," she said. "Mr. Ishida, has your opinion of your sister changed? Now that you know what kind of person she was, do you regret going to all this trouble for her?"

"I never saw it as trouble," I said. "My sister was just a normal girl. When she was your age, she was as naïve as you are."

Seven Stars' expression hardened, and her eyes narrowed. I realized I was being insensitive—of course she resented being compared to my sister.

"Mr. Ishida, did you know my mother almost killed me once?" Her words hit me hard.

"My father had tried to leave us for Miss Ishida. Of course, my mother didn't take it well. She drove my father and me to a deserted area outside of town after spiking our drinks with sleeping pills. She wanted to kill all three of us using the car's exhaust. But things didn't go according to plan, because I woke up."

I stood still, speechless.

"My father promised us so many times that he would end the affair, but he never did. And I'm a nasty person, Mr. Ishida. I think your sister deserved her death. She shouldn't have kept forcing her way into our lives. She even left something of hers in our house, hoping to be discovered."

I cleared my throat. There was only one thing I could think of. "It was the knife, wasn't it?"

She pursed her lips. "So you knew."

"I bought it for her," I said. "It was a birthday present."

"You have weird taste, Mr. Ishida."

"It was practical."

Seven Stars paced around my tiny living room, her arms still crossed. "The knife is still inside our kitchen cabinet. I'll bring it here."

I shook my head. "Just leave it there. If you want, you can use it."

"Why would I want to use what's not mine?"

"My sister is dead. When a person passes away, their belongings are no longer theirs. Since I gave her the knife, let's just say it's become mine again, so I have the right to give it to you. You can decide whether you want to accept it or not. You can even get rid of it, if you'd like."

"Fine. I'll consider it." She had stopped moving and leaned against the wall. "I heard your sister was a good cook."

"She was."

"One day, I'm going to be a better cook than her. Would you consider going out with me then?"

"Perhaps."

She clicked her tongue. "You're lying."

"Good that you know."

Seven Stars bit her lip and lowered her head. Her hair fell into her face. "Don't be conceited. Ten years from now, I'll be in my twenties and drop-dead gorgeous. And you'll be a sad uncle in your thirties. I'm going to forget all about you, but you're going to remember me. You're going to regret ever having turned me down."

I smiled. "I know."

"No, you don't. If you knew, you wouldn't be rejecting me."

Her tone was flat, as if she were talking about something mundane. I had no idea what was on her mind. This girl, I could never read her.

"Are you getting back together with your Tokyo girlfriend?" she asked. "What if she doesn't want you any more?"

I shrugged. "I'll worry about it when the time comes."

"Maybe she already has a new boyfriend. She could be married by now, and have given birth to a cute baby girl."

"Hey, I've only been gone for six months," I said, laughing. "It's not like I disappeared for years."

She looked up and mumbled, "I know."

I walked over and stood beside her. "Honestly, you're young and beautiful. What do you see in me?"

"Actually, I've asked myself the same question. What *do* I see in you?" She sighed. "I've thought about it a lot, but I don't have an answer."

Seven Stars unzipped her schoolbag, removed a white plastic bag, and poured out the contents. A pile of Ritter Sport Cornflakes chocolates landed on the floor.

"What—"

"You said they were your favorite, didn't you?" she said. "But don't eat them all at once. You'll get fat."

I was shocked at both the insult and the gift. "You didn't steal them, did you?"

"Hey, that's not fair. I promised you I would never steal again, didn't I? How dare you accuse me of that. I paid for every single one of these."

"Thanks, but . . ." I scratched my head. "This is too much."

She laughed, and I laughed too. After we stopped laughing, we looked at each other for a moment. Suddenly, she inched forward and planted her soft lips on mine. It happened so quickly, I didn't have time to react. I stared at her, dumbfounded.

"Goodbye," she whispered before walking to the door.

Seven Stars left without looking back. I took it as a sign that she didn't expect an answer.

After she was gone, I crouched down and gathered all the chocolates. There were fifty-eight in total. Flashy indeed. I unwrapped one and took a bite. It was already half-melted.

Deep down, I'd known she was serious about me. And I couldn't deny I was drawn to her. It was completely different from what I felt toward Nae. If my relationship with Nae was gentle and uplifting, then what I had with Seven Stars was the complete opposite. Things between us were intense and destructive, like a raging storm.

3 2

The
Train
Station
and a
Chinese
Movie

On my last day of work, I dropped by Mr. Katou's office on the way to Yotsuba. I'd wanted to pay him one last visit, but I was told he'd resigned from his job.

The receptionist flashed me a professional smile. "Mr. Katou wished to spend more time with his family."

"Do you happen to know where he's living now?" I asked.

She shook her head. "I'm sorry, I have no idea."

From the tone of her voice, I could tell she wouldn't give me any information even if she'd had it. Since the office was near Segayaki, I went to his old house, hoping the new owner might know something.

I pressed the doorbell and waited. A petite middle-aged woman opened the door.

I greeted her, "Good morning. I'm looking for Mr. Katou."

"I'm afraid he's no longer living here," the woman said. "He moved out several weeks ago when we bought the house."

"Do you happen to know where he went?"

She shook her head. "After we signed the contract, he gave us his office number. But when I called a few days ago, I was told he had resigned and left Akakawa."

"I see." I bowed to her. "I apologize for taking up your time."

"Please don't worry about it," she said before closing the door.

Because I'd left my apartment early in anticipation of spending some time speaking to Mr. Katou, I ended up reaching Yotsuba nearly two hours ahead of my first class. With some time to kill, I called the kimono lady on the phone at the reception desk.

"Good morning, this is the Katsuragi Hotel," a woman's voice answered. "How may I assist you?"

I cleared my throat. "I'm looking for Mrs. Katsuragi."

"This is she. May I know who's speaking?"

"It's Ren Ishida."

There was a pause before she responded, "Yes, Mr. Ishida. What can I do for you?"

"I was hoping to contact Mr. Katou, but I have no idea of his current whereabouts. He's resigned from his post and left Akakawa. Do you happen to know where he might be?"

"I'm afraid not."

"He mentioned his wife was going to stay with relatives in Hakone, so he might be there as well. Perhaps you know someone there?"

She sighed. "I have no clue, Mr. Ishida. And to tell you the truth, even if I did, I wouldn't say anything. The fact that he didn't let anyone know where he was going means he wants to be left alone. It would be a terrible mistake to rouse a sleeping tiger, don't you think?"

I kept quiet.

"Please heed my earlier advice and stay away from him. This will do you no good."

"I'll keep it in mind."

I put down the phone and walked upstairs. What the kimono lady had told me made sense. For such a high-profile man to disappear from a small town like Akakawa could only mean he didn't want to be disturbed. I decided to give the matter a rest.

THE PRINCIPAL CALLED ME into his office to give me my last paycheck.

He passed me the envelope. "Thank you for your hard work."

I bowed and took it from him. "Thank you for taking care of me."

"Say, Ishida, do you have any plans tonight? It's our tradition to go out drinking whenever a staff member is leaving. I should have told you earlier, but it slipped my mind."

"Sure, let's do that."

He led me out and announced to the rest of the staff that we were hitting the bar that night. Everyone cheered. Most of them had anticipated the drinking session.

"Time flies, doesn't it? It's already your last day," Honda said. "We're going to the bar by the train station. It's called Blue Note. Do you know which one it is?"

I nodded. "I've passed by it a couple of times."

"We always go to the same place. It's close by and affordable, and the owner is the principal's old high school friend. Are you a big drinker?"

"Not really."

Honda leaned in toward me. "Listen carefully, this is the deal. They're not going to let you off until you're drunk. You need to pretend to be intoxicated and do something embarrassing, like sing loudly or do a funny dance."

I laughed. "I would rather get drunk than do what you just suggested."

"Or you can pretend to fall asleep. Unless you'd prefer to actually be drunk."

"I could do that," I said, "pretend to fall asleep."

"Good. I'm going to play the hero and get you back to your apartment." He patted my shoulder. "Is there anything you need to bring home?"

"Thanks, but I've been doing that over the past few days. Everything else fits into my bag."

"All right, enjoy your last day of teaching."

SEVEN STARS CAME TO my class and acted as if nothing had ever happened between us. It was your standard student-teacher interaction, except that she handed in a strange composition entitled "The Train Station" as her homework assignment. I could tell it wasn't something she'd written using the prompt I'd given.

The Train Station
by Rio Nakajima

A woman recounted her dream to her male companion.

"I could still remember it clearly after waking up," she said. "In my dream, I was stranded at a quiet train station. Service was delayed due to heavy snowfall. I sat on an old wooden bench, waiting for the time to pass, feeling cold and lonely."

She turned to him, hoping for his response, but he seemed uninterested.

"And then I saw you," she continued. "You were sitting alone on the bench next to mine, waiting for your train, too."

Still, he said nothing.

"You looked at me, so I worked up the courage to talk to you,"

she said. "You were friendly. I was having a great time. I wished the train would never come."

He mustered a smile, even though he wasn't sure whether that was the response she was looking for.

"Not long after, I heard the sound of the train approaching. I woke up without knowing whose train arrived first."

The story ended there, but the ending didn't read like an ending. "That was all?" I asked Seven Stars after the class was over.

She nodded. "Yup."

I'd put her composition at the bottom of the pile, so she would be the last student to leave the classroom.

"This is an intriguing story, but not what I was looking for," I said. "The homework I assigned was an argumentative essay."

"Really?" she asked playfully. "Are you going to ask me redo it?"

"You don't need to, since I'm leaving. Today is my last day."

Her smile disappeared. "I know."

"You know a lot of things, don't you?" I leaned back in my chair. "I'm curious. Whose train arrived first?"

She shrugged. "That, I don't know. The woman woke up before she could find out."

I'd expected such an answer from her. "That must be vexing."

"You're wrong, Mr. Ishida. You don't understand a woman's heart. She's glad she'll never find out. She doesn't even want to know. Either way, it's going to be sad, since one of them has to leave first. It might be fine for the one leaving, but the one who is left behind must feel very, very sad."

Seven Stars pulled the paper from my hand and crumpled it up. Opening the window, she threw it out.

"What are you doing?" I asked.

"You're overthinking this. It's just a story I wrote, no big deal.

Don't worry so much about it." She leaned closer and touched my forehead with the tip of her finger. "See, you have wrinkles here."

She took her schoolbag and walked out. Her high ponytail swung with every step she took. And that was the last time I ever saw her, the girl with the beautiful fingers. Never again in my life would I meet such a precocious girl who could sweep me away like a violent tidal wave.

I LEFT THE OFFICE with the rest of my colleagues around ten. The bar was only a few minutes away on foot, but the December night was cold. We walked as fast as we could.

When we reached the place, there were only four other patrons. Unidentifiable jazz music played in the background. The sound was faint. It probably came from a stereo hidden somewhere behind the counter.

A man welcomed us and showed us to the biggest table in the middle of the room. He appeared to be the owner. The principal bowed to him, and they went to the counter to chat. The rest of us took off our coats and seated ourselves, the principal joining us shortly. The bartender brought a few bottles of Nikka whiskey, some mixers, two buckets of ice, and a tray of shot glasses.

"Isn't this too much?" one of the teachers asked.

"It's okay," the principal said, "we haven't gone out to drink in a long time."

One of the young female staff brought a set of larger glasses and filled them with ice cubes, liquor, and bottled iced green tea. The principal gestured for us to pick up our drinks and led us in a toast. Once we'd put down the glasses, another staff member refilled without pause, coaxing everyone into another toast. The principal seemed in high spirits. He laughed loudly and exchanged banter with everyone.

After a couple of rounds, most faces around the table had turned red, yet no one was slowing down. If anything, everyone was getting more pumped up, especially the principal.

"Is he drunk?" I whispered to Honda, who sat next to me.

"No, he holds his liquor well," he answered. "But it's his mission to get everyone drunk before he lets us off."

"Honda and Ishida, what are you whispering about?" the principal shouted. "Stop talking amongst yourselves and drink more."

Another staff member filled our glasses until the liquor overflowed and invited us for a toast. Honda and I had no choice but to oblige.

After a while, I noticed the young woman who did most of the pouring didn't mix the drinks equally. The glass on the far right would have the most whiskey, while the glass all the way to the left would have almost no alcohol in it. I kept taking the one on the left and drank copious amounts of iced green tea with only a waft of liquor scent.

I glanced at my watch. It was already past midnight. The majority of my colleagues were drunk, but most were still drinking and pouring for each other nonstop. Some of them started sipping the whiskey on the rocks. The bar owner returned with more.

Watching my colleagues chatter to each other at the dimly lit bar reminded me of a Chinese movie I'd seen at the Cinema Komori. The movie theater was old, but within walking distance of my house. Unfortunately, it had since been demolished and turned into a McDonald's.

I went to that cinema with my first girlfriend on our first date. We kissed during a scene when the two leads stood in a bar similar to this one. It was just a brief peck on the lips, an amateurish kiss, but I was still so nervous. Good thing the cinema was dark, or my girlfriend would have seen me turn red.

And that movie, what had it been about? An extramarital affair, if I remembered correctly. I was sure the female lead had young children. What a choice of film to watch on a first date. And what had the title been? I couldn't recall. It had something to do with music and it started with an *A*—Allegro, Adagio, Andantino?

I gave up; I couldn't remember. Was I getting old, or was I just drunk?

The teacher sitting across the table stared at me. He looked quite intoxicated. We had never talked, and I felt uncomfortable under his intense gaze.

"Are you looking at me?" I whispered.

"Yes, it's your eyes," he said. "You don't look like your sister, but you have the same eyes as she did. Do you know that?"

His voice was clear enough for everyone at the table to hear him. I drained my glass. "Is that so?"

The atmosphere became tense. All this while, the staff had tried not to talk about my sister in front of me. But now, the barrier was broken. After an awkward silence, the principal spoke.

"She was a sweet girl, wasn't she?"

I nodded.

We continued to drink for a while, but no one said anything. The uneasiness lingered.

"We've had enough for the night," the principal finally said.

Everyone murmured in agreement. I looked at Honda. His face was completely red.

"Are you all right?" I asked, patting his shoulder.

He looked at me and muttered something unintelligible. He continued to drink, then put down his glass and fell asleep on the table.

"Someone needs to take care of Honda," Abe said.

I was about to volunteer when Maeda said, "I'll take him back. I can drive, and I know where he lives."

"I'll help you carry him to the car," I said.

"Don't worry, I'll do that," said one of the male teachers. "My car is parked next to his."

He stood and helped Honda leave the bar. Maeda followed behind, holding Honda's briefcase. The principal went over to the counter to settle the bill.

"Is it true that Maeda likes Honda?" one of the teachers asked.

"Of course it's true," another teacher answered. "She's been eyeing him for such a long time."

"What about the no-relationship rule?" the first teacher asked.

A female staff member waved her hand. "Is there such a rule? Someone must have made it up."

I remembered Maeda being the one who'd told me that. Had she known Honda was seeing my sister? Anyway, that had nothing to do with me. Grabbing my bag, I left the bar with the rest of the staff. Once outside, they took turns shaking my hand and giving me parting words.

The night got colder as we walked to the main street. The bus service was no longer available, so some of the group, including me, had to flag down taxis. A yellow sedan came. Because it was my last day, they forced me to take it. I thanked them and promised to keep in touch before climbing in.

When the taxi stopped at the intersection, I stared at the red light. I must have been drunk, because it seemed to last forever, as if someone had pressed a switch to freeze time. But when the light turned green, time made up for it by moving faster, blurring the streetlights together.

WHEN I ARRIVED AT my apartment, the sight of a man standing outside my door gave me a fright. Was I hallucinating? I blinked a few times. Walking closer, I realized it wasn't my imagination. Speaking of the tiger.

"Good evening," Mr. Katou greeted me. He held a dessert shop paper bag in his hand. "I apologize for coming here unannounced."

"Don't worry about it." I opened the door, hoping I didn't reek of alcohol. "Please, come in. I hope you weren't waiting too long in the cold."

Mr. Katou followed me into the apartment. He wore a thick, long dark-gray coat, but it still wouldn't have kept him warm on such a cold night.

"Was it hard to find this place?" I asked.

"Not really," he said. "I've been here before."

I waited for him to explain, but he didn't. I should have probed him for more, but I could tell from the way he shifted his glance, he didn't want to talk about it.

"Please, take a seat," I said. "What can I get for you? A cup of coffee?"

He nodded. "That would be great."

Mr. Katou took his coat off, revealing a crisp white shirt underneath. He sat down and rubbed his palms together. He must have been waiting for some time before I returned.

I went to the kitchen to make coffee. While waiting for the water to boil, I splashed icy tap water on my face. It woke me up, though I couldn't do much for my queasy stomach. When I returned, Mr. Katou had already placed the paper bag on the low table. I put the coffee next to it.

"Please, help yourself," I said.

He reached for the mug. The coffee must have been too hot, but he still took a sip. He held the cup in his hands for a moment before setting it back down.

"You've found yourself a pleasant apartment," he said. "It fits the image of one of my favorite poems, 'Shizuka Na Tsukiyo Ni.'

'On a Silent Moonlit Night.' It's by a poet named Akitsuki. 'Aki' for 'autumn,' and 'tsuki' for 'moon.' Have you heard of him?"

"No," I answered, wondering if he was talking about the book he kept reading over and over. "I'm not familiar with many poets."

"Neither am I. Previously, I only knew the famous ones, like Basho and Issa, but few years ago, I chanced upon Akitsuki in my wife's personal collection. I enjoy his works. They calm me down and silence the noises around me. I wanted to get hold of more of his books, but he only has one, which is probably why most people have never heard of him."

"Uh-huh."

He took a deep breath and pushed the bag toward me. "Actually, I came to deliver this."

I wondered what he could possibly have for me. "May I?"

"Please do."

Opening the paper bag, I found a small porcelain urn.

"I found this in Miss Ishida's room when we moved out," Mr. Katou said. "I apologize for keeping quiet for so long, but I couldn't decide the right thing to do with it. I heard from my office that you were returning to Tokyo, so I thought it would be best to pass it on to you before you left. After all, you're Miss Ishida's next of kin."

I held the urn in my lap. "Did anyone else know about this?"

He shook his head. "Only my wife and I."

"I went through that bedroom a couple of times."

"It was well hidden under one of the wooden floor panels," Mr. Katou said. "When Miss Ishida was taking care of my wife, she confided to her about the miscarriage. The clinic in Kuromachi helped to arrange a discreet cremation."

"I see." Trying hard to maintain composure, I asked, "How is Mrs. Katou?"

"She's started to speak again and responds when we talk to her. The new environment seems to be helping her regain strength."

"That's great."

He nodded. "My wife has always blamed herself for our daughter's death, even though I was also to blame. I was too preoccupied with my work to pay attention to my own family. You knew it too, didn't you? Miyuki . . ." His voice turned hoarse. "She was never sick."

I swallowed hard. "I had a vague idea."

"My wife isn't well." Mr. Katou rubbed his eyes. "Have you ever heard of Munchausen syndrome by proxy?"

"No—what is that?"

"It's a mental illness, and a rare form of child abuse. It happens when a child's caregiver, usually their mother, fabricates or causes symptoms in them to gain attention."

A lump lodged in my throat. It was a conclusion I'd hoped was wrong.

"I figured it out too late, and because of that, we lost our daughter. After Miyuki was gone, my wife refused to talk. I took her to several psychologists, but they couldn't do anything as long as she shut herself in. I didn't know what to do. I guess she needed a change of scenery, and for me to acknowledge what had happened instead of masking it with work."

"I'm so sorry for your loss," I said. I decided not to tell him about my last conversation with Mrs. Katou.

He mumbled words of thanks before getting up. "It's late. I'd better get moving."

I stood and accompanied him to the door.

Putting on his coat, Mr. Katou said, "My wife asked me to send her regards."

"Please give her my regards, too." I hesitated for a moment, then decided to say something. "And thank you for the medical documents."

His eyes widened, but he didn't say a word. He only nodded before walking down the stairs. I took it as an acknowledgment.

The cold wind blew, and tiny bumps appeared on my arms. I pulled up my collar and returned to my living room. Sitting in front of the low table, I clasped my hands in prayer.

"Pigtails, may your soul rest in peace."

I took the small urn and carried it to my room, where I kept my sister's urn. I placed the urns side by side on the floor and poured the ashes from the small container into the large one, careful not to spill anything.

"I hope the two of you can rest peacefully, now that mother and daughter are finally reunited."

After putting the urns in my wardrobe, I took a shower and went to bed.

That night, I slept soundly. It was probably the perfect combination of drunkenness and fatigue. The next morning, I read in the newspaper that there had been a mild earthquake during the night. But I didn't recall hearing or feeling anything. I'd sunken into the quiet, bottomless pit of sleep; even an earthquake couldn't rouse me.

3 3

Farewell
at
Capriccio

I left my apartment five minutes before ten with a Takashimaya
Department Store paper bag. It was less conspicuous than walking
around with an urn in the street. But my worry was unfounded, as
I didn't run into anyone. People woke up late on Sunday.

I spotted Honda's black sedan parked across the street. Walking
over, I knocked gently on the rear window. He peered over the
newspaper and unlocked the door.

"Were you waiting long?" I asked, getting in.

"No," he said. "I just got here."

He must have seen the paper bag, but he didn't say a word
about it.

I put on my seat belt. "The drive is around two hours, right?"

"Yes. You can sleep, if you'd like," he said, turning on the engine.

Honda flicked the radio on. It was tuned to a jazz channel. I
recognized the melody as John Coltrane's "My Favorite Things."

As the journey began, the music enveloped us both in warm
nostalgia. The next song was a number by Charlie Parker, followed
by Duke Ellington. One familiar sound after another. Listening to
the music, it occurred to me the station must have been set when

he'd dated my sister, and he'd never changed it. Just like he'd never gotten rid of the rabbit trinket.

Honda turned the steering wheel. His gear-shifting was almost unnoticeable. I held the paper bag tightly, especially when we sped up and made turns. This had happened before. Six months ago, on the way from the crematorium to the Katsuragi Hotel. So much had happened since then.

We passed through several farming towns before reaching the mountainside. Honda switched to a lower gear as we started up the steep, curvy road. No wonder the place was quiet. This route wasn't easy to drive.

A half-hour later, the car slowed near a long bend. Honda parked it at a spot where the shoulder was wider. When I opened the door, the clean mountain air filled my lungs. I felt refreshed just breathing it in. We climbed the barricade and admired the scenery. From where we stood, I could see the little town at the bottom of the mountain.

"Do you think the wind is strong enough?" Honda asked.

"Hopefully," I answered.

I opened the paper bag and took out the urn, slowly tilting it. The wind blew away the ashes. When only a small portion of the ashes remained, I poured that into the lid and the wind whisked it away. I closed the empty urn and put it back into the paper bag.

"I came here alone once," Honda said. "When Keiko returned the engagement ring, I was heartbroken. I drove all the way here and threw the ring from this exact spot."

I kept quiet, unable to think of anything appropriate to say.

"At that time, I only thought of this mountain. Maybe because I have fond memories of coming here with her."

"My sister was a fool, wasn't she?" I said. "I'm sorry about what happened."

"Well, feelings are something you can't force. Either you have them, or you don't. But coming here sure brings back memories." He stared off into the distance. "Have you heard the news about Nakajima?"

I shook my head. "What about her?"

"She handed in her withdrawal form a few days ago. I was in the principal's office when she came in and I overheard the conversation. She's going to try modeling. It surprised me a little. I mean, the industry is such a gamble."

"But it suits her, don't you think?" I said, smiling.

He nodded. "It's good to be young. Anything feels possible. As you grow older, you forget how to dream. Before you realize it, one day you wake up and look in the mirror, wondering who the middle-aged man in front of you is."

I laughed. "It can't be that bad."

"But, like you said, it might be achievable for her," he added. "She does have a certain charm."

"And she's stubborn enough to keep pursuing it."

A flock of black birds flew by, screeching loudly. Passing through the clouds, they soared into the distant sky.

"Do you know what kind of birds those are?" I asked.

"They're a type of cuckoo," Honda said. "In Australia, they're called rainbirds. They're thought to sing before stormy weather—it has something to do with their migration pattern."

So those were rainbirds.

"No matter how far they travel, they'll always return home," Honda continued as another flock showed up.

"Isn't that salmon?" I asked.

"Really? Maybe both salmon and rainbirds," he said, and looked up. "The sun is getting high. Shall we make a move now?"

"Of course."

We climbed back over the barricade.

"About the Italian restaurant," I asked Honda, "is it nearby?"

"Yes, it's on the way back. We can go there for lunch."

"Actually, I was planning to go alone," I said, choosing my words carefully. "Before she passed away, my sister and I had planned to go there together."

"I understand. I'll drop you there," he said with a smile. "There's a bus stop near the restaurant. You shouldn't have any problem getting to the nearest train station."

We got into the car and drove off.

I thought about how nice it would have been if my sister had chosen Honda instead of Mr. Nakajima. He would've treated her well. And if she'd ended up with him, she would probably still be alive.

But as Honda had said, feelings couldn't be forced. If my sister could've chosen whom to fall in love with, I was sure she would've picked Honda. But he wasn't the one in her heart.

The car stopped in front of a cottage-style building. The place looked more like an inn than a restaurant. A wooden sign bore the name Capriccio Ristorante.

"This is the one," Honda said, glancing at my paper bag.

"Do you mind if I leave the urn with you?" I asked. "I'm not going to keep it and it's hard to carry it around."

"Of course," he said. "You're returning to Tokyo tomorrow, aren't you?"

"Yes, first train in the morning."

We sat in silence for a moment.

Finally, Honda said, "Ishida, you need to stop blaming yourself for Keiko's death. She wouldn't want you to do that."

I swallowed hard. "I know."

"Well, then." He grinned and offered his hand. "This is a temporary goodbye."

"I like that." I gave him a firm handshake. "A temporary goodbye."

"And remember what I said about your girlfriend. Don't make the same mistake I did. Tell her what you really want to say."

I nodded slightly and thought about Nae. She deserved an answer.

I got out of the car and stood at the roadside. I waited there until I could no longer see Honda's car. It suddenly occurred to me that Honda and Mr. Tsuda were both math teachers. Could it be more than coincidence? I hoped I was wrong, but it was too much to be random chance. My sister had probably tried to replay her past, hoping for a different outcome, and ended up disappointed. When you ask too much of others, of course people will start to fail you.

I pushed the door and walked into the restaurant. The bell tinkled and soon after, an elderly lady came out from the kitchen.

"Welcome," she said. "Are you dining alone?"

"Yes, my companion couldn't make it," I said.

"That's a pity. I'll get you the best table in the house."

She led me in and I realized the restaurant was empty. She gave me a table for two with a panoramic view of the valley and handed me a menu.

"Can I get you a glass of water?" she asked.

I nodded. "That would be great."

The lady disappeared into the kitchen and I gazed at the empty chair in front of me. I imagined my sister sitting there, looking at the menu, and asking me what she always did.

"Hey Ren, what are you ordering?"

I asked her in return, "What would you suggest?"

She glanced through the menu and bit her lip. "It's hard. Everything looks delicious."

"What did you have last time, when you came with Honda?"

"Bruschetta, beef lasagna, and tiramisu."

"I'll have that."

"No." She shook her head. "Let's try something new."

"Why don't you choose for both of us? Pick anything you want."

Her eyes widened. "Really?"

I nodded. "If after that, you still have something you want to try, we can always come back another day."

My sister smiled but didn't say a word.

I watched her go through the menu, mumbling here and there. Sometimes, she would look at me and ask for my opinion. But most of the time, she was in her own world. Keiko Ishida, she always had the excitement of a child.

"Are you ready to order?" The elderly lady's voice startled me. She had placed a glass of water on my table.

"What do you recommend?" I asked.

She tilted her head. "Do you have any preferences? Pizza, pasta, risotto?"

"Probably pasta."

"May I suggest the fettuccine Alfredo? It's fettuccine pasta, tossed with Parmigiano-Reggiano cheese and butter," she said. "It's popular with our regulars."

"I'll take that, then," I said, though seeing how empty the restaurant was, I had doubts about who might qualify as a "regular."

"What about the first course? Our crostini is good."

"Sure, I'll follow your recommendations."

"And would you like a glass of wine, or dessert?"

"Just a cup of coffee will do. No sugar."

The elderly lady scribbled on her notepad. "One crostini, one fettuccine Alfredo, and one coffee, no sugar. Is that correct?"

"Yes."

She disappeared into the kitchen again, and my sister began to take form.

"You should have ordered dessert, too. A meal isn't complete without it," she complained. "It's like the final note of a song, or the conclusion of a journey. Ren, you're missing the punch line."

I sighed. "If you want it that much, you can add on the dessert."

"It's too much for one person."

"It's fine, I'll help you finish it."

But knowing her, she would polish off the whole thing.

"Sorry, Ren, I couldn't control myself," she would say with a satisfied grin. "It was too yummy! Next time, let's order two."

I laughed. "Seeing you eat killed my appetite."

"Hey, that's rude."

I knew my sister loved sweet things. Parfaits, candies, shaved ices, stuff like that. Nae loved sweet things, too. Perhaps all girls loved sweet things.

The elderly lady came with the crostini. She seemed eager to start a conversation. "Is this your first time here?" she asked.

I nodded.

"How did you find this place?"

"My sister recommended it to me."

Her eyes lit up. "That's nice of her. Please send her my regards."

"I will," I mumbled.

"All right, I won't disturb you any longer," she said, probably sensing I would prefer to be alone. "Enjoy your meal."

I smiled and started eating.

The food was as good as my sister had said it would be. The crostini were perfectly toasted. Generous amounts of herbed goat cheese and sautéed baby spinach formed the perfect topping, and I could taste the tanginess of the lemon zest.

The fettuccine Alfredo came just as I finished the last bite of the crostini. Like the appetizer, the main course didn't disappoint. It had more butter than I'd anticipated, but was still delicious. I polished it off without leaving a single drop of sauce. The elderly lady looked pleased when she delivered my coffee and cleared the dirty plates.

But what moved me wasn't the fact that the food was done well. It was the warmth I sensed in it. I could feel the passion and dedication poured into every single course.

"What's most important is feeling," my sister used to say. "When you cook for someone you care about and you put your heart into it, your feelings will come through."

I buried my face in my hands, unable to contain the sudden burst of emotion. At that precise moment, I realized why I had the same unpleasant feeling whenever I thought about Mr. Tsuda. He wasn't a man who could've made her happy. I'd always known he was going to cause her pain.

And she did get hurt. Not once, but twice. I should have saved her. Or at least, I should have saved her when it happened again.

"Ren."

I felt a gentle touch on my shoulder. When I raised my head, my sister was looking at me.

"Are you all right?" she asked.

"I'm sorry," I said. "I'm sorry I didn't do anything for you."

"That's not true. You've done plenty for me, Ren." She reached for my hands and held them in hers. "Listen to me. I'm all right. I lived a fulfilling life. It wasn't perfect, but I have no regrets. I made my choices and accept the way things turned out. What happened to me has nothing to do with you."

I sat still, unable to look at her.

"Can you promise me you'll stop blaming yourself?" she asked.

After a long while, I nodded. "All right."

"Thanks, Ren," she whispered. Her dark brown hair shone in the sun.

I felt an ache in my chest. "Mother told me why you came to Akakawa."

My sister looked up.

"Did you manage to find your real mother?" I asked.

"No, but I didn't try very hard." She paused, taking a deep breath. "It took me a while, but I realized the only family I ever needed was you."

Even though my sister was smiling, I could see sadness in her eyes. Or was it loneliness?

I thought of her room in the Katou household, and her desk at Yotsuba. Neat and orderly, with no personal touch. As if she had never been there. From the moment she had come to Akakawa, she had already planned to disappear.

"Are you going to leave?" I asked.

She stared at me. "Why do you ask?"

"I don't know." I averted my eyes. "It just feels that way."

My sister squeezed my hands. "I promise we'll meet again one day. You know I always keep my promises, don't you?"

I kept quiet, and she let go of my hands. Her outline gradually faded. She disappeared with a smile across her face.

"YOUNG MAN, ARE YOU all right?" the elderly lady asked. She had returned with the check.

"Yes, just a lack of sleep." I placed a few bills on the wooden tray. "Can you tell me how to get to the nearest bus stop?"

"It's about a ten-minute walk," she said. "After you exit the restaurant, turn right and follow the main road. You can't miss it."

I thanked her and left.

Following her directions, I walked up the steep road. Before long, I saw a public pay phone by the side of the road, one I didn't remember seeing when we'd driven to the restaurant. Why was there a phone booth here? The area was so quiet, who would ever use it?

Perhaps it was fate.

I pushed on the dusty glass panel of the paint-chipped door. Reaching into my pocket, I retrieved some coins and inserted them into the slot. The display lit up, and I punched in the numbers I knew so well.

Taking a deep breath, I waited for Nae to pick up the phone.

AUTHOR'S NOTE

I used to read a lot as a kid—at least a book a day. I would spend my recess periods in the library with my best friend. I loved getting lost in the new and fascinating world of each story, and I knew I wanted to be a writer.

However, when I went off to college, studies became my priority. As I struggled with mounting academic work, I no longer picked up books I hadn't been assigned. By the time I began my first job in marketing, reading had become a thing of the past.

Then, one day, a colleague recommended a book to me. "I'll lend you my copy," he said. "I'm sure you'd like it."

I politely turned him down. "I don't have time to read."

But he insisted I give it a try, so I relented.

That book ended up changing my life. It rekindled the wonder I'd once felt, and the dream I'd once had.

Thank you for picking up *Rainbirds*. I hope you've enjoyed reading it as much as I enjoyed writing it. And if you have, I ask that you share it with someone. A friend, a family member, or a colleague—especially one who has not been reading for quite some time.